Magical★Explorer

Volume 1

Reborn as a Side Character in a Fantasy Dating Sim

Iris

ILLUSTRATION BY
Noboru Kannatuki

YEN
ON

New York

Magical★Explorer: Reborn as a Side Character in a Fantasy Dating Sim, Vol. 1

Iris

Translation by David Musto
Cover art by Noboru Kannatuki

MAGICAL★EXPLORER Vol.1 ERO GAME NO YUJIN KYARA NI TENSEI SHITAKEDO, GAME CHISHIKI TSUKATTE JIYUNI IKIRU
©Iris, Noboru Kannatuki 2019
First published in Japan in 2019 by KADOKAWA CORPORATION, Tokyo.
English translation rights arranged with KADOKAWA CORPORATION, Tokyo through TUTTLE-MORI AGENCY, INC., Tokyo.

Yen On
150 West 30th Street, 19th Floor
New York, NY 10001

Visit us at yenpress.com ★ facebook.com/yenpress ★ twitter.com/yenpress ★ yenpress.tumblr.com ★ instagram.com/yenpress

First Yen On Edition: December 2021

Yen On is an imprint of Yen Press, LLC.
The Yen On name and logo are trademarks of Yen Press, LLC.

Library of Congress Cataloging-in-Publication Data
Names: Iris (Light novel author), author. | Kannatuki, Noboru, illustrator. | Musto, David, translator.
Title: Magical explorer / Iris ; illustration by Noboru Kannatuki ; translation by David Musto.
Other titles: Magical explorer. English
Description: First Yen On edition. | New York, NY : Yen On, 2021–
Identifiers: LCCN 2021039072 | ISBN 9781975325619 (v. 1 ; trade paperback)
Subjects: CYAC: Video games—Fiction. | Role playing—Fiction. | Magic—Fiction. | Fantasy. | LCGFT: Light novels.
Classification: LCC PZ7.1.I76 Mag 2021 | DDC [Fic]—dc23
LC record available at https://lccn.loc.gov/2021039072

ISBNs: 978-1-9753-2561-9 (paperback)
       978-1-9753-2562-6 (ebook)

10 9 8 7 6 5 4 3 2 1

LSC-C

Printed in the United States of America

Chapter Select   CONTENTS

Magical★Explorer

Illustration: Noboru Kannatuki

Graphic Design: Kai Sugiyama (Tsuyoshi Kusano Design Co., Ltd.)

Erotic video games—eroge—are, for the most part, chock-full of things to ridicule.

And there are plenty of reasons to lampoon them, too. Let's start with the protagonist's family, shall we?

Most of the time, the eroge protagonist's parents aren't around. Coincidentally absent. Whether it's an excuse to have a childhood friend or little sister character wake him up every morning, or to simply turn a blind eye to how he can easily bring girls back to his room, the full explanation remains a mystery. In-game justifications for this phenomenon vary. Sometimes, his parents are away on an overseas business trip, while other times, he's living on his own or in a dorm. Occasionally, the parents will be dead from the very start.

On top of his parents being absent, he gets to have a beautiful younger sister to take care of him, too? It sounds ridiculous, but it's par for the course in the world of these games.

Indeed, slightly peculiar living arrangements are the norm for an eroge hero.

The things to poke fun at don't stop at their family situation. Their special Eroge Protag Privilege ability is just as silly.

For example, in titles where the protagonist cross-dresses as a woman to attend an all-girls school, his secret will never get out for some reason. In fact, his identity stays so safe that you'll have to assume it's down to him having special powers or something. In one particular eroge, the main character manages to get through a whole swim class without getting found out. Though, in that case, a ghost attends the class in his stead, so it's bit more understandable.

Right, a ghost takes his place. Of course the truth wouldn't get out. Makes total sense.

All that being said, however, the story will commonly play out with his identity getting discovered with such contrived timing that you'll be shouting at your screen. The wig tightly secured to the main character's head during an intense gym class easily slips off in a scuffle with one of the heroines later on.

Oh yeah, a tussle with a heroine will do that. Very reasonable.

Not to get too off topic, but to the average person, the entire premise of *Guy Dresses as Girl and Attends an All-Girls High School* would be extremely unusual and difficult to accept. In the world of eroge, however, it's so normalized that even the most casual of fans can immerse themselves in this scenario free of skepticism. Only those truly new to the genre will find this strange at all.

Another example of Eroge Protag Privilege is the hero's high popularity.

Beautiful women flock to the main character like moths to a flame. Pretty little sisters and stepsisters affectionately refer to him as big bro. A gorgeous childhood friend comes to wake him up every morning without permission, only to recoil and slap him in embarrassment after throwing off the covers to reveal his morning wood. An elegant student council president, gifted with superb intellect and the beauty to match, turns meek and modest when the sex scene comes around. Don't forget the petite, baby-faced teacher who clearly looks like a kid despite having graduated college. They'll all convene around and lust after a guy who lacks any redeeming qualities outside of a basic degree of cordiality. These girls must all be succubi or something. Or maybe the protagonist is actually an incubus?

Granted, it's not just the main character who's abnormal—the same goes for his potential partners, too.

Lovey-dovey heroines with speech patterns that would be an instant turnoff in real life. Girls skilled enough in combat to baffle a professional martial artist. Housewives who look just as young as their high-school-aged children. Heroines. Who look. Like. Elementary schoolers.

However, no matter how young the girls may look, the games make sure to include a disclaimer reading *All characters appearing in this game are over the age of 18*, so that the esteemed gentlemen playing can choke their chickens free from worry.

The stories in these games are similarly screwy. Even when put up against the narratives of TV shows, anime, or manga, eroge are on a completely different level.

Here's a good example: In one game, a male protagonist lives with his father and his siblings, all of whom are male. A men-only household, in other words. Next to them is a home where a mother lives with her daughters. So a women-only household. Now, the father of that house full of men wants a daughter more than anything in the world, and the mother next door in the women-only household wishes she had a son. The two parents rack their brains before they have an epiphany—

—yup, they swap a son with a daughter.

Totally reasonable for an eroge. A brilliant plan, really—brilliantly foolish. Just like that, the main character is traded away and suddenly ends up with his own harem.

Genre buffs would probably eat it up, praising the wonderful narrative setup. The average person, on the other hand, would probably be left wondering who came up with such a contrived plot device.

The same thing holds true for that title from earlier where the protagonist disguises himself as a girl. A harem gets dropped into his lap. While I can't speak with authority on the subject, there are also eroge known as *nukige* that prioritize sexual content above all else. This subgenre features overly lewd scenarios that even veteran players might find hard to stomach.

To make a long story short, eroge exist in a kind of exaggerated version of reality, where common sense doesn't hold true.

Even if you ended up in that reality, outside of a select few titles, you wouldn't have any problems as long as you were the main character. He's the center of the eroge world and extraordinarily popular, after all.

But what if you found out that you weren't, in fact, the center of that universe? One wrong move, and that fantasy could turn into hell itself.

"Oh no, you gotta be kidding me…"

The image reflected in the mirror was both me and not me. Or rather, I should say that the person in the mirror moved exactly how I wanted him to but didn't *look* like me.

To top it all off, I had seen his mug before…

"This is totally that eroge protagonist's...loser friend who's always hanging around...!"

I collapsed to my knees.

The friend of an eroge protagonist usually leads a life of misfortune.

Some of these characters fruitlessly repeat the same eccentric behavior over and over again and earn the ire of the heroines, while other best friend types get embroiled in the protagonist's two-timing and end up playing matchmaker on his behalf.

More than anything else, however, the most common characterization for this character, not to mention the main source of his misfortune, is that he isn't popular with girls.

Best friend characters are *extremely* unpopular. Beautiful women won't even get near them. The reason is simple—imagine what would happen if a girl the player was interested in hooked up with the protagonist's best friend instead. Complaints would flood the development studio, and the player base would dwindle.

It's quite possible that even I would send a fist through the screen if an obnoxious asshole who kept butting in ultimately stole a cute girl away from me. Or I would immediately spam the game's support page with all sorts of nasty abuse, then follow up by leaving enraged reviews on message boards and the like, so all we players who'd been wronged could dry our tears together.

Now then, the character of Kousuke Takioto reflected in the mirror is versatile enough that his qualities range from extremely hapless to downright cursed. Of course.

Kousuke appears in *Magical★Explorer* (*MX* for short), a tactical simulation game often derogatorily referred to as a click game because you have to click through menus to do anything. The player character rotates between campus life and battling through dungeons as part of school or other events, strengthening themselves and their party members along the way. Additionally, *MX* lets you craft weapons, armor, magic, and magic catalysts. Using the crafting system, you can equip unique weapons and can even open up a shop to shoot for becoming the city's top alchemist merchant.

Being an eroge, obviously it contains plenty of romantic elements, too. It wouldn't be an exaggeration to call them the primary focus of the game.

In-game, these beautiful and powerful heroines are involved in your daily life to an abnormal degree (so long as you're the protagonist), with erotic episodes popping up so often, you'd think it was a blessing from on high (so long as you're the protagonist). You can even successfully sneak into the women's bath and catch a glimpse of all the leading ladies at their sexiest (so long as you're the protagonist).

The main character's friend, Kousuke Takioto, is what you'd call a comic relief character—tearfully biting down on his handkerchief as he jealously side-eyes the protagonist flirting with all the different love interests. A foil through and through.

While he has lines like *"That girl is super cute, right? Well, actually..."* and *"She's supposed to be the prettiest girl in the Academy,"* the main character inevitably snatches away anyone he's interested in. It goes without saying, but none of them are reserved for Kousuke Takioto.

Far from it, since all the girls in the game hate his guts. He's pretty good-looking, but between his poorly-timed dirty comments and downright boneheaded behavior, it's clear why he's so reviled. A few of the heroines don't outright hate him, but these exceptions comprise a small portion of the overall cast.

Thus, when we view the romantic elements from Kousuke Takioto's perspective, we find he is a supremely unfortunate individual.

His misfortune extends to the game's combat as well. All male eroge characters are prone to having unremarkable combat abilities in the first place. It makes sense. The ladies and gentlemen playing eroge are after the beautiful young heroines they wish to make their own.

When sought-after heroines are powerful, their popularity increases. The higher their popularity, the higher the merch sales. Above all, however, the developers love their female creations and want to make them as strong as possible, so it's natural they'd be so effective in combat.

Despite all those caveats, Kousuke Takioto's combat ability isn't terrible. Nevertheless, the fact that he's geared toward experienced players, the fact that he doesn't have his own unique weapon, and more than anything, the fact that heroines get such preferential treatment makes him seem underappreciated in comparison. Most people remove him from their main party by the end of the game. I was no exception, of course. I wanted to use the heroines instead!

"Gaaah…"

The Kousuke Takioto reflected in the mirror heaved a sigh.

"I guess I should try confirming if I really am Kousuke Takioto for now…"

I grasped at the smallest of straws as I removed a scarf around my neck that was essentially the unlucky best friend's defining character trait. Nonetheless…

"Is reality truly so cruel?"

Why had this happened? It seemed I really was Kousuke Takioto. This body was not my own. And the reason for my metamorphosis… remained unclear, along with any way to get back to normal.

Besides, instead of focusing on why this had transpired, I needed to think about what I was going to do next. It would be one thing if I understood why I had transformed, but I doubted it would clear up anytime soon. It would be more constructive to consider how I was going to live from here on out.

"This is the world of *Magical★Explorer*, right?"

It wasn't Japan. The *MX* world had been developed through a combination of magic and machinery. A fantasy world, home to elves, beastfolk, and dwarves, too.

In that case—

"I should…be able to use magic, right?"

No, I would *definitely* be able to use magic. A few moments prior, while confirming I was indeed Kousuke Takioto, I had found a school admission information guide. This guy was enrolled at Tsukuyomi Magic Academy.

Who could get into a magic academy without being able to use magic?

"Magic, huh?"

If it was possible, I absolutely wanted to try. Actually, wouldn't I end up getting expelled if I couldn't? How was I supposed to do it, though?

"In the game, you just click the mouse button, and it comes out on its own…"

I had no game screen, and I definitely couldn't click any mouse buttons. I couldn't even look at my own stats. I would have liked to at least see how much HP and MP I had, but that wasn't happening.

However, Kousuke Takioto had only been able to enroll in the Academy because he could use magic. Maybe there was a chance he had a textbook on spellcraft lying around?

I got up from my chair and went into the living room.

Consistent with his in-game characterization, Kousuke Takioto didn't appear to be a bright student by any stretch of the imagination. Only around half of the problems on the tests tucked inside the pages of his notebooks and textbooks were marked correct. Meanwhile, the photos of famous and important people adorning the covers of his magic history and language books had been doodled over, poorly.

I thought to myself, *What the hell, man? Take school seriously*, but then, starting from last year, his textbooks suddenly lost all their scribbles. Instead, written all over them were a variety of magic circles and formulas.

I closed the magic history textbook. Then I picked up an overly pristine magic tome that featured an illustration of a monkey holding a book in its hands on the cover.

"Magic for Monkeys?"

I flipped through the pages of the book, which was so free of any doodles or creases that it had probably never been opened before. This brought up some questions, but without any clear answers, I decided to disregard them. I guess I'd try reading it for now.

If this book was to be believed, all creatures born into this world possessed mana, which was present even in the atmosphere. This lined up with what I had read of the in-game lore.

Utilizing that mana brought forth the wonder of magic—the creation of fire, the summoning of water, and the invocation of the wind. It was even possible to create earth and metal.

However, since these marvels consumed a proportionate amount of mana, magic-users needed to possess an equivalent or greater amount of mana in return. The primary difference between the average person and a magic-user was the size of their mana reserves. Apparently. Though, if things were the same as in the game, then Kousuke Takioto proudly possessed enough mana to make even a teacher at the Academy blush. It was about the only thing he *could* be proud of.

"Aw, I tried copying exactly what's written there, but is this it? I do have this weird feeling all of a sudden, though..."

If I were to describe it, I'd say that, much like my eyes and ears perceived light and sound, it felt as though my whole body had become a new sensory organ of its own. I could feel what I assumed was some mysteriously warm magical energy radiating from my figure, but at the same time, it felt like a similar presence existed separate from my form as well. This outward energy softly brushed up against me. It honestly tickled.

"Hmm, why did I start perceiving this energy so clearly the moment I became aware of its existence?"

I couldn't come up with an explanation. It wasn't surprising, given I didn't really know anything about this mana stuff in the first place. *That's it, I should try using some magic.* If I could, then I would be able to say for sure if what I felt was mana or not.

"Ummm, *Light*."

According to the book, the illumination spell Light used a small amount of mana, so even non-magic-users could cast it. But to be honest, I doubted whether I'd be able to cast something this simple. When had I ever experienced magic before? Contrary to my expectations, however, the phenomenon happened instantly.

"No way... You can't be serious..."

A light floated before my eyes. I sliced my hand through the air around the glow, checking to see if there was a cord or some other power source attached to the light, but my hand only met air. Then I slowly brought my hands toward the glow.

"Ha, ha-ha-ha, ha-ha-ha! This. Is freaking. Awesome!"

I wasn't able to touch the luminescence, however. Nor did it give off any heat. My hand simply went through it, right down the middle. Its shape remained unchanged, however, and it didn't move an inch. When I stopped the supply of mana, the mysterious glow immediately vanished.

I turned out all the lights in the room and closed the curtains. Then I cast the spell again.

With a flash, the mysterious, gleaming orb illuminated the dark interior. I cut off the mana flow and recited the incantation to extinguish the light. Upon doing so, the orb disappeared immediately, and the interior grew dark again. When I repeated the Light incantation, its glow returned to the room.

"I don't believe it..."

Unlike an electric-powered light source, the orb emitted no heat. It was solely composed of mana. Sure enough, immediately after I cut off the mana supply, the glow would disappear. Casting the spell again lit the area up in a flash.

I grew more impressed each time I cast Light. This mysterious power called magic excited me.

If someone else had seen me, they probably would have wondered what the hell I was doing. After all, Light was the very first enchantment a magic-user learned. It was apparently taught around kindergarten or early elementary school, so it wouldn't be strange for someone to scold me for getting worked up over something so basic. How could I not, though?

What if a person from a world without electricity suddenly saw a television or the Internet for the first time? If they didn't piss themselves right then and there, they'd at least freeze up at the sight. However, in our world, the existence of electricity was normal, something we grew accustomed to from a young age. Not surprising at all.

Magic must be the same way. It would probably be discouraging if I saw just how many people in this world would ridicule me for being so worked up about such an elementary enchantment. Still, I wanted to chew them out—you try coming here from a world without magic. To you lot, it might just be Light, but to me, it's an electricity-free, levitating source of illumination.

"Daaaaaaaang..."

I cast Light and immediately extinguished it, then I repeated the process again. Each time amazed me just as much as the first. A thought then began percolating in my mind.

I extended my hand to the luminescence and tried to completely envelop it. Then, slowly opening my hand, I gazed at the unwavering glow. As I did this, I felt the smolder inside me gradually grow into a burning fire.

I wanted to use spells to try out all sorts of new things.

Light wasn't the only form of magic. Offensive magic, defensive magic, recovery magic, support magic, meme magic, sexy magic—there were innumerable different kinds. And I could use all of it. Kousuke would have a rough time pulling it off alone, but through the assistance of friends or items, I'd be able to fly, swim freely underwater, or even breathe like a fish. If I was able to properly utilize battle magic, I could even take on dungeons.

Right, of course! This world had dungeons!

I could go adventuring in those dungeons. And if things really were the same as in *Magical★Explorer*, this world was home to a great many of them.

The Academy, which served as the main setting of *MX*, was built in a region that had an especially large number of labyrinths. Additionally, thanks to magic teleportation circles, I could challenge dozens of them. There were the bread and butter of video games, namely cave- and ruins-style dungeons, but also Japanese-style mazes built like ninja houses, as well as completely wide-open and undivided grassland areas, ravines, volcanoes, snowy plains, and floating islands in the clouds. Additionally, some dungeons were themed around a reflective glass-surface lake—the sort you see used in anime all the time—plus even more fantastical varieties, like crystalline structures that sparkled like gemstones.

I could journey to all those environments and more.

Indeed, I was now in a fantasy world. And I could see the fantastical with my own two eyes!

Wait now, think bigger. Dungeons aren't even half of it.

It was the same for the world itself. There were so many fascinating sights to take in. Like Earth, this world had its own versions of cars and smartphones. The plot lays out that their power comes from mana and magic stones.

I could also use magic tools. I wondered how these tools worked and what was possible with magic stones. There were countless mysteries I wanted to uncover, and in the realm of *MX*, researching these things could give me answers. This wasn't a dream, but true reality.

Not only that, but within this world, there was a large continent that humankind had yet to explore, which contained places at its center that could never exist on Earth. These whimsical locales included a floating castle, a large underground labyrinth, an underwater palace said to house a dragon, as well as a forest that contained a towering World Tree the size of a small mountain. However, the game itself mainly focuses on dungeons and the Academy, so those places are only referenced, with the player only having access to a limited selection of areas.

But I wasn't restricted by the game. I was free.

I could accompany the protagonist and the heroines on expeditions to all these fascinating destinations.

This realm was also home to beastfolk, elves, dark elves, dwarves, dragonfolk, and other races that did not exist on Earth. It was possible to interact with these people, too. If we became friends, I might even be able to go on adventures with them, as well.

Excitement coursed through my veins as my thoughts jumped from one new thing to try to the next. There was one problem, though.

"If I'm going to go adventuring through dungeons and around the world...I'm going to need to get stronger."

Powering up, huh? For that to happen, I would need to do some serious training.

If Kousuke Takioto was true to his in-game characteristics, he had glaring weaknesses. Nevertheless, if players managed to overcome his shortcomings and use him well, he had totally unique abilities and could become unbelievably powerful. Above all else, however, I had knowledge on my side. While I doubted I would be able become the absolute mightiest, I knew I could at least grow tougher.

Actually, wait a minute—was becoming the absolute strongest truly out of reach?

In eroge, generally, the player-controlled protagonist and the heroines popular with users and the production team received the most favorable treatment.

"Could I surpass them and make the best friend character the mightiest of all? You know, it might actually be possible."

Despite all those overpowered characters, could I actually emerge on top?

Of course, I had no illusions about this. Those girls were monsters. One of the main heroines could manipulate tempest winds at will and fire off wide-range blades of air sharp enough to chop iron-hard shells into pieces. Another could instantly heal anyone, no matter how severe their injuries. There was even a heroine with a lightning-fast special combo attack so powerful that it could shred the last boss to pieces. Up against these inhuman heroines, it was no exaggeration to say I had a steep hill to climb.

"But, I mean, if I'm already aiming to get stronger, I might as well..."

Despite understanding the difficulty of the road ahead, I wanted to shoot for the stars. That didn't mean I wanted to try to undermine the heroines, though. It would be egregious to get in the way of the girls I loved while they were working hard to make themselves more powerful. I simply wanted to surpass them and become the strongest myself.

Protagonist? Overpowered heroines? Ha! If anything, having people worth surpassing only made it that much more exciting.

If I truly was the game's Kousuke Takioto… If I truly was him, then I would have a unique ability that could compete with the overwhelmingly gifted protagonist and heroines, the developers' favorites. Furthermore, I had more of the mana I'd need to put my special skill to good use than the Expansion Four Kings, the Big Three, and even the protagonist.

And above all else, I had game knowledge.

An understanding of the game's ins and outs was the most overpowered ability of all. To become the strongest, I knew where I could unlock my potential and where to find the most overpowered equipment. I even knew which dungeons contained the most profitable magic tools and treasure, and I understood where I could learn the strongest skills in the game.

It seemed I had the minimum requirements to become all-powerful completely covered.

"That settles it."

I didn't know why I had come to this world. But if I had to live here, I was going to train myself and aim to become the mightiest character of them all.

I'd outstrip the Big Three and leave the protagonist in the dust.

Then, be it dungeon, a floating castle in the sky, or the World Tree, I'd freely travel wherever I wanted.

I was going to savor everything this world had to offer!

Chapter 2 〔 **The Friend Character's Finicky Ability**  〕

Now that I had decided to enjoy this new life, I began putting my plans in motion, but the reality of the situation was pretty tense. Kousuke Takioto was saddled with both a tragic past and a tragic present.

"Let's see... His parents both passed away last year, and his paternal grandfather died long before that. Since he's totally estranged from his relatives on his mother's side, his paternal grandmother is his only blood relative and his current guardian, but she's now sick in the hospital. The illness has exacerbated her dementia, so she's no longer able to act as his caregiver."

Kousuke Takioto's life was excruciatingly hard, more than the protagonist would have been able to bear. Though I guess I couldn't talk about his life like it didn't involve me anymore.

"Still, aren't this guy's circumstances a little *too* grim? I mean, if he has such a bleak background, why'd they turn him into a comic relief character?"

Thinking back on it...when one of the heroines brings up her own family situation, I remember that Kousuke looks a little sad for a moment. He immediately goes back to his usual stupid grin, so I thought it was a bug or something at the time, but that might have actually had something to do with this hidden backstory of his.

Now then, what was I supposed to do here? First of all, while this world resembled Japan, it wasn't the same place. Who was I supposed to turn to? The police? City hall? The Academy?

Fortunately, I'd passed the test to get into the Academy, but I doubted I would be able to afford the tuition. Forget tuition; at this rate, I was going to starve to death in a ditch somewhere.

"What am I gonna do...?"

As I stood there, bewildered, a chime suddenly rang. From what I could tell, there was a guest at my door, but I was in no mood to answer. *For the time being, I guess I should go to the police. Or maybe I should search this world's Internet for info about where to go?*

I chewed on these questions, but the doorbell's chime interrupted my train of thought.

Getting up with a sigh, I headed toward the entryway.

"Yes, yes, how can I help—*wah?!*"

I was unable to stop a strange noise from escaping my mouth.

Standing there was a woman who I recognized all *too* well.

"Good day. Kousuke Takioto, correct?"

I gulped.

"M-Ms. Hanamura..."

Smiling as she stood in my doorway was Marino Hanamura, the principal of Tsukuyomi Magic Academy, which served as the primary setting for *Magical★Explorer*.

Now, even though a gorgeous woman I recognized from an eroge was inviting me to dinner, I didn't think it would be wise to accept the offer at the drop of a hat. At the very least, it was best to make sure I knew where I was going.

"I'm sorry; this was the only place available...," Marino Hanamura apologized.

Apologizing about a place like this? She was absurd. The prices in this restaurant were so high, you could practically see bills with lots of zeroes sprout wings and fly up to heaven.

"Not at all. I'm stunned there's such a wonderful place so close to my house, really."

Marino Hanamura was the principal and director of the Tsukuyomi Magic Academy, who showed up around the protagonist and his friends occasionally. She didn't get involved deeply with them, though. However, she did pull strings and maneuver behind the scenes.

Since her character bio had her as a major figure in the magic world and working as academy director, I'd assumed she was rich. That said, I didn't expect her to be *this* rich.

Sighing slightly, I tossed one of the cubed cuts of meat into my mouth. It was as soft as sponge cake, and one bite was enough to fill my mouth with its savory juices. The carefully prepared soy-sauce-based marinade flooded the inside of my mouth with bliss. No way did the

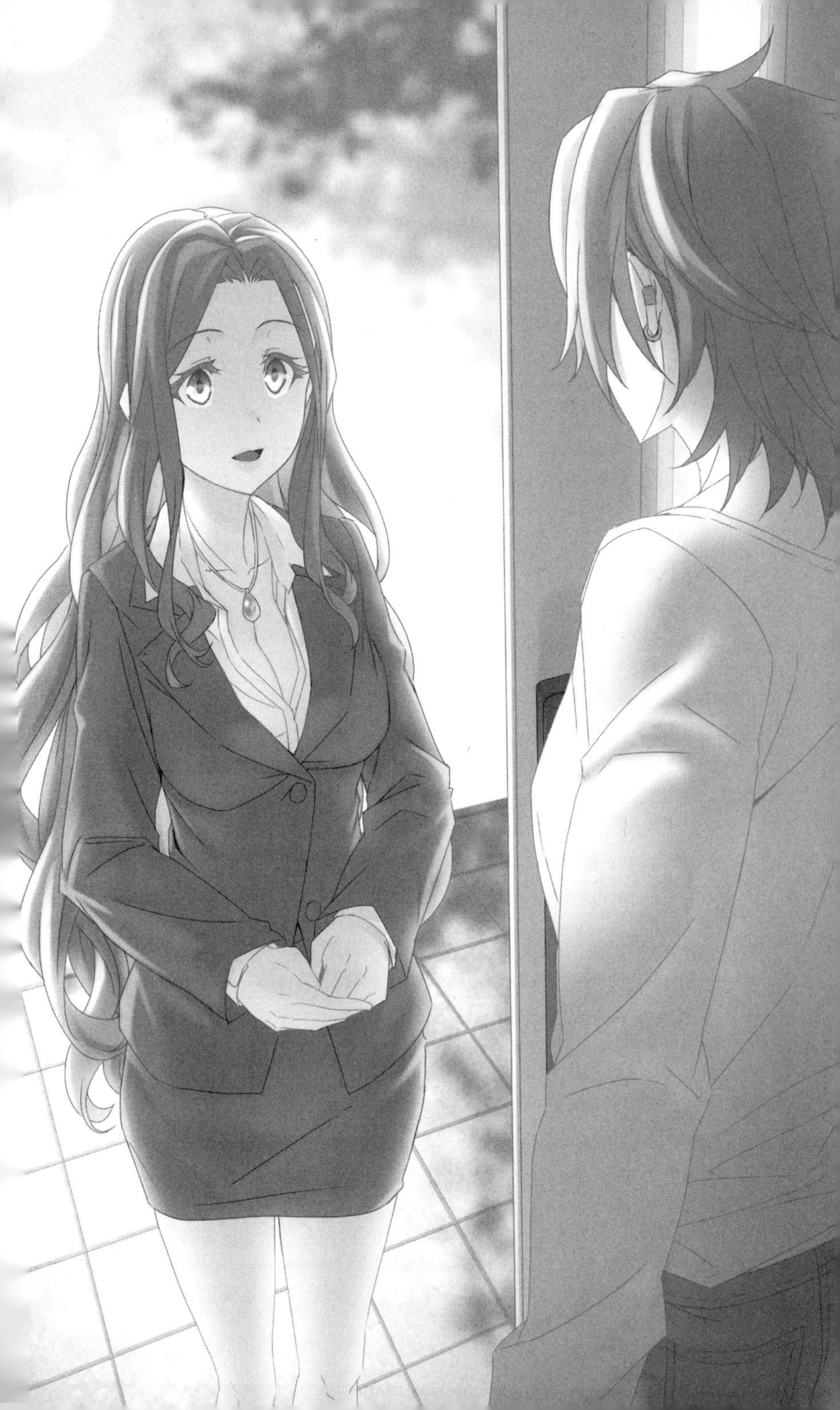

strips of shoe rubber I'd understood to be meat before this meal remotely compare.

While taking in this luxurious feast unlike anything I'd ever had, I stared hard at Marino. Meticulously upkept skin which perfectly concealed her age. Faintly wavy hair that made you want to run your fingers through it. Purple eyes that drooped down slightly, giving her a kind and gentle appearance.

"Is something wrong?"

I'd been too obvious. Marino Hanamura cocked her head in confusion as she questioned me.

However, I couldn't just say, *I can't believe there's an eroge character sitting in front of me* or *You don't look at all like you have a daughter old enough to teach in the Academy.* Seriously, beautiful older women were an eroge mainstay, but she still looked far too young. If she were wearing a uniform, she could have easily been mistaken for an Academy student.

"Oh, no, I'm just a bit starstruck to be sitting with a celebrity of the magic world like yourself…"

Deflecting with a random excuse would have to do for now. If this world lined up with the game, she was definitely a celebrity.

"My, my, no need to be so nervous. Besides, from now on, I'll need you to be much more relaxed with me."

I puzzled over her words, unsure what she was talking about.

Her eyes narrowed, and her face grew serious.

"Kousuke Takioto."

"Y-yes?"

I snapped to attention, feeling a subtle intensity hidden in her tone.

"I'll get straight to the point. I'm taking you in as my child."

"……?"

Um, what did she just say?

"You're going to be my child."

"…Huh?!"

What was going on? She wasn't making any sense. What was with these huge back-to-back developments?!

"Forgive me for not notifying you before moving forward, but parental custody has already been transferred over to me, per the Magic-User Guardianship Law."

Custody transfer? Now, hold on just a second. What the hell was she talking about? I'd just been wondering if I needed to transfer custody elsewhere or whether I needed to declare myself an independent, but to do that, I could simply go to city hall, get a residence certificate or whatever, and… Actually, just how did that stuff work in this world anyway?

Never mind, this wasn't the time to worry about that stuff. Marino Hanamura? Becoming my guardian? The Witch of Tsukuyomi?! Rumored to have blasted an S-Rank monster into dust all by herself?! The witch with lustrously smooth skin, who looked no older than the average college student, despite having an adult child of her own?! The character who had caused players to bombard the game's user support page in despair because she hadn't been given a route of her own?! The lady who never did end up getting the heroine treatment and never appeared in any of the extra events?!

"I hope we can get along."

"I—I hope so, too…?"

After that, she offered words of compassion to Kousuke Takioto for his continuous series of misfortunes. That said, it was me inside, not him. I didn't feel any hint of sadness in the slightest.

According to Marino Hanamura's explanation, she was a relative of my mother's—her cousin, to be precise. My maternal grandfather had promised to look after me, but my mother had apparently left her will with Marino, so she had ended up as my guardian. She would now be handling my school tuition and living expenses.

"You're going to be living at my place from now on. Do you have your things in order?"

"At your…house? Not the school dorms?!"

I couldn't stop myself from pointing out the absurdity.

Tsukuyomi Magic Academy was a government-funded educational institution for magic. Not only was it filled with talented students, but both the scions of the country's elite and their equals abroad came to study there. It was a prestigious institution, enough to make you wonder how a dunce like Kousuke Takioto had managed to get accepted there in the first place.

Since there were so many international students, the school needed on-campus dorms. In the game, that's where Kousuke Takioto lives. Not only that, but his room is right next to the protagonist's.

"Of course, you can live there if you want. It's just that we're going to be family now. My house is close to the school, but more than that, I want us to live together so we can get to know each other better."

…Hold up just a minute here. I was utterly confused from the get-go.

Not only did the whole *Becoming Kousuke Takioto* thing make no sense to begin with, but then I learned about his traumatic backstory missing from the game, and now I was going to be freeloading at the house of this beautiful witch?

What the hell was up with these eroge-style plot developments?

Well, actually, if this was the same world as in *MX*, then it was, in fact, an eroge world. However, I was nothing more than decorative support character—a nobody whom a stiff breeze could knock over. Yet here she was, requesting that I come live with her. Except, at her house…

"But you have a daughter, don't you? Won't she hate having me there…?"

Though still young, Marino Hanamura's daughter was a teacher at the Academy and a character that confers a very important skill to the protagonist in the game. Her backstory involves something about carrying on her dead father's research or something. Actually, if Marino was my mother's cousin, that made her daughter my second cousin.

"Besides—" I tried to continue, but Marino raised her hand to interrupt me.

"I do indeed have a daughter, but I made sure to get her approval on everything. Also, you don't have to be extra considerate about that stuff, okay?"

I mean, she says that, but… If I wasn't in the dorm, wouldn't that cut off the protagonist from advancing a bunch of story events down the line?

Naturally, I couldn't blurt that out. Seeing me conflicted over the situation, Marino gently shook her head.

"…You'll need some time to think this over. There's one thing I'd like you to keep in mind, though. You're always welcome with us."

She appeared to have misunderstood my concerns and was trying to be thoughtful. My real worries lay elsewhere, but I couldn't see any reason to correct her, so it was probably better to roll with it.

"My apologies."

"Oh, stop. What are you apologizing for? You don't need to be so considerate, and I won't stand for you acting so stiff and formal, got it? Now, the dorms don't open up until a week before class starts. That means it'll be two weeks from today until you can move in. We'll put this on hold in the meantime. I'd like you to decide between the dorms and my home before then."

"I understand."

"Also, whether you're living with me or not, I'd like to introduce you to my daughter."

I couldn't really argue with that. At the end of the day, I was going to have to introduce myself to her daughter, Hatsumi Hanamura, at some point. We were relatives, after all.

"When would be the best time for...? Um, I mean, when should I come over?"

Marino glared with displeasure but smiled as soon as I relaxed my speaking style.

"Whenever you're ready. You could come now if you'd like, but I'm assuming that's a bit too soon. Right, that reminds me. Wherever you decide to live, you can send your belongings to my house for now."

I nodded with understanding.

"I'll pay for the shipping costs when they arrive. I'll contact someone I know in the business, so when you're all set, just let me know, okay?"

Her statement made me realize something.

"By the way, I don't have your contact info... Not that I have a cell phone anyway, I guess."

When I was figuring out if I really was Kousuke Takioto or not, I looked around for a cell phone or a suspiciously similar substitute, but unfortunately, nothing came up. In the game, Kousuke and the protagonist exchange contact info, so I'd assumed he either had one already or had bought one prior to that event. Oh well. Once school started up, I would be able to use a different method of communication, which would end up getting used more than phones.

"Oh, right, I forgot. You haven't carried one since last year, have you?"

Let's see—by "last year," she must have meant when my parents died. The reason for their deaths was a mystery to me, but something must have happened to Kousuke.

"Let's go buy you one now."

"Oh, no, I don't really need a phone anyway."

Personally, I didn't feel the need for one. I didn't have anyone to get in touch with anyway.

Marino's shoulders dropped as she looked at me with pity.

"You got a phone call right before demons killed your parents, right? I know because I got one, too. I understand how traumatic that must have been for you."

"Hmm?!"

Just how miserable was this dude?! I really didn't have anything I could say to comfort him.

Now that I thought about it, Kousuke Takioto never picks up the phone when the protagonist calls him. He always claims he was asleep or something, but his absences must really come down to his trauma with phone calls. She said demons killed his parents, didn't she? That explains how ballistic he gets whenever the topic comes up.

"But it's better to carry something that can make a phone call in case of an emergency, so I'd like you to have one regardless. If anything happens, I'll come rushing over."

The sympathy was hard to bear. Honestly, it's downright abnormal for Kousuke Takioto to be such a class-clown character at school given his tragic circumstances. He must have some screws loose. I remembered him saying some truly shocking stuff every once in a while, but he probably couldn't help it with a backstory like that. Anyway.

"Um, you'll buy me one? I'll keep it on me…"

Marino looked at me with deep concern as she encouraged me:

"You don't have to push yourself too hard, okay?"

From my perspective, I wasn't pushing myself at all.

We headed straight for the mobile store after we finished eating, and I got myself a cell phone. Though I was taken aback when my new mother entered the store and immediately asked them to show her the most expensive model they had.

Shortly after this, we returned to my house, and I consulted with her about what I needed to do next. Did we need to immediately start preparing for the move, and did we need to handle the governmental paperwork? We thought things over, but I didn't expect her ultimate answer…

"Sorry, I'd really like to spend more time together, but I have some work to do…"

With that, she left, and I was alone.

If I were to defend her, I would insist that she must be plenty busy herself. That was understandable. She was the head of the Academy and an influential presence in the magic world, to boot.

That said, she did come to me with the bombshell news that she was my new mother, only to say the same day that she'd be busy with work, so we would be unable to see each other for a little while. Definitely a strange decision.

For me personally…it wasn't that big of a deal. Whether I'd been reborn into this body or we had simply swapped consciousnesses, Kousuke's misfortune didn't feel real to me.

But man, imagine being told after experiencing countless tragedies that you had a new mother and would need to move out, only to have her immediately rush off to work and leave you alone with your unfathomable anxieties.

Honestly, it was a miracle the in-game Kousuke Takioto didn't end up becoming a total shut-in. It was hard to believe this was the same character who is always saying things like *"For real?!"* and *"C'mon, man, give me a break,"* or even *"That chick's a total babe, right? Let's hit her up. You act like a thug, and I'll be the dashing hero who comes to save the day."*

"I really pity this guy…"

This was enough thinking about Kousuke Takioto, though. I had myself to worry about.

"You know…this is way too much, right?"

My new mother had left behind a thick envelope. A wad of bills peeked out of the top. Per Marino, this was supposed to be "one week's worth of living expenses." One thing was for sure—

"She's lost her grip on financial reality."

I took the bundle of bills out of the envelope. The amount of money in the wad would have been equivalent to several decades' worth of my own high school allowance. I could have ordered top-class sushi delivery for every meal and still have enough left over to buy a car.

Marino had smiled, insisting that I "go ahead and keep the change!" but how would I even manage that? Was I supposed to buy brand-name handbags and luxury watches or something? What other expensive goods were there…? I guess in this world, there were magic tools and the like.

"…Hold on now."

I had something absolutely extraordinary on my hands, didn't I?

Two things that ordinary people would die for yet could go their entire lives without obtaining—

Money and authority.

The wind seemed to be at my back, urging me onward as I aimed to become the strongest in the world.

Deciding to use the wad of cash I'd been given to power myself up, I immediately set to work. First, I needed to get a detailed handle on the current state of the game world and devise a plan.

"No way there's a game wiki or anything, right…? In that case…"

They never put out strategy guides for eroge, so the Internet was pretty much the only place you could find walkthrough information for them. Produced and financed solely by heroic volunteers from the player community, these wikis listed everything from dialogue choices in chats with the heroines to walkthroughs for each ending, all the way to enemy stats, item drop rates, and damage calculations.

"If I could at least have that spreadsheet… Oh well, I don't even know if I'd be able to use it here."

Using the wiki data as a reference, my spreadsheet housed detailed data I'd personally gathered as well as notes on the optimal leveling methods. It had everything from speedrun-related data to RNG manipulation tables, except, well, with the game becoming reality, I doubted any RNG manipulation was going to be happening. There was no way to return to the title screen.

"Though as it stands, my problem is more fundamental than any walkthrough data… In the game, I just had to press a button to use magic, but now I have to forcibly circulate my mana."

In which case, my first step would be to read this book and learn all the fundamentals of magic. I picked up the tome sitting close by.

Magic for Monkeys.

Making some tea, I sat back in my chair and continued quickly skimming through the book. Its pages contained everything from explanations on the concept of magic to basic spells and simple forms of practical enchantments. It was as if the book had been specifically written just for me.

"Let's see… It says here that 'strengthening one's mana can be accomplished via collecting magic particles and pushing one's magic to the limit.'"

In the game, your mana can go up or down even without using it up to its limits. You can raise your level, use special items, or improve it via equipment. Which of the two explanations was correct? What I needed to know more than anything else was whether everything this book said was true, or if things here remained faithful to the original game mechanics. Maybe both were correct.

"This'll need testing."

That would come later. For now, I continued reading to deepen my knowledge base so I could come up with the most efficient testing method.

After finishing the book, next came testing and experimentation. First, I decided to see for myself whether the book's information was true or not. I picked out a few spells that seemed like they would be harmless even if they were cast incorrectly and went out into the garden to give them a try.

It went about as I expected. Most of the enchantments gave me no trouble. However, I ran into a predictable roadblock with a select group of beginner spells.

"...Yup, I don't have any aptitude for emission magic..."

The in-game Kousuke Takioto isn't simply proficient at self-enhancement and mana donation skills, he's unparalleled with them. In exchange, however, he is almost entirely unable to use emission magic.

"*Water Gun.*"

Small balls of water materialized as soon as I cast the spell, but they moved very slowly and eventually succumbed to gravity. Needless to say, they completely missed their target and had almost no force behind them. If I worked hard at it, I might improve, but considering I'd do more damage enhancing myself and throwing a nearby rock, it didn't seem worth it. Maybe I could use the spell for cleaning if I had to. Just as I'd anticipated, my magic proficiencies were in line with the Kousuke-of-the-game's proficiencies.

"Phew."

Letting out a small sigh, I bit down on my scarf. Since becoming Kousuke Takioto, the more I learned about him, the more I came to understand the wonders of his signature accessory.

"I bet the length of his scarf helps him get the most out of his enhancement spells, huh?"

Taking his character traits into consideration, this could become my most powerful piece of equipment. The same way it is in the game.

"In that case, I should use this money to buy a new scarf. This current one is fine, but there's got to be something higher-quality out there."

Yup, that settled it. Was there anything else I wanted? Well, if I had to pick something else…it'd be books. My current lack of knowledge was staggering. Though on the book front, I actually had someone who would get me them for free. Rather, I'd *just* met someone who would.

"I'll ask Marino for a few."

I imagined she'd be willing to lend me some books.

However, it was best if I saved the shopping and the books for a later date. Time was of the essence. That meant what I needed to do now was…

"Practice my enchant and enhance magic."

Returning to my room, I rummaged through my dresser. After picking out and changing into running clothes, I used a tablet to check the map of the area surrounding my house. When I exited, I activated my enhance magic and took off in a sprint.

I was very fortunate to have a big park close to home. In a similar stroke of good luck, it had a runner's path as well. With many streetlights along the path to accommodate late-night runners, it made for a pleasant running location.

Still, the people running by must have wondered what was up with me. In fact, the person I'd just passed did a double take. If I were in his position, I probably would have done the same.

Cutting through the wind, I was darting at close to twice the speed of everyone else. My pace was a product of my enhance magic. At my current rate, I could have shattered any of Earth's short-distance running records with ease.

That wasn't the only thing drawing people's attention, though. I could see them staring hard at my scarf flowing in the wind behind me.

They must be looking at me and thinking, *Why's he wearing a scarf while running?* If this were the Tokyo Marathon, with all the participants dressed up in costumes, they probably wouldn't have batted an eye. Despite the strangeness of my getup, I was wearing the scarf for an important reason.

As I ran, I sent mana through my scarf. It suddenly went from flapping in the wind to a stiff standstill, hardened like a sheet of iron.

Enchantment—the magic Kousuke Takioto is most skilled with. Through furnishing his scarf with a colossal amount of mana, he is able to move it at will, as if it is a part of his own body. In the game, these skills are called Third Hand and Fourth Hand.

Not only is his scarf highly versatile, he can even alter its fundamental properties with mana. He can make it as hard as iron and use it as a shield, or if he enchants it with water, it can become a small, fire-repelling wall. Additionally, since he moves it just as easily as his arms and legs, he can hold a sword in each of its ends on top of both of his hands, allowing him to use a four-blade style of combat. Plus, by enchanting it with ice, he can get through the summer months without needing any air conditioning. What a fantastic ability.

The game version of Kousuke Takioto is able to move this scarf at will, using it to block or parry his opponents' strikes. These skills would be vital if I wanted to improve my close-quarter combat abilities. By the end of the game, he grows to be able to employ them at will, but I needed to reach that same level of proficiency myself.

I wondered how long I had run. I got the feeling it had been about three miles, but I wasn't fatigued at all, which I assumed was an effect of the enhance magic. At this rate, I could see myself running ten times that distance without issue.

I wound down my run as these questions about my seemingly limitless amount of stamina weighed on my mind. My mana reserves were clearly the same as Kousuke Takioto's in the game. Despite using so much of it, neither the enhancement spells I'd used on myself nor the magic I'd placed on my scarf had come close to using it all up.

"I'd like to know my limits... Actually, if I don't, I won't know the conditions I need to meet to increase my mana."

Normal usage wasn't nearly enough to quickly drain me of all my mana. I needed an efficient way to dry it all up. Speaking of mana, was there any magic that could quantify and show me my stats? That would really help me out.

"Oh well, I just gotta do what I can."

For now, I guess I'd practice my enchant magic.

After doing some digging, I discovered that cloth crafted from monster materials was the easiest to enchant and the most magically conductive. When you factored in the feel of the material on your skin, the options grew really limited.

Scanning all the enchanted tools in the area, I let out a sigh.

The magical tool general store had a large number of products. However, if you asked me if I actually wanted any of it, the answer would be no. But don't get me wrong, that was only because I was after something so unique.

"Hmmm, a thirteen-foot shawl, you say? We don't have anything *that* long, I'm afraid…especially at this time of year. Once you get to that sort of size, it might be better to just buy the fabric yourself."

I'd expected as much. A normal scarf or stole would have been considered long already at six feet. Something more than twice the length was guaranteed to drag down on the ground.

"That's a good point," I said.

After being directed toward the handicraft area, I went over and heaved another sigh.

I picked up a piece of pure-white fabric. Next to it was a gray fabric, and beside that were blacks, reds, and yellows. All of it was simple, plain cloth. The more magically conductive a fabric, the more limited the color options, and the higher the price.

"I guess I'll go with this one for now."

After much deliberation, I bought two pieces of all-red cloth. It had been woven with thread taken from monsters. The two pieces together cost about as much as I would have received from twenty years of my old student allowance. I prayed that its quality would match its price.

Returning home, I immediately took out the purchased fabric and wrapped it around my neck. Then I stood up to check how well it sat on my shoulders.

"Thirteen feet might be too long after all…but it conducts mana unbelievably well. Arachne thread lives up to its reputation."

I could simply trim the length down later. The conductivity was fantastic, so I really had no complaints. There was, however, one slight drawback…

"If I stop supplying it with mana, it really drags down on the ground. It would probably get caught on something, too. I've got to think up a way to counteract that…"

Deciding I would worry about it later, I shelved the question and shot mana through the fabric. Then I began training to move independently from the shawl.

However, it proved more difficult than it had been with my old scarf.

Was it too long? I wasn't able to move it around as easily as I had been with my previous scarf. If the surface area was the issue, I didn't have many options, since it was over twice the length and width of the old one. Although in the long run, it was probably better if I used something large and long like this.

"Just have to train with it, I guess…"

I immediately changed into my running clothes and wrapped the fabric around my neck as I had with my scarf. Then I began training to move the stole freely while I ran.

Running along, I circulated my mana and moved the fabric. Using Third Hand on the right side of the stole, I made a forty-five-degree slash, while simultaneously making a sweeping motion with Fourth Hand on the left side.

My goal was to make it possible to easily move each end of the fabric as I attacked with both my arms and legs. In the game, Fourth Hand and Third Hand aren't available right from the start. Once Kousuke explains that he *"got used to moving them around,"* the skills unlock for him to use. By the endgame, he's a regular Asura demigod with this four-sword style. Unfortunately, due to his special circumstances as the protagonist's best friend, he's still resigned to being an ill-defined character.

At any rate, I needed to get comfortable with this ability fast. Before starting school, if possible, and before I moved into the Hanamura house.

If I couldn't get a handle on it, Kousuke Takioto would have trouble during his mock battles against the heroines. Though, if things progressed as they do in-game, I was supposed to lose all those battles anyway.

On the other hand, I was planning on smashing through all those event flags anyway, so it was possible I could basically not fight at all.

"I still need lots and lots of practice…"

Finishing my light convenience store meal, I focused my training next on circulating mana through the fabric while I ran. After I was done, I read the magic textbooks in my room, and as I drilled the information into my brain, I considered my next move.

"Looks like the best place to start is leveling up and getting more skills."

My reading made it clear that this world had a level system just as it does in the game. Overall level, constitution level, magic level, resistance level, stealth level, and more. All of these categories except for overall level were divided up even further, but it would be impossible for me to cover them all, as there were nearly twice as many level types as there are in the game. The presence of these detailed subdivisions apparently hadn't actually been confirmed; their existence was all just a supposition based on a tepid research hypothesis that essentially went, *Hey, you know, they're probably there?* The only thing they knew for sure was that there was a broad range of level types out there.

How did they know that for sure? Thanks to a magical implement, you could roughly confirm your levels. However, this tool wasn't something you could easily get your hands on, and it didn't appear to be widely used.

As I pondered levels, I heard the doorbell. I kept my magic circulation going as I headed for the entryway.

"Hee-hee, I finally finished work."

There stood Marino Hanamura, greeting me for the first time in several days. I invited her inside and didn't hesitate a moment before following.

"Do you always do this, Kousuke?" Marino asked, grabbing the fabric I was filling with mana. It felt a bit like I was a dog being led on a leash by my owner.

She stroked the stole. It no longer felt like fabric, though. Teeming with magic, it was hard as steel, and I could move it around independently.

"Not always. Recently, I've being keeping it up constantly as a form of training, though."

"...Your enhance magic and mana pool are quite abnormal, huh?"

I nodded.

Frankly speaking, Kousuke Takioto is the party member with the greatest amount of mana in the game. More than double the amount the main heroines who fire off powerful ranged magic attacks nonstop have. Of course, if you were to go back through on New Game+ and feed characters stat power-up items like candy, any character could reach that amount.

With his vast reserve of mana, it would be easy to assume Kousuke

Takioto can wantonly fire off magic nonstop from a distance, but that isn't the case. Mainly focused on close-quarters combat, he's unable to use area of effect magic. He's a very strange and unique character, the kind you don't usually see in other games.

However, his mana pool is vital to his success in combat. The game handicaps him by tying any of the actions he can take to burning mana. He consumes mana even when he isn't using magic to attack. In this way, his design is unique because he has more mana than anyone else yet still finds that amount insufficient. However, with his outstanding Third Hand and Fourth Hand skills, you could say he's an advanced-level character, quite effective when used properly.

Now that I thought about it, all his actions cost mana because his Third Hand and Fourth Hand require a constant supply of it. The very skills I had been practicing.

Though I imagined him as continually exhausted and out of resources in the game, I didn't get that same impression from using his skills in real life. It could be because I was doing everything under normal circumstances. Maybe the tense atmosphere of real battle changes things. I would need to investigate this possibility later on.

"If you could master this...that would be incredible. Focus on defense, and you could turn the stole into a multi-foot steel shield; focus on offense, and you would have enough power to split boulders in two."

On top of that, I could equip each Hand with weapons or protective gear, and I could enchant those with a variety of different elements, too.

There were, in fact, several other game characters who possessed similarly strange characteristics. Of course, their unique qualities varied slightly from Kousuke Takioto's.

"Can you put more mana into this? Or maybe you could stretch it out into a shield?"

In response, I sent even more mana into the scarf. Then I altered the fabric's shape, fanning it out.

Marino touched the cloth and gasped in admiration.

"This could even stop my magic to some degree... But instead of spreading it out, what if you tried to make it as rounded as possible?"

"What do you mean?"

"This shape won't be able to dampen the impact from a strong attack. Not only that, but if you're attacked in the same area over and over again, it'll eventually break. You should make it rounded to try and deflect attacks away instead."

It's true that many of the shields you saw in games were arched in some way, but I didn't realize that was to help deflect attacks. However, it might be an even better idea to add hooks to the scarf so that it could catch enemy swords. On the other hand, if they struck with too much force, I could get overpowered and be sent flying, so maybe it was better to deflect their blows instead? Depended on the battle, I suppose.

"How long can you keep this up for?"

"I'm at ten hours at this point, I think? My goal was to aim for the full twenty-four, though…"

That being said, I'd only been keeping it up during my normal, everyday life. Adventuring and fighting would certainly give me other situations to use my mana, too.

Marino gave an exasperated sigh.

"Your enchant skills and mana pool might have me beat."

"Maybe that's true, but I can't use emission magic to save my life…"

"Hee-hee, then you'll just have to find yourself a good party at the Academy as soon as you can. Even the deepest level of the Academy Dungeon shouldn't be too difficult for you."

Marino was right to emphasize the importance of a good party. Still, there would be times I would have to fight solo, so I needed to think of ways to cover my weaknesses if worse came to worst.

"I hope so anyway…"

There was another problem with parties—who would be willing to join me?

"What's wrong?"

"Oh, no, just wondering if I'll be able to get party members together or not."

Joining up with the protagonist would be a surefire way to get strong allies. I wasn't sure how good an idea that was if I was ultimately going to overthrow him, though.

But maybe that was the best course of action. I'd beef up the protagonist a bit and have him defeat the Demon Lord. In the game, both the battle with the Demon Lord and the dungeon crawl to reach him are total slogs.

In any case, I had room to experiment. If the protagonist looked like he would grow stronger even without me around, that meant solo training would be an option. Then all that was left would be getting a group of promising party members together. I'd be able to find some…right?

Marino grinned. "I'm sure you'll be just fine."

My move into the Hanamura residence was the most fortunate moment of my life. It wasn't because Marino Hanamura was a beautiful woman who looked young enough to be in high school. Well, I couldn't say that wasn't part of it, nor could I deny that I got a little excited whenever she touched me.

No, the actual reason was that now I would be able to pick the brain of the Witch of Tsukuyomi, a titan of the magic world.

"So using magic increases one's mana pool after all, then."

"Yes, I believe the constant magic enchantment you've been doing is the most effective method of widening it. Though I don't think anyone else besides you could handle it."

An average magic-user would use up all their mana immediately if they tried using magic like I did. I was only able to manage thanks to my ridiculous amount of mana and my aptitude for enchant magic.

"But seriously, you're quite the hard worker, Kousuke."

"Really?"

Marino prefaced her next statement by admitting that she wasn't really one to talk, then added:

"You're always so focused on magic."

She chuckled. Her tone sounded half-teasing, half-exasperated.

"You think so?"

"I do. You don't need push yourself so hard, okay?"

Apparently, she hadn't been irritated or fooling around but genuinely concerned for my well-being. Still, from what I knew of my limits, I was nowhere near them.

"I'm not really working too hard. Magic's just fun."

I was simply fixated on how entertaining it was. The same thing had happened back in Japan, too. I'd get caught up in a good book, get hooked on a video game late into the night, or play soccer until the sun went down. It was easy to concentrate on something you enjoyed doing.

"Right, well, if you have any questions, feel free to ask me, okay?"

I had every intention of doing that.

"Okay, now that we've got that out of the way..."

She then launched into an hour-long lecture on magic as we rocked back and forth inside the spell-powered car. Upon arriving at our first stop—

"We're going to have to part ways for a little bit. Sorry my work is getting in the way."

—Marino apologized. She told me that she absolutely had to meet with someone today, so she wanted me to wait for her a little while.

"No, not at all. If anything, I'm the one who's getting in the way here."

Clothes, food, and a place to sleep—I would be relying on her for all my needs from this day forward, all without earning any money myself. There was also this stole of mine. She'd sewn my piece of fabric into a proper stole for me. You're telling me she could sew on top of everything else? Just how talented was this lady?

Marino's youthful features loosened into a smile. Then she extended her hand and gave me a gentle flick on the forehead.

"You're family! Get in the way as much as you want!"

"Well, you're just as much family, too, so the same goes for you."

At these words, she pouted with bashful delight before her puffed-out cheeks dissolved into a grin. *Someone, anyone, please tell me just how old this woman is supposed to be.*

After parting ways with the ridiculously cheery Marino, I trekked down an unfamiliar road, following wherever my feet took me.

"Five hours... What should I do until then?"

The city I was currently in served as a port that connected different countries of the world, so it was filled to the brim with races from all over. There were elves with slightly pointed ears and people with animal ears you just wanted to reach out and touch.

With all these people visiting from abroad, the development of a gift shop and souvenir trade was inevitable. Here in Wakoku, Kousuke Takioto's home country, magic was especially well-developed, so many customers came to buy magic tools here. There were plenty of places I could find to kill some time.

I saw a variety of enchanted tools at the magic catalyst store I decided to visit, from wooden and iron rods to staffs made out of some strange metal called mithril. There were catalysts in the shape of books, along with bracelet and ring types. The tome-shaped magic catalysts appeared to have a magic jewel set on each cover, and they were bizarrely thick and heavy, too. Other intriguing items included a catalyst shaped like a parasol and another shaped like a lollipop.

Browsing all these weapons made me suddenly consider which one I wanted to use in the future. In the game, Kousuke Takioto fights with a sword and shield. Since he's a frontline combatant inept at using long-range skills, he clashes with monsters like a hotheaded idiot, always charging straight at any enemy he sees.

His exclusive skills Third Hand and Fourth Hand were compatible with almost any close-ranged weapon. In that case, what equipment was Kousuke Takioto best suited for?

Most of the gentlemen frequenting the game's wiki concurred that it was best to make him abandon offense and specialize in defense.

A shield in his right hand, a shield in his left hand, a shield in his Third Hand, and a shield in his Fourth. Kousuke Takioto's offensive power is a little lacking, especially since he doesn't have a unique weapon. Naturally, he would pack quite the offensive punch if he was equipped with a sword in each of his four hands, but in exchange, his defense would go straight down the drain. In that case, the players reckoned, why not turn Kousuke into a wall and make him single-handedly take on every attack?

When he initially learns Third Hand, his defense is practically impenetrable. Since monsters focus mostly on physical attacks at that point, many players use him to get through that part of the game.

However, his dominance as a tank is short-lived. Around the early midgame, an Overpowered Tank Heroine and a Zombie Heroine show up to take over his role. Kousuke Takioto's power is roughly on par with Overpowered Tank Heroine's. Despite that, she has access to easily obtainable, unbelievably powerful equipment, which Kousuke Takioto lacks. Not only that, but she has the most important factor for any eroge character. A trait that would be forever out of Kousuke Takioto's reach. That's right—

—Overpowered Tank Girl is extremely cute.

Unbelievably cute.

I bet all the players asked themselves, *Why should I use this skeevy comic relief dude instead?*

It would be fair to say that Kousuke Takioto is destined for the bench. I had done exactly that myself. Also, given his bizarrely powerful enchant magic, many players end up leaving him behind in the Magical Instrument Development Lab. Having him there drastically increases the lab's production speed. However, a character doesn't grow much when you leave them there, so they don't gain any levels. Ultimately, this results in players assigning him to the Magical Instrument Development Lab for the entirety of the game, forever barred from the battlefield.

The character of Kousuke Takioto himself says that he wants to grow stronger and defeat monsters. Yet in the end, the omnipotent player usurps his freedom, forcing him to devote all his time to developing magical tools in the lab. It's like he's a wage slave at a toxic company, really. Despite his usefulness, the protagonist and the heroines treat him like a total idiot in the story. Truly a pitiful young man. And after the miserable and tragic life he's led, too.

"Sir, is there something wrong?"

The brown-haired staff's concern told me that the heartrending sadness of Kousuke Takioto's circumstances had shown on my face.

I should save these thoughts for somewhere else.

My meetup spot with Marino was at a hotel with a name I had become very familiar with.

"Hanamura Hotel…"

The silver building loomed over me. It dwarfed the surrounding buildings, towering over the area. Built with a wealthy clientele in mind, the hotel was both dazzling and modern yet struck a harmonious balance with its surroundings. I wondered how much it cost just to maintain the beautiful garden beside it.

"The Hanamura Group, huh?"

The Hanamura Group was a major player in the spheres of magic and politics, and the voice of president Ryuuen Hanamura held significant sway in many different countries. I could have sworn that Marino Hanamura had once left the family, but based on the fact that she still used the Hanamura name, she was clearly still a member. She practically carried the whole magic world on her shoulders; not only was her skill in spellcraft without question, but she also had connections and enormous wealth.

And now I had become Marino's son. My actual mother had been a member of the Hanamura family as well, though I still didn't know much about her. This was true both in the game and in my current reality. I could at least surmise that she'd fled from the Hanamura family, or something along those lines.

"…I still have some time; might as well hit up a café."

The moment I mumbled these words and turned around, it happened.

The brilliant flash of light was the first thing to reach my five senses. Not even a second later came the deafening concussive blast. A gust of hot air scorched my skin. Black smoke and a burning smell filled the air, and the area descended into chaos. People ran out of the black smoke, trying to escape, their screams resounding through the streets. As flames rose up from the building, I couldn't do anything but stare in awe.

A nearby restaurant had exploded, from the looks of it.

People swarmed out of the restaurant, everyone struggling to get out first. Some were holding arms that had gone limp while others were using another person's shoulder for support. One individual was covering their mouth with a handkerchief. I had to do something, but right when I tore my gaze away from the building, someone caught my eye.

"…What's up with him?"

Amid all the people fleeing, their faces twisted with fear, one man showed no emotions. That was already plenty strange enough, but he didn't look around at all, either, appearing completely calm and collected.

His movements were just as strange as his lack of expression. Instead of going to the corner where all the other people had taken refuge, he was scurrying toward the hotel as if he had some objective in mind.

Panicked citizens were also fighting to get outside the same Hanamura Hotel that Marino and I had booked for the night. They stared, bewildered, from the café next door, some of them grabbing their phones to start a call, while others opted to use their phones to take videos of the burning scenery.

As people streamed out of the hotel doors, the expressionless man made his way inside. I covertly followed behind him.

The inside of the hotel was bedlam. Both the guests and the staff were in disarray, with incensed shouts and the wails of children echoing all around. The man completely ignored the chaos, continuing on for several minutes before coming to a halt.

In front of the man was a door, beside which stood a red-haired man dressed a suit. They started muttering something to each other, but their voices were too low for me to make out anything they were saying.

I heard the sound of the red-haired man clicking his tongue in frustration. He continued conversing with the suspicious and expressionless man, but soon after, he opened the door for them to both go inside. I quietly slipped in after them.

They'd entered a large room. There must have been a big buffet dinner of some kind going on. Recently abandoned food and plates still sat on top of the many tables that had been laid out. Now much of that food had been cruelly scattered on the floor, staining the expensive-looking carpet. Several men in suits also seemed to be crowding around something.

Darting to an adjacent table, I lifted up the tablecloth and hid myself underneath it. Then I strained my ears to listen.

"You traitor!"

It sounded like the incensed voice of a young girl reprimanding someone. As I listened to her endless stream of abuse—she was calling them worthless human beings, totally ungrateful, and the like—I lifted up the tablecloth. There, I saw a girl surrounded by the men in suits and gulped...

The men in suits had encircled three people. A pointy-eared handsome elf man and another pointy-eared elf girl stood with weapons in their hands in front of a third girl, trying to shield her.

Wait, that girl they were protecting...

...she was one of the game's main heroines!

She had long golden hair and green eyes. Her brow was furrowed, and her lightly pointed ears quivered in anger. There was no mistaking her.

That elf was Ludivine Marie-Ange de la Tréfle, the ultimate main heroine who was featured on the game packaging and always ranked near the top of every character survey!

Due to her lengthy, hard-to-remember name, her friends and the players all called her Ludie.

However, for those stricken with Ludie Syndrome—the ability to derive unique pleasure from her constant verbal abuse—being able to say her whole name was a badge of honor. Naturally, I'd memorized her whole name, and I could even say the full official name of a certain thorny, flat-chested, and pink-haired main character from a popular light novel series from years past. Now that I thought about it, why was I so skilled at remembering overly long character names but awful at memorizing things for school?

Now then, what type of heroine was Ludie?

In the original game, she has a fear of men, or more accurately, a fear of humans in general. She is usually aloof and speaks harshly to others, particularly when conversing with men. As such, when you get close to her, she angrily demands that you get away from her. However, she's only like that in the beginning. After a certain in-game event, her attitude does a complete one-eighty, and she starts dating you.

Not only does she become clingy and affectionate, but she also grows super devoted to the player character.

Although, to get to that point, you need to trigger a special event and resolve an incident for her.

Also, she still treats all men besides the protagonist cruelly even if the player gets that event, and she regards Kousuke Takioto in particular as less than dirt. This attitude only seemed to spur on the players' possessiveness, however, because she was unbelievably popular. In later patches, the number of available heroines more than doubled from the original twelve, but that still didn't so much as dent her popularity.

What was Ludie's reason for hating men so much, you ask? I might have been watching the very origin of that hatred playing out before me.

The cornered elves had strange-looking guns pointed at them. The expressionless man from the café joined the group and trained his own gun on the trio.

"Milady, you've got it all wrong. I haven't betrayed you at all. I've always been on this side of things, see?" replied a bald-headed man to Ludie's accusation. He'd apparently been working for her. She clenched her teeth, and her face contorted in anger. Even as the men slowly backed her up against the wall, the fire in her eyes showed no signs of snuffing out.

Seeing her now, I was reminded of a post written on the developers' blog: *We had a very good reason behind why Ludie hated men so much. But if we had gone with that backstory, she wouldn't have been a virgin. Then the higher-ups came to us and said, "If you do that, we're going to get enough angry letters to cover Mt. Fuji. You absolutely, no matter what, come hell or high water, have to make her a virgin. I don't care if you die and get reincarnated, you get teleported to an alternate dimension, or if some evil god possesses you, you have to make sure she's a virgin" lol. Well, a lot happened before we shipped, and she ended up being a virgin in the final build of the game anyway, lol.*

Given the content of that post, the scenario writer had clearly come up with a character backstory that would have incited rage from the player base.

Additionally, the events of Ludie's past, revealed to the player after they befriend her, lined up with the situation in front of me. The image of Ludie tearfully revealing that she had been betrayed by someone whom she had confided in had been seared into my brain. That exact moment was playing out right before me.

Now then, what was I supposed to do?

If I saved her here, it could have a substantial effect on the story. The organization opposing her appears as a major enemy throughout much of the early to midgame, but those events might not trigger anymore. Still, though, was I just supposed to let this happen?

Okay, hold on a second. First of all—before taking any of that into account—was I even strong enough to save her?

Could my current equipment defend against these men and their unfamiliar weapons? All I had on me was a stole and my backup scarf. If those guns could pierce through my stole, then...

Not only that, but I hadn't ever been in a real battle before—could I even help? The closest thing to fighting experience I had was grade school judo, and outside that, I was totally clueless. Could a guy like me save her?

Furthermore, if things here played out as they do in the game, Marino was supposed to be the one to save Ludie. Not me. The in-game dialogue made that perfectly clear.

If butting in now would make the situation worse, that would give Marino more to deal with at best and could lead straight to a bad ending at worst. The smartest move here was to turn around like I'd never seen a thing.

"Why don't you just give up?" the bald man barked at Ludie. Instead, she shook her head.

"I have Claris on my side! We may be at a disadvantage, but the longer this gets drawn out, the more the tides will turn against you!"

She must have been referring to the woman standing diagonally in front of her, sword in hand. I didn't remember seeing her in the game. The bald man glanced over to Claris before shrugging his shoulders.

"Oh, no, you don't think we came here without a plan, do you?"

"What is that supposed to...? Huh?!"

The moment the bald man spoke, something passed in front of Ludie, and Claris collapsed to the ground.

It was the handsome elf standing next to Claris, who had appeared to be on Ludie's side of the situation. Claris lay clenching her stomach, having sustained a punch to the gut. The elf man then drove his foot into her.

"Aaaugghh!"

He slammed his foot into her again and again. Each time he did, Claris's face twisted in anguish, and she let out a muffled scream.

"No, this can't be. No...not you, too, Aurelien."

Recoiling from the betrayal, the previously haughty confidence drained from Ludie's face. She now looked on the verge of tears. Even from my hiding spot, I could tell how much her arms and legs were shaking as she pulled back despite having nowhere left to run.

Legs hitting the wall, she looked behind her. She realized she had no path of escape left.

"Heh-heh-heh, bwa-ha-ha-ha-ha-ha!"

Aurelien cackled loudly as he watched her struggle. Gripping his stomach as he laughed, he seemed thoroughly amused, almost unhinged.

"That's the look I wanted to see! *Ha-ha*, why do you think I put up with years of your bratty entitlement? It was all for this moment. It was worth it, too!"

As Ludie's expression twisted into pure despair, she erratically shook her head like a doll about to run out of batteries.

The bald man and his comrades slowly took a step forward while keeping their guns trained on her.

"Whoa, whoa now, don't shoot her yet. I wanna have some fun before killing her," Aurelien warned, grinning widely. All the nearby men except for the bald one gave a small cheer of delight.

I took my backup scarf and wrapped it all around my head to conceal my face, then adjusted it slightly to secure my line of sight. I sent enhancement magic surging through my scarf, my stole, and the rest of my clothes.

The bald man's group slowly crept forward. Aurelien grinned.

At about thirty feet away, I could see a line of tears streaming from one of Ludie's eyes. Then, from the other eye, I saw a droplet fall to the floor.

It was a strange feeling. My brain was ready to boil over in rage, but somehow, my thoughts were clear as day. I know it seems contradictory, but I have no other way to describe the feeling.

Now it was go time.

Considerations like, *It's dangerous, so I should pretend I didn't see anything*, or *I can't save her because the story will change*, had been completely erased from my mind.

Aurelien kicked Claris aside and began making long strides toward Ludie. The moment he reached out a hand toward her, I rushed at him.

I aimed for the bald man right in front of me. Lifting up a table within reach using my Third Hand, I chucked it directly to where he was standing. The glass dinnerware sitting atop the table shattered just as Aurelien ripped up Ludie's skirt. With their attention on her body, the men were slow to respond to the airborne table.

Several of them were sent flying. Running over to Ludie's position, I immediately grabbed another table with my Fourth Hand, then hurled it to where all the men had clumped up together.

"Who are y—? Aaaaugh!"

One of them was knocked back mid-shout. As I ran, I picked Claris off the ground with my Third Hand before shifting her into my arms. Without a second to spare, I hardened my Third Hand and repelled the bullets speeding toward me.

"*Hrng!*"

A shock resounded through my head. Intense pressure seized my neck.

I hadn't been able to fully repel their attacks. Despite my Third Hand completely negating most of the assault, one of the bullets had bludgeoned me in the head.

I'm glad I wrapped my head up with my scarf...

I immediately regained my balance and charged toward Aurelien. Brandishing my Fourth Hand high above the dumbfounded elf, I smacked it across his cheek as hard as I could, fully intending to pound him into dust.

"Gaaaugh!"

I quickly spread my Fourth Hand and Third Hand out wide, and shifting Claris to one hand, I picked up Ludie with the other. Then, after expanding my stole to safely cloak the three of us, I sent a massive amount of mana through the fabric to fully harden it.

Bullets pelted my stole like hail. I could hear the sound of them making contact, but it didn't move an inch. It wouldn't get torn apart anytime soon. That said, this was a clear stalemate. I turned my focus from the stole toward the two elven girls.

Ludie still seemed confused, staring at me dumbfounded. On the other hand, Claris was conscious but severely wounded.

Now that these two were in my arms, what options did I have left? I was already anxious enough on my own.

"Hey, can you use healing magic?" I asked Ludie in my right arm, who flinched in surprise before shaking her head.

"Dang..."

I'd figured as much. She specializes in long-range offensive magic, so she normally shouldn't be able to use healing magic. Neither could I, of course. In a normal playthrough, around midgame, you'll get items by clearing certain events, which can allow both Ludie and me to learn healing spells, but wishing for those now wouldn't get me anywhere.

While pondering my next move, I felt a slight heat on my back.

"Whoa, whoa, give me a break here..."

Now they were resorting to fire magic. My stole shield seemed to be holding out, but I wanted to put a stop to their assault as soon as possible. Getting pelted with attacks like this was risky, and I wasn't even sure how strong this stole shield was in the first place.

Considering the situation, though, risking it all on my stole was the only real option.

There was a chance it would be able to ward off every attack my opponents could throw at it. However, if I kept this up and devoted everything to defense, it'd be all over when my mana ran out. While it seemed like I had plenty left in the tank, without it, this fabric was normal fabric, and I'd be totally useless.

Nevertheless, I couldn't go on the offensive, either.

"…I didn't take this shortcoming into account. What the heck am I supposed to do here?"

My thoughts leaked out in a whisper. Having shaped my stole into a dome to cover us, I'd completely obscured our surroundings.

The stole wall was certainly sturdy. However, by extending it out to shield us, I had cut off our entire line of sight. It was as if a pitch-black umbrella had been opened up right in front of us. If only it had been a see-through plastic umbrella, then we wouldn't have had a problem.

Ah, that's it! By that same token, this meant our enemies didn't know what we were doing, either. It was the perfect opportunity to come up with a plan. If I could just prepare something to try and catch them off guard…

But what was that supposed to look like? Regardless of whatever plan I could come up with, the only magic in my arsenal was using my stole for Third Hand and Fourth Hand. I hadn't really practiced anything else. If I wanted to smash them, I would either need to get in close or find something to throw at them. If I did that, though…

When I turned away from my stole to look at the two women in my arms, Ludie met my gaze with an anxious stare of her own.

Going on the offensive here would put them in danger. If I kept my stole shield active here, that wouldn't be a problem, but… Wait, hold on a second—

Grabbing her tightly, I lightly shook Claris.

"Hey, you, I need your help."

"*Nnngh…ngh…*"

If Claris was able to cast defensive magic, then that changed everything. Just having her protecting Ludie would be enough to leave them here momentarily while I switched to the offensive.

Still wincing in pain, she slowly opened her mouth.

"*Ugh… Who, are you…?*"

I couldn't stop myself from clicking my tongue in annoyance. There wasn't any time to get into that stuff. What if they fired their magic at me all at once and my shield gave out? Or attacked us some other way? The nasty images popping up in the back of my mind exacerbated my frustration.

"No time for introductions. Just tell me yes or no. Can you use any magic that can protect yourselves from those guys behind me?"

"...*Augh!*"

She trembled violently, and an agonized look came over her. She appeared to have broken some bones. I regretted that I'd shaken her so carelessly, but it was too late for that.

"Claris!"

Ludie turned anxiously to Claris, who gazed at Ludie as she spoke:

"I think, I can...manage. But I...won't last...long..."

"I'm leaving it in your hands, then. I'll need you play dead while you're using your magic."

Then I turned to Ludie.

"You're going to act like you're preparing a defensive spell by charging your mana and pretending to cast Aegis. Shout the incantation out. Don't actually cast it, though. You're going to use...some sort of attention-grabber instead."

Ludie tore her eyes away from Claris and stared at me with concern.

"An attention...grabber?"

"That's right. You can use Flash, right? Light will work, too. I want to surprise them. I'll handle the rest."

I felt bad, but these two were going to be my decoys. Right now, the assailants' primary concern was offing Ludie and Claris—not the sudden arrival of Kousuke Takioto.

In which case, they were sure to aim straight for the girls in front of them. I assumed some would come my way, but not too many to handle.

Then, while Ludie convinced them she was using shield magic, she would cast a spell to grab their attention. All I could do was pray everything would go down smoothly.

"Okay, let's do it. Claris, you use shield magic the moment I leave. Then Ludie, you pretend like you're the one casting it, and once their first barrage lets up, you cast some sort of light spell or whatever to blind them for a moment for me. Got it? Sorry, but we don't have time to waste. Ten seconds."

As soon as I finished my explanation, Claris leaped into action. I could hear her grumbling about something and could tell she was charging her mana.

"Ten, nine, eight…"

Ludie also began preparing her incantation.

"Seven, six, five."

Meanwhile, I began my own preparations to diffuse and alter the mana in my stole. Claris then lay down on the ground to play dead.

"Four, three, two."

I grabbed Ludie's arm to help her stand up. Then—

"One! Ludie, get up! Shield magic, now!"

The moment I forced Ludie to her feet, her voice boomed:

"Aegis!"

Just as the light element shield magic went up, I removed the enchantment from my stole. The men had spread out so that they were no longer bunched together into discrete groups. My charge forward caught them off guard for a moment, but the bald man quickly regrouped and shouted his orders.

"Aim for Tréfle!"

They were targeting Ludie, just as I'd expected. However, the guy closest to me still turned the barrel of his gun my way.

I immediately extended my Fourth Hand to defend while my Third Hand sent him tumbling. Just then, the interior of the room flooded with blinding light. Ludie had cast her attention-grabbing spell. It didn't seem to have had much of an effect besides brightening up the room. Nevertheless, it had succeeded in creating an opening. Storming toward the men focused on Ludie, I grabbed one with my Fourth Hand and catapulted him away.

"Gwaaaaaah!"

Watching as the man attending to Aurelien's injuries was propelled into the air, I erected a wall with my Third Hand. As I defended myself from the flurry of bullets they shot in response, I started taking them out immediately.

First, I used my stole to hurl tables at the men, double-checking to make sure each of my targets had been incapacitated. Next, I quickly rounded them all up together. Filling a nearby tablecloth with mana, I stretched it over their heads before expending a substantial amount of mana to cast hardening and immobilizing enchantments on the cloth.

That was one problem solved.

Sighing, I turned my attention toward Ludie and Claris and gasped.

Hot damn. I forgot that her skirt got all torn up.

My eyes rested on Ludie, who was currently in quite an immodest and unbecoming state.

The moment she noticed my wandering eyes, her face went beet red, and she tried to hide herself with her hands. However, she failed to conceal her adorable, white, ribbon-adorned panties. They complemented her beautiful, pale skin so well that I almost wondered if they were *too* adorable for her. Almost. On top of that… Actually, I should probably stop there.

"D-don't look!"

F-fair enough. What the hell was I staring at?!

Averting my gaze from the blushing and teary-eyed elf, I frantically searched for something to cover her up. Unfortunately, all I found was a torn and trampled strip of what had once been her skirt. It only served to heighten my sense of shame. That was when I realized something.

Of course. I didn't need to rummage around for her skirt, I had this stole wrapped around me, didn't I?

I quickly removed my stole and rushed toward her, keeping my eyes off her all the while.

"Uh-oh."

I wasn't sure if it had happened because I wasn't looking or because I was so flustered. First, I stepped on one of the plates scattered on the floor and began sliding forward. Then the stole in my hands wrapped itself around my head in a truly miraculous way. Though I could no longer see in front of me, I knew I was tipping over.

This is bad, I thought, but it was too late. I stretched my hands out in front of me to try and brace myself.

My hands felt an impact, but there was no pain. Instead, they met a warm and soft elasticity.

That was true for both my hands. In my right, it felt slightly firm with a blissful degree of softness, with something attached at the tip. The thing in my other hand felt very lively, like a quivering bowl of jelly…baffled, I squeezed my hands again.

"Eeeeeeeek!"

"Aaaah!"

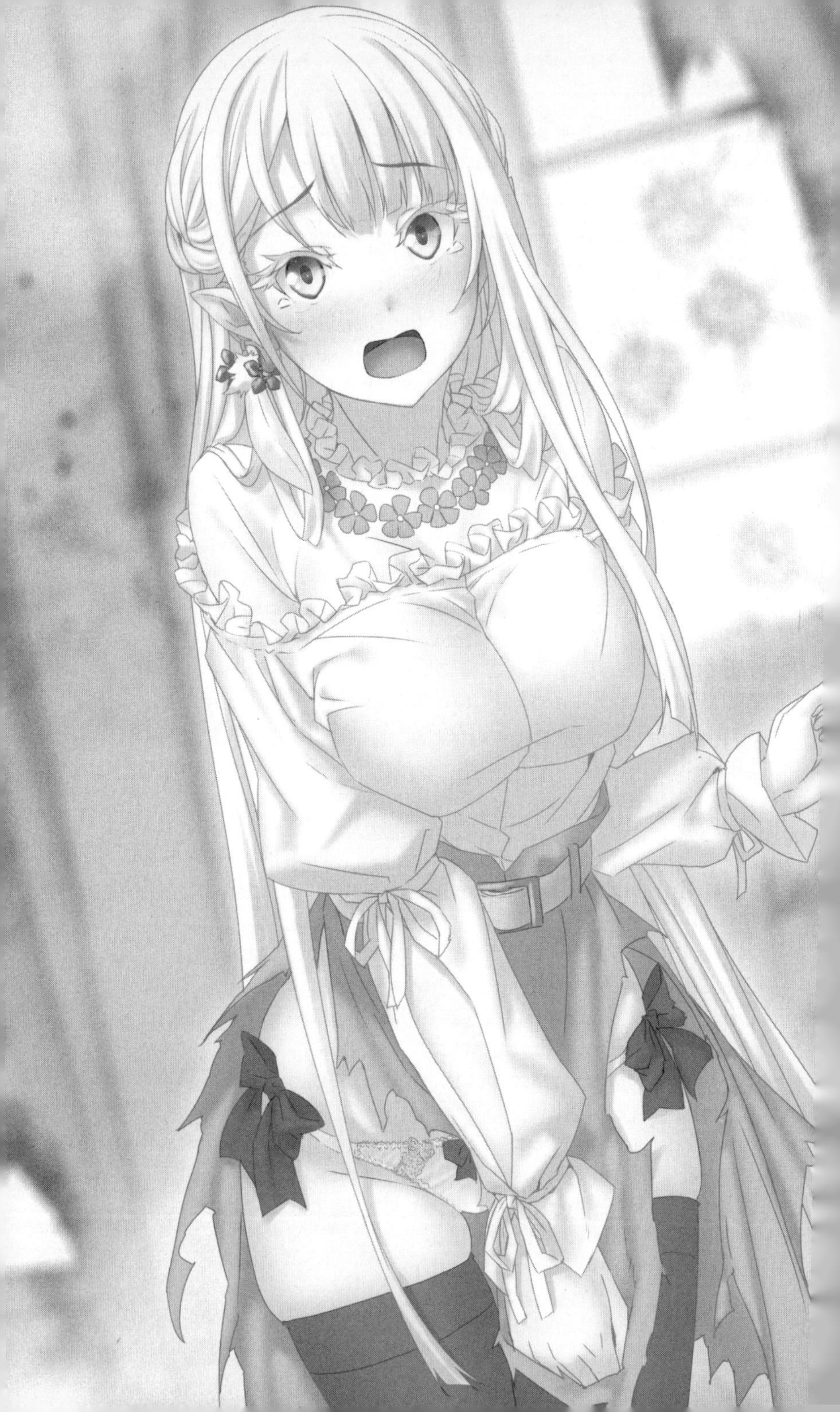

Two female screams echoed right into my ears. That's when I finally realized what I had been touching. At that exact moment, my stole slipped down from around my face, revealing the scene before me.

"Oh no…"

In my hands were Ludie's breast and Claris's butt. I looked at Ludie's still-beet-red face and immediately let go of her. Jumping to my feet, I threw my stole toward her lower body. Then I ran away as fast as I possibly could.

"I-I'm soooooorrryyyy!!"

When I came to my senses, I was sitting on a toilet seat. I had really panicked back there. I couldn't remember anything that had happened after fleeing from Ludie and Claris.

"I did something really awful at the end there…"

What was up with me doing some real eroge protagonist-type shit? Falling over and grabbing a girl's chest and butt is totally in the protagonist's wheelhouse, not mine. Comic relief characters like Kousuke Takioto are supposed to say pervy things to the leading ladies and get the snot slapped out of them. Though he's the type to make sure he's got a front-row view of a girl's panties while she's kicking him into the dirt. That's the Kousuke Takioto I remembered.

Wait, what the hell kinda tangent was I going down here? I needed to get my thoughts back on track.

I was glad I'd been able to save them. Things may get hairy down the line, but I had absolutely no regrets about doing what I did. If I hadn't rescued them, I know I would have regretted it up until the day I died. That being said…

"I must have really changed up the plot, huh…?"

At this point, the game's story technically hadn't even started yet. The game starts the day before the first day of school, and there was over a week left until then. With this in mind, it was possible that the modifications I'd made could cause the narrative to drastically diverge from the original script.

Ludie herself doesn't even show up in the game until a little after school already starts. As soon as she arrives, an event triggers where the protagonist's party fights alongside her, but…would she even be delayed in starting school now?

In the normal narrative, she claims circumstances at home had pushed back her enrollment, but it's likely this incident has something to do with it. Since it still happened in this version of events, however, it was possible her enrollment would be delayed as usual.

"It's possible that me saving her might have some weird effect on things…"

Part of Ludie's in-game characterization is that she idolizes Marino Hanamura. That idolization must stem in part from Marino rescuing her in the normal scenario. It might not be the exact reason itself, but it has to be a contributing factor.

But since I was the one to save Ludie this time, how were things going to play out? In the worst-case scenario, she might not even enroll in school at all and head straight back to her home country instead. As a main heroine and one of the developers' favorite characters, Ludie was especially strong. It would be a huge boon to have her in my party.

"Oh well, nothing I can do… Instead of worrying about that, it would be more productive to consider my next move…"

I'd learned a lot from the recent battle. The first thing I needed to address was my weaknesses—when I'd been focused on defense, it had been impossible to examine my surroundings. It had been as if there were cloth umbrellas obscuring my line of sight in every direction. I needed to be able to erect a wall while still maintaining my field of view.

"Normally, that would seem totally impossible, but this is a world of magic, so…"

Since skills existed in this world, Mind's Eye and Clairvoyance might be useful to have. I should be able to get Mind's Eye after an upperclassman leads me to a certain location, so I should give it a try.

Now that I thought about it, I could already bump into her if I was lucky. The upperclassman, that is.

The next issue was long-ranged attacks, which countered my abilities. While I'd understood they would be a weakness of mine from the beginning, experiencing real combat had driven home just how vital long-ranged combat would be during future encounters. It would probably be a good idea to carry some kind of bow, gun, or shuriken.

I could figure out which one I was suited for at school and focus on honing my skills with it. However, worrying about other weapons would come after mastering my Third Hand and Fourth Hand. There was no point abandoning my training halfway. Besides that, money was also a concern.

"Money... I've really screwed up now..."

I had already used up almost all my money buying the stole, and then I had to go and leave my most expensive possession lying at Ludie's feet. Despite its importance, I was in no mood to get it back.

"There's a chance my identity's still a secret..."

Since my scarf had been wrapped around my head, my face should have stayed hidden. Was it best to try acting like I knew nothing about the whole thing? That was impossible. If Ludie ended up enrolling in the Academy, it would only be a matter of time before I would get found out. My fighting style was way too unique.

"I should avoid fighting in front of Ludie to keep my secret as long as possible. That's my only option. In the meantime, I should think of how to deal with the fallout when she eventually finds out..."

Bow down on the floor in front of her and beg? Well, when the time comes, I'll make sure to get my stole back. Now that I thought about it, I'd given it to her to use as a replacement skirt, but couldn't she have wrapped herself up in one of the tablecloths lying around? Too late now.

Anyway, a backup stole was on its way to my new home, so I was sure everything would work out. Wait—

"Oh shoot, what time is it? Did I miss my meetup with Marino?!"

I quickly took out my cell phone to check, but I couldn't see the time at all.

"Wh-whaaaat? You can't be serious..."

My brand-new cell phone had a large crack running through the screen, and no matter how many times I pressed the power button, the crystal display remained black.

Quite a bit of time had passed since the incident, and after reuniting with Marino thanks to some help from the hotel staff, we were now rocking back in forth in our hotel limousine while heading through town on our way to dinner. Marino had been worried sick and had wrapped me up in a tight hug the moment we saw each other. She was pretty stacked.

"Hey, Kousuke?"

I peeled my eyes away from the car window and turned toward Marino. She wore a grave expression, and she was rubbing the bracelet that served as her magic catalyst. She looked ready to fire off magic at a moment's notice.

"Yes?"

"You said you were close by that explosion, right?"

"Indeed I was."

I'd told her about the explosion but had left out everything that happened in the hotel. If I mentioned my exploits there, I would have had to bring up the part about falling on those girls' chest and butt.

"That explosion wasn't all that happened today, actually. There was a terror attack on our hotel... You know about that, right?"

Of course I did. I'd been at the scene of the crime.

"There were quite a few terrorists involved, but did you know that one of them seems to have gone missing?"

"Huh? I thought I'd gotten everyone..."

No way! They weren't able to capture everyone?! If one of them was still at large, then...they must be hiding out somewhere? I fled the scene, leaving Ludie and Claris behind, thinking they were safe!

"Are those girls okay?!"

Marino closed her eyes and shook her head.

"...Unfortunately, a suspicious individual groped their boobs and butt..."

It couldn't be... I'd run away, and some depraved pervert had taken that chance to assault them. How horri...... Wait, what was this strange sensation lingering in both my hands?

Marino giggled and broke into her usual smile.

"I heard you fell, but one misstep and that would've been real sexual harassment."

"I'm sorry."

Marino grinned at my apology, but her smile faded as she continued:

"But they still haven't caught one of the perpetrators. I'm not talking about you, of course; I mean one of the men who attacked those girls."

"That's not good…"

"Tread carefully, okay? That said…why didn't you fill me in about everything that happened in the hotel?"

"…Tailing after a suspicious guy on a whim, not contacting you before getting into a fight…purposefully sticking my neck out into a dangerous situation… I figured you'd be really angry with me."

"Well, aren't you sharp…?"

Marino grinned as she pulled me close and ground both of her hands into the sides of my head. It didn't hurt at all.

"Next time, don't be so reckless and get in touch with me instead! Still…that was very brave of you."

Then Marino drew me in tighter and patted me on the head. It was honestly pretty embarrassing.

"You did a good job, really. And you know what? The girl you saved is the Tréfle emperor's second-eldest daughter."

"Huh… Whaaaat?! No waaaay!"

I separated from Marino's grasp and feigned surprise. Of course, I knew about all of that. I'd watched the game's end credits more times than I could count. I knew how much Ludie liked pickles, how she put salt and pepper on her eggs, and most important of all, I knew all about her different kinks.

"*Tee-hee*, surprised?"

"Who wouldn't be? But are you sure it's okay for me to know about something that big?"

She had just disclosed the identity of one of the female victims. I'd been at the scene in person, so sure, it might have been fine to tell me. At the same time, these were details that didn't need to be shared. I had no intention of asking about it myself, and if I hadn't been told, I'd planned on keeping this knowledge a secret. The truth would no doubt have gotten out eventually, though.

"I actually debated on telling you…but I decided letting you know would be best down the road."

Down the road?

"What do you mean?"

"Things aren't set in stone yet, so I'll have to explain everything to you a bit later… Looks like we've arrived."

Our car stopped, and a brawny man opened the door for us. I thanked him and exited the car with Marino.

Inside the building, there was nothing but lavish and decadent food as far as the eye could see. Smacking my lips in delight, I explained to Marino why I'd been in that banquet hall and what happened after the fighting was over.

"Hmm, I get it now. On top of leering at Ludivine's immodest figure, you went and groped her chest, too. Lucky you."

"Yeah, I got really luc—wait, what're you trying to make me say here?!"

"...You didn't grope her on purpose, did you?"

"Of course not!"

It was simply that, if you asked me whether I wanted to touch her chest or not, the answer was obviously yes, and if I you told me to prostrate myself on the floor for a chance to do it again, I'd spread-eagle on the floor in heartbeat. Still, what happened back there had been an accident. Besides, I didn't like the idea of forcing myself onto women like that.

"......You're absolutely certain it wasn't intentional?"

"It really wasn't!"

Hearing my reply, Marino's hardened expression melted away into her usual benign smile.

"That's good. Also, it seems they'd like to give you a proper thank-you."

"'They'?"

"Ludivine and the elf whose butt you groped."

That was true, sure, but I wished she could have phrased it differently.

"...I don't think I can look them in the eyes. I'd rather just say I appreciate their gratitude and leave it at that."

"Things won't be so simple, I'm afraid. Why, Ludivine is planning on enrolling in our school!"

"Whaaaaat, you're kidding me?!"

Duh. With her beautiful features and her proficiency with wind magic, she'll get nicknamed the Wind Princess. She'll even have the LLL fan club form in her honor, too. Honestly, if it hadn't been Ludie back there, I probably wouldn't have been so quick to get out of there... All right, I probably would have done that anyway.

"That's right! Well? Surprised?"

My acting had done the job. Marino nodded, looking immensely pleased with herself.

"I am... I can't believe we're going to attend the same school. Oh no, how am I supposed to face her after I touched her like that...?"

"Don't worry. She still seems a bit bothered by it, but she isn't angry. In fact, she was the one who said she wanted to thank you."

I would've been in big trouble otherwise. Given her social status, if she had ordered me to take responsibility, I don't think anything short of seppuku would have done the job... I was getting scared just thinking about it. The next time we met, I should probably refer to her as Your Highness, just to be safe.

However, I probably wouldn't be seeing her until after school started. I had some time before that. Until then, I just had to think up a few ways to approach the situation, simple as that. It was best to take your time with this stuff.

I confidently nodded to myself and brought my bowl of soup to my lips.

"With that in mind, I'm planning on having Ludivine and her retainer over to our house soon, so be ready to meet with them, okay?"

What?

"Cough, cough, cough..."

Marino's words echoed in my head, making me choke on my soup.

Um, was this a joke?

You can generally boil down people's problems to money and relationships.

This sentiment is not only true anecdotally but is also clearly backed up by surveys and statistics.

The same holds true even when playing games. Especially in eroge, where the majority of the protagonist's troubles stem from his quest to get closer to the title's various cuties. I suppose that's to be expected of a romance game, though. What's funny is that eroge players themselves often fret over money and people, too.

For starters, eroge are very expensive. It's common for a single game to cost close to a hundred dollars, so your average pencil pusher can't afford many of them. Deciding which titles to buy is a gut-wrenching process.

After choosing their product, then come the "people" problems. First-edition copies of eroge often come with various retail bonuses such as wall scrolls or plastic folders. However, in many cases, these bonuses don't showcase the whole cast of heroines; instead, each bonus features a single girl.

In other words, you're forced to choose a heroine before even playing the game! Of course, buying them all was a possibility, but for the average individual eyeing an almost one-hundred-dollar piece of software, purchasing enough copies to get every retail bonus is a tall order. Before the game goes on sale, we gentlemen must thus choose which of the heroines appeals to us the most.

Once the game starts, we are thrown further into a quagmire of personal relationship anxieties. I am referring, of course, to the decision of who we will pursue first. Comparing all the beautiful women on the box, you must decide on which order you'll go through their routes. What an opulent problem to have. Although sometimes, you'll step on such a big land mine that the resulting trauma will cut off another heroine's route. That really only ever happens in the absolute best games out there, though.

Now, it's never made clear in-game, but the various obstacles facing Kousuke Takioto are more serious than even the protagonist has to deal with. This holds true for both his backstory and his unique abilities. The personal relationships within his new family, too, must put a lot of stress on his mind.

"Um, so…"

"……"

She didn't even flinch as she stared at me. Marino's daughter shared the same eye and hair color as her mother. However, she wasn't at all outgoing and sociable like Marino. Of course, her expressionless and taciturn personality was all part of the game characterization. More importantly, though: Marino, I get that you're busy with work, but I wish you hadn't left the two of us alone together.

As I worried about how to handle the situation, Hatsumi Hanamura suddenly spoke up.

"…I've heard about your current circumstances."

"I—I see."

".........."

"Um... Hatsumi?"

".........."

Without saying a word, she simply continued to stare at me, and with what appeared to be displeasure, at that.

If I had to guess, this is probably part of why Kousuke Takioto doesn't move in to the Hanamura house in the game.

He hadn't been able to endure Hatsumi Hanamura. Of course, as the daughter of the enchantingly beautiful witch Marino, she was gorgeous herself, but it was impossible to figure out what she was thinking. She was also gloomy and difficult to approach. By contrast, Kousuke Takioto was a loud and obnoxious jokester character who must be really suffering on the inside.

The bottom line was that Kousuke Takioto and Hatsumi Hanamura were like oil and water. I didn't really blame him for deciding to live in the dorms instead.

If I didn't know this was the world of *Magical★Explorer*, I might have made the same choice as Kousuke. Of course, I couldn't deny the possibility that this beautiful mother-daughter combo might have enticed me to live with them, either. However, this perverted gentleman in particular was very familiar with the world of *MX*.

"Hatsumi, I look forward to living with you from now on. Pardon my forwardness, but I'd like to borrow a book on magic, particularly on spatial magic, if possible."

This house was home to the Witch of Tsukuyomi, Marino Hanamura, and the professor Hatsumi Hanamura. They obviously had plenty of magic books, but they even had their own research lab. I'd also discovered that the house had its own enhancement facilities. While the Academy also had those facilities, they could only be used during certain times, and dorm students had a curfew on top of those restrictions.

True, this house may not have been the most comfortable living arrangement. To a magic-user, though, this was the absolute best environment you could be in. So why would I need to leave and go live in the dorms? I should make use of everything at my disposal. That said, I still didn't want to inconvenience them.

"...This way."

Hatsumi spun around and began heading down the hallway.

She led me to a huge library, bigger than any you would find in a typical home.

"Around here."

She showed me to a section of the library. Amid the multitudes of magic books, there were also unfamiliar magic tools lying around, along with what could only be described as bundles of pages in desperate need of binding.

"Is it okay for me to look around like this? You have research data and stuff around here, right?"

That I already knew. In the game, she's studying a somewhat unique type of magic, and she eventually instructs the protagonist on how to use it.

There might have been important academic materials of hers mixed up in the mess. Stuff like valuable statistical data or research secrets... Was she really okay with flaunting this to a stranger?

"...You know about my research?"

"You're continuing your late father's research, right?"

Hatsumi nodded.

It's not elaborated on in-game, but apparently, her father had been killed. On the developers' blog, they'd written: *We had thought up a ton of lore for her backstory, but the adults in the room made us cut all of it, lol.* Hence why I didn't know the full details myself.

"The really important stuff isn't in here."

I nodded at her reply.

"Thank you very much. Well then, I'll be reading in here for a bit."

I then turned my back to Hatsumi.

Under normal circumstances, I probably should have chatted with her to get to know her. Unfortunately, I didn't see our conversations going anywhere fast, and it must have been difficult for her to try talking with me as well. We didn't seem to have much chemistry, either.

I took several books off the shelves and placed them on the table. Then, to continue training my mana manipulation while I read, I activated my Third Hand and Fourth Hand before struggling to flip a book's cover open. I'd confirmed this for myself during my days experimenting, but the larger the area I was enchanting, the more mana it required. The more I extended the length of the stole, the harder it became to make precision movements. However, little by little, through my daily training, I'd started becoming more dexterous with my Third and Fourth Hands.

I'd read several pages when I heard something—the sound of several boxes getting thrown around. I turned to find Hatsumi setting several large packages down.

"...Don't mind me."

I wonder what she came here for? With her on my mind, I continued reading. However, I didn't sense her leave the room.

When I moved my eyes from the page to Hatsumi, I saw that she was making coffee for some reason. When our gazes met, she quickly stood up and walked over to where I was.

"Here."

"Th-thank you."

After I took the cup, she gave a small nod and returned to putting away her packages. Then, of all things, she started doing what appeared to be work.

...Why did she decide to start working here?

"Oh, this tastes great."

It tasted slightly different from regular coffee. It was rich in flavor, low in acidity but very bitter, and with a distinct aftertaste. Due to its intensity, people who couldn't handle bitter coffee surely would have hated it. On the other hand, coffee enthusiasts who preferred low acidity would have considered it a perfect cup and leaped at the opportunity to drink more.

I peeked over at Hatsumi. She was focused on the paper in front of her, silently writing away. I could talk to her about the coffee later.

I returned to the book I was holding in my Third Hand.

Some number of hours must have passed by the time Hatsumi got up and came over to me.

"Let's go eat."

Looking at my new phone, I saw it was well past noon, right around the normal end of the school or work lunch hour.

"You weren't waiting for me, were you?"

"No. Leaving now means places are less crowded."

She'd planned on going out to eat, apparently. Now that I thought about it, the Hanamura household didn't employ a housekeeper. It was a smaller home than I would have thought, but it still had much more room than its three residents could ever need. Given how busy Marino looked, it wouldn't seem strange for there to be someone around the house to do the cooking and the cleaning.

"I was planning on showing you around the area on the way back, if you'd like."

I instinctively shook my head at her offer.

"Oh, Marino...told me all that stuff, so I'm fine."

The moment the words left my mouth, I noticed an ever-so-slight shift in Hatsumi's expression. It was nigh imperceivable, so I wondered if my eyes were simply playing tricks on me.

"I see. Let's go, then."

She brought me to a small café about a five-minute walk from the house. There wasn't much space, with only a few tables and a small number of counter seats.

Hatsumi and I sat down at an empty table and scanned the menu.

"Do you have a recommendation, Hatsumi?"

"...Everything's tasty. If I had to pick one, I'd say the fried Blood Horned Rabbit."

I couldn't say for sure, but I imagined the smile I gave must have looked very stiff and forced.

If my memory served me correctly, the Blood Horned Rabbit was a monster. She had recommended it, though, and to be honest, I was a bit curious, too.

"I'll go with that, then."

Both ordering the same dish, we waited for our food to arrive, falling silent immediately.

What was I supposed to talk about? Back in the library, I could have avoided the issue by escaping into the pages of a book, but Hatsumi was sitting directly across from me, so reading a book right now would be unbelievably rude. I guess I could try referencing something we both had in common.

"Um, you also graduated from Tsukuyomi Magic Academy, right, Hatsumi? What was it like? How about the students? It's gotta be like a who's who of the magic elite, right?"

"...There were some incredible people there... But I had almost no friends in school."

"*Ha-ha...*"

It felt like the mood had soured even further. Coming from her, though, it sounded very plausible.

"But it's the perfect environment if you're after strength or scholastic learning. I can say that with certainty."

"I'll be sure to study hard."

Our food was brought out to us while we discussed my random conversation starter. The mood may have chilled, but the meal was nice and warm.

As we began eating, I continued our conversation, turning the topic toward how Academy classes were structured.

"Wait, so you're saying the higher I raise my rank, the more types of courses I can choose from?"

"Yes. First, you have your general subjects and magic fundamentals classes in the morning. Those students who meet a sufficient level of proficiency can take supplementary classes in the afternoon."

I gave an understanding nod. It's almost the exact same way in the game. When you level up your stats, the number of classes available for you to take increases. Here, too, the more you improved your abilities, the more classes you had to choose from. And I could only assume that the more classes that became available, the more knowledgeable about magic I would become.

If what you could gain from these lectures lined up with the ATTEND CLASS option given to the players in-game, however, then going to lessons wouldn't prove too valuable. Particularly in Kousuke Takioto's case.

"Is that so...? Incidentally, are a majority of those extra classes concerned with offensive magic, by any chance?"

"...I suppose so. They taught me high-rank offensive magic."

Yup, I was right. If that was the case, I probably couldn't get anything out of the courses. To be precise, I might have been able to *use* offensive magic, but my dubious power level in that area wouldn't make it worth my while. Honestly, I didn't need to work hard on my grades; I just had to graduate. I could fill up that time with my own self-training and dungeon exploration instead.

With that decided, I constructed a simple schedule in my head. After school started, most of my actions would revolve around improving my physical fitness, strengthening my mana, and developing counter-measures against long-range attacks. Wait, wasn't I doing all that already?

"...I can teach you," offered Hatsumi.

I cocked my head in confusion for a moment before quickly realizing she was referring to the extra magic classes.

"Let me explain. The truth is, due to my natural predisposition, I can't use most kinds of magic. Even if you were to teach me practical magic, I'm not sure I'd be able to use any of it well."

Hatsumi replied with a quiet and sullen "too bad." She stopped tearing through what was left of her meal and stared at the plate in front of her with an absentminded expression.

"Instead, I actually had some questions about this constitution of mine I wanted your take on... I was hoping you'd help me out with that instead."

Hatsumi suddenly raised her head. Then she gave me a thumbs-up.

"Leave it to me."

I got the vague sense that, quiet and impenetrable though she may have been, Hatsumi wasn't a bad person at all.

The monster meat, meanwhile, was more delicious than words could ever describe.

The special privileges of living in the Hanamura household didn't end with having the mother and daughter teach me magic. The enchantment facilities were another perk, and I didn't have to deal with any annoying curfew, either.

Yet another advantage was that I now had access to some new places to check out.

"Oh, that waterfall? Sure, of course! Wait...how do you know about that waterfall?"

I ended the phone call before she could prod me any further. I'd easily gotten permission from the landowner. After that, I went to Hatsumi's room and knocked on her door.

"Hatsumi, I'm going out to run and practice my magic. I'll be back before dinner."

"...Okay."

Leaving her room behind, I slipped into the running shoes I'd bought with my leftover cash.

"All set."

I began running down the still-unfamiliar streets with a vague sense of the right direction. Marino had given me a small tour of the area, but she hadn't shown me the route to my current destination. I could figure out the rest of my way on my own.

"Hah, hah, hah, hah, hah..."

I kept my pace up as I jogged along the street, dodging people as I went. The initial paved concrete footpaths eventually gave way to dirt and grass until finally, I entered into a grove of trees to reach my destination.

After a few minutes of dashing through the woods, I first noticed the sounds around me change. Amid the rustling of the trees, there came the pounding of water. As I advanced deeper into the woods, the sound of colliding water grew louder and louder.

At last, a waterfall greeted me, signaling I had arrived at my destination.

The rapids looked about fifty feet tall and just under one hundred feet wide. The thin and expansive cascading water sparkled in the reflected sunlight, and I caught myself with my mouth half-agape, entranced by the beauty before me. A reserved beauty, you could say. Meanwhile, the water pounding at the base of the falls from its height created a white mist, like a localized fog.

As I'd approached the waterfall, I'd realized I could see a rainbow at certain angles. The small rainbow that was currently visible stretched out over the cascade like a gift wrap bow.

I continued down the slightly precarious trail and stepped behind the falling water.

"......"

I was speechless.

I would liken it to a curtain of water. The view from behind the torrent was breathtaking. From one side of the curtain flowed a thin, pale veil of water, and from the other, light poured in through the lush and verdant foliage. The trees seemed to swim as they shook in the wind, and pale-green leaves floated down gently from their branches.

The magnificence was overwhelming. One look was enough to clear the mind and refresh the spirit. The grandeur made me want to gaze at it forever.

Fwish. Fwish. Fwish. Fwish.

Even amid the roar of the waterfall, I could hear the reverberation of something cutting through the air.

My eyes fell on a girl holding a naginata polearm. She must have noticed me standing there, but her swings never faltered. Staring hard at the curtain of water, she focused wholly on wielding her naginata.

Truth be told, I had a hunch that she might have been here. She ends up bringing the protagonist to this place in the game. To be completely honest, I'd *hoped* she would be here.

She was the heroine I wanted to meet most of all.

Each swing of her blade sent droplets flying off her cheeks. I wondered how long she had been standing there and practicing. On closer inspection, I could see beads of sweat forming on her flawless visage.

Magnificent scenery stretched out in front of me, yet my eyes were fixed on her.

Her beautiful, lustrous black hair shone like polished onyx, framing a face so symmetrical that it looked like a perfect mirror image. Her bewitchingly keen eyes glinted like the edge of a cursed magic blade. I could feel her vaguely evanescent expression sucking me in.

If there were a goddess in this world, then she must have been standing right in front of me.

I'd been staring at her intently the whole time, but she showed no response, as though she didn't care at all. To her, I was some foreign substance, underserving of a single moment of her consideration. Completely shutting me out of her consciousness, she ignored me as if I were just another part of the scenery.

Her black hair danced with each flourish of her polearm. It was unbelievable how fast she could brandish her blade with the slim, fair-skinned arms peeking out from her martial arts gear.

As I went to wipe the sweat dropping down my eyelids, I realized I was trembling slightly. Whether it was from awe, excitement, or joy, I couldn't say.

Probably all of the above. However, the strongest emotion of all was undoubtedly the joy I felt from getting to see her. I gazed on at her as she continued, still swinging her lance.

I couldn't contain my glee. After all, she was the character I had probably poured the most energy into raising in the game. The character I trusted the most, the woman I never left on the sidelines, sending her to battle regardless of if she was disadvantaged or not, and the character who cut through all the strongest bosses like butter. She was right in front of me.

She was really there. In the flesh. One of *MX*'s Big Three, the vice president of the Morals Committee, nicknamed Water Dragon Princess due to her skill with water magic—Yukine Mizumori was standing before me.

Suddenly, her endlessly repeating practice swings came to a halt. Then she shifted from the overhead stance she'd been using up until then and brought her polearm down to her side.

"Phew."

Right as she exhaled, something flashed for a moment. When I looked again, the naginata was jutting out in front of her, and the curtain of water had been sliced vertically in two.

I hadn't been able to detect the jab with my eyes.

But the naginata's dance wasn't done yet. First came a slash upward and a slash downward, then a sweeping cut.

Observing this splendid combo attack, I slowly felt heat pulse throughout my form. Suddenly, I couldn't stay still, like I had to do something. I wanted to take off running. The urge seized my entire body.

I soon realized the origin of this impulse.

Turning away from Yukine Mizumori, still brandishing her naginata, I exited out from behind the waterfall. Pouring all my strength into my legs, I set off running like a rocket.

My heart was feverish. Blood and mana careened through me like a river flooding over in a hurricane, my whole body aflame.

Ah, dammit! I cursed inwardly.

Her spellbinding beauty, an envy that made me want to scream, and a jealousy smoldering within me. All of it jumbling together had lit a fire inside me. I wanted to be able to brandish a weapon just as splendidly as her. I wanted to be that strong. No—I wanted to be even stronger.

These thoughts echoed through my mind.

I climbed a bit farther up and exited out into an open area. There, I circulated all the mana I could muster and sprinted off. I ran incessantly and carelessly, as if to quench the blaze inside me.

Just how much had I sprinted? The shining sun had begun to dip below the horizon, and the nearby area had gotten dark. I couldn't stay here training any longer. There was no light to speak of, but more importantly, I'd promised to be back home before dinner time.

"Time to head back…"

Muttering this to myself, I dashed off toward home.

It was absurd that I hadn't been able to see her naginata move at all. Even with how far away I was, I still hadn't been able to see it. What did I need to do in order to wield a weapon that well? Not only that— how could I ever compete with such speed?

I supposed I could try acting before my opponent. More specifically, I could move first to preempt my opponent's attack. Outside of striking first was turning my stole into a big shield instead.

I went into the house and took my shoes off at the door. Still lost in thought, I headed straight for the bath.

First, I wanted to improve my eyesight. From there, I wanted to eventually be able to reflexively react at Yukine's speed and manipulate my stole as quickly as she'd swung her naginata.

I removed my shawl and my sweat-soaked shirt.

I'd heard that professional athletes trained their eyesight and practiced improving their reflexes. Maybe it was best for me to do the same. And maybe I should also try gaining a bunch of different skills—!

The moment I went to grab the doorknob to the bath, I heard the door click open.

"……"

"……"

Standing before me was Hatsumi, her naked, fair skin flushed with a subtle pink. She must have just been getting out of the bath. Her wet hair clung tight to her skin, and water drops trickled down her face and body. Wisps of steam rose off her whole figure, its warmth plainly visible. I'd guessed as much, but she had an extremely voluptuous pair of melons, with adorable, pink-colored, just begging to be sucked on… Um, then there was her not-too-thin yet not-too-meaty torso and her thick, childbearing hips. She'd just barely been able to cover her most precious place with her towel, but… Yeah, I was in real big trouble here.

As I worked to eternally etch the picture in my mind, I frantically shut the door.

"*Hnaaaah!*" Hatsumi screamed, her voice totally unlike anything I'd heard from her before, and guilt swelled up inside me.

"Sorry, sorry, I'm so sorry!"

Then I heard the loud thudding of footsteps coming down the hallway.

"What happened?!"

Marino had apparently been home. After rushing straight over to the bath, she gave me a once-over before a huge grin spread across her face.

"Eeeek! ♪"

Her scream had a jovial tinge to it. Wait, she was screaming, too? Why?

I suddenly looked down at my own body. A firm and healthy physique to be proud of. Part of me wanted to brag about my well-defined chest and abdominal muscles. I wouldn't, though. Below those, I saw something bigger than what I'd been used to back on Earth. Yes, *that*.

I get it now—I was completely naked.

I'd left my clothes in the changing room. There wasn't a single strip of cloth covering me.

"Gaaaaaaaaaaaaaaaaaaah!"

I quickly covered my crotch with my hands. One disaster truly begets another.

"Kousuke, you're moving so faaaast! ♪"

What was this woman talking about? Marino covered up her face with both hands, but she kept staring at my nakedness through the cracks between her fingers.

Shit, shit, shit, what was I supposed to do here? It was no use. All the thoughts flying around my head made it impossible to think straight.

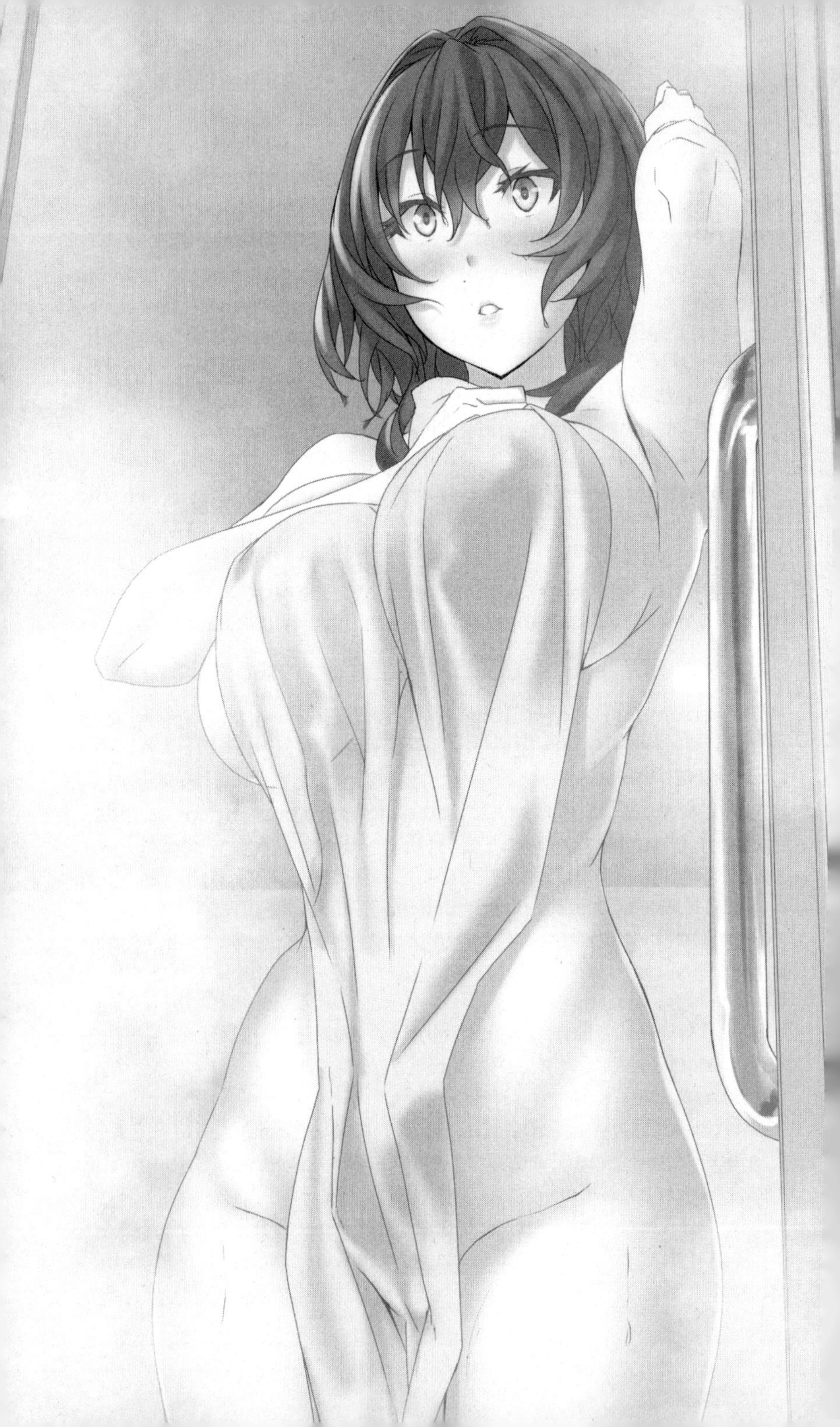

The door suddenly swung open again to reveal Hatsumi exiting in her underwear. Then magic came shooting forth from her hands. There was no way I could defend myself in time. I didn't even have my stole with me anyway.

"Welp, I'm done for."

Light flashed before my eyes.

I'd experienced many things for the first time since coming to this world. Using magic was definitely an example, as was riding in a mana-powered car. And today, for the first time in my life, I was prostrating myself on the floor. Though I'd planned on doing so in front of a certain member of royalty soon anyway.

Hatsumi had been scowling at me for a short while now. It didn't appear she was going to let up anytime soon, either. All I could do was keep my forehead planted fast against the floor.

There had to be some way to get her to forgive me.

That was it, I would take a page from eroge. They usually have a scene that involves peeking in on a girl bathing. Honestly, if an eroge had the protagonist living with a girl and didn't feature a scene like that, I'd question if it really deserved to be called an eroge at all.

What did the characters from those games do to beg for mercy?

Right. What exactly was there to glean from the kind of exaggerated reality where girls will straight up give you permission to bathe with them? Besides, didn't all those guys have Eroge Protag Privilege anyway?

"…………"

The silence was unbearable. Still, I was the one at fault here. I'd gone into the changing area without checking if the bathroom was empty. I was so wrapped up with other thoughts that I didn't think twice before walking inside.

"Dinner's ready!" echoed from the kitchen. Naturally, I didn't move a muscle and kept my head pasted to the floor. I felt like the friction would rub my bangs clean off, but I had no choice in the matter.

"*Sigh*… Kousuke, pick your head up."

At her command, I slowly lifted up my head. She wasn't scowling anymore.

"Let's go eat."

She appeared to have forgiven me for now.

In the dining room, the table was laid out with an arrangement of food any Japanese child would enjoy—Salisbury steak, mushroom potage, and rice. We all sat down, gave thanks for the food, and began eating.

Hatsumi didn't look upset. She simply ate her steak in silence. I stayed keenly clued in to her mood as I ate.

Much to my surprise, Marino was a great cook. I told her, with all honesty, that the food was tastier than any hotel restaurant or inn dinner service meal I'd ever had, and she immediately replied with an "Oh, stop, you ♪" before refilling my plate. It was all delicious.

The Salisbury steak was particularly good. The handmade patty was unbelievably juicy, flooding my mouth with every bite.

"I had thought about making your favorite foods, Kousuke, but... you know, you say you like anything, right? That's why I made a big spread of Hatsumi's favorites. You know what? She's got a very childish palate."

Hatsumi reacted to her mother's words by shaking her head with uncharacteristic fluster.

"Now that you mention it, last night...she had fried chicken and omelet rice for dinner."

When I thought about it in that light, both were dishes especially enjoyed in childhood.

"Ngh?!"

Her face tinged slightly red, daughter glared at mother. In the game, Hatsumi comes across as a bit robotic, but I didn't get that impression at all anymore.

"I actually love that sort of food, too. If there's any places where you like to eat around here, Hatsumi, I'd love to have you show them to me."

"......"

Hatsumi silently continued working through her meal. She would probably take me to them eventually. That's what I chose to believe anyway.

Feeling a little bit relieved, I was having my fill of the potage when Marino let out a small gasp. She'd suddenly remembered something.

"Oh, right, right. Ludivine is coming here tomorrow."

"Is that right? Well, now......... Wait."

What did she just say?

"She'll be around shortly after noon, I think. Make sure you're home, okay?"

She'd dropped this bombshell as casually as if she were telling me she was going to be home late from work.

After I finished dinner, I racked my brain back in my room. I'd known she would be coming by eventually. However, I hadn't yet thought up any ideas on how to approach her.

First, I needed to get an overview of the situation—Ludivine Marie-Ange de la Tréfle was the second daughter to His Majesty, the Emperor of the Tréfle Empire. And what I had done to this noble and high-born woman was: fly in to her rescue, leer at her panties, and grope her boob.

"...I'm headed straight to death row."

First up, I'd prostrate myself. I would deliver to Her Highness Princess Ludivine my most heartfelt apology for my multiple dis-courtesies. I had to somehow earn her pardon, or my future looked bleak.

Now, how exactly was I going to do that?

Hypothetically speaking here—let's say an average girl came and touched my private parts. Would I forgive her? Depending on the situation, I might need to reward her... Maybe Ludie would forgive me after all.

"Like things'll go that smoothly."

Countless schemes were floating around in my head when there was a sudden knock at my door.

"Kousuke."

"Hatsumi? Come on in."

She scanned my room before she caught her breath for a moment.

I'd left everything I didn't expect to need behind, so it was pretty tidy. Of course, there wasn't anything that might need hiding, either.

"Is something wrong?" I asked, addressing Hatsumi as she looked closely around my room.

"No, nothing wrong. I just had something to ask you."

"What is it?"

"...Kousuke, um, do you like elderly people?"

"Huh?"

"You prefer mature older women, don't you?"

Okay, what the hell was she going on about?

"Mom's pretty old, you know?"

"All right, can you fill me in on how exactly you came to that conclusion?"

Yes, yes, take a seat right here. Let's take this from the top.

"Well, you and Mom are so buddy-buddy. I thought maybe you were making a bid to become my new dad."

That would never happen. Also, did she honestly think Marino would fall in love with her close cousin's son? That kind of stuff only happened in eroge. If that were the case, though, I absolutely wanted to hear about it. Of course, Marino was absolutely my type with a capital *T*, so maybe... Hold up, where the hell was I going with that?

"First off, that's definitely not what's happening here. Personally, I didn't really think I was treating you and Marino any differently, to be honest..."

"But when you talk to me, you're so formal."

She had a point. That said...

"Marino gave me a strict order not to talk so formally... It's a habit of mine, so it just comes out naturally, really."

Marino would puff out her cheeks and sulk whenever I would act cold and distant with her, so I didn't have much of a say in the matter. Puff out her cheeks? Wait, just how old was she, again? Still, she sure looked cute doing it...

"You don't need to be formal with me, either. I want you to refer to me more affectionally. Call me Big Sis."

So she was after that big sis status, huh? There hadn't been any events to get closer with her in-game to give me an impression beforehand, but her characterization was all over the place.

Setting that aside for the moment, I wanted to go with Sis at the very least. Big Sis sounded embarrassingly childish. Yeah, that's what I'd call her.

"Um...gotcha. Sis."

She nodded half-heartedly, as though she'd gotten a fish bone stuck in her throat.

I expected her to then leave my room, but she didn't. Instead, she made herself comfortable, and we chatted idly until it was time for bed. Needless to say, I hadn't come up with a single idea about how I would face Ludivine.

Maybe if a typhoon made landfall right on top of us, Her Highness Ludivine would cancel her visit.

The thought crossed my mind as I lay in bed. Unfortunately for me, however, the view from outside showed clear skies and sunny weather.

I opened up my window to let in the fresh air. The spring wind that blew in was a little cool, just enough to finish rousing from my slumber. Then I quickly changed and left the house to go running.

I decided on a course that would bring me near the waterfall. I'd thought as much when I was getting shown around the city, but there were a lot of intersections in the main drag, plus a lot of traffic lights. Conversely, the woods were on private land, so there was almost no one there. Free from stops at red lights, I could jog without interruption.

"...*Hah, hah, hyup, hyup, hah, hah, hyup.*"

Kousuke Takioto had possessed quite a lot of stamina from the start. Thanks to my daily runs, however, I felt as though I had even more endurance than before. What I needed next was explosive momentum and the ability to move regardless of my exhaustion level. When exploring a dungeon, a monster could ambush you at any moment.

Along the way, I stopped to stretch my legs at the waterfall; there, Yukine Mizumori was again swinging her naginata. As always, she struck an imposing and beautiful figure, though with a subtle hint of ferociousness as well. I watched her form for a little while but then left her behind. I needed to release all the pent-up motivation I'd felt when I observed her, so I continued on my sprinting route.

After another hour or so of running, I returned home. I immediately headed for the bathroom but remembered to knock this time, of course. The only people who repeatedly peeped on women bathing were fools who refused to learn their lesson or eroge protagonists.

Finished with my bath, I walked down the chilly hallway floor and headed into the dining room.

"Morning, Kousuke."

"Good morning, Marino."

Dressed in an adorably frilly apron, Marino truly looked no older than a teenager as she made breakfast in the kitchen.

"You're always up so early. Hatsumi could learn a thing or two."

"I'm only waking up early to go running, though. Sis is off from school anyway, so no harm in sleeping in, right?"

Marino's hands came to an abrupt halt, and she turned around to face me.

"'Sis'?"

I nodded.

"She asked me to call her that yesterday...that's all."

Marino replied with a simple "I see," giggling at my answer. She then looked back down at her hands. Soon followed the rhythmic sounds of her chopping.

"Sorry, but can you go wake Hatsumi up? That girl's been asleep for long enough."

"Huh? Is it okay for me do that?"

"Of course. You're her little brother, right? Just go in and shake her a bit. She'll get right up."

Marino chuckled loudly as she continued working her hands. Still hesitant, I headed toward Hatsumi's room.

"Sis? Are you awake?"

I knocked on the door and called out, but there was no answer. I tried calling out again.

"Sis?"

I knocked again. Still no reply.

Marino did tell me it was okay, I thought, timidly cracking open the door.

Hatsumi's room had close to the same layout as my own. With all her possessions placed in another room, there wasn't much in the way of personal belongings, and its tidiness made it look very spacious.

"Siiiis. Sis?"

Approaching the big white bed, I peered down at Hatsumi's face from above. Her eyes were shut tight, leaving her long eyelashes visible. I took a big gulp, looking at the pale-white and alluring nape of her neck, which was no doubt a result of her job being largely confined to indoor areas. Since she showed no signs of rousing, I slowly reached my hands out to her.

"Sis."

I rested my hands on her shoulders and gave her a light shake. However, she still seemed dead asleep. Trying again, I gave her a harder shake.

"Mn, mnhh..."

Her delicate lips trembled slightly, and she began to move. Then she slowly opened her eyes.

"Morning, Sis."

".........Good morning."

Removing the covers as she sat up, she stretched her arms above her head. This simultaneously served to accentuate her voluptuous chest. It appeared she wasn't the type to wear a bra to bed, since her emphasized cleavage did not seem to be contained within one.

Eyes still half-open, Sis groggily spaced out until she seemed to suddenly remember something and put her hands on her clothes.

That was close.

Catching a glimpse of her pretty little belly button, I immediately turned in the other direction.

"A-anyway, I'll be in the dining room."

Excusing myself, I quickly fled the room. Clearly, Hatsumi was not a morning person.

With everything that happened that morning, it was little wonder that I couldn't think up how I was going handle the afternoon. It was too late to try calming myself down and considering my next move, too.

Seated before me was someone who had graced my computer screen to serve me many a time, in all senses of the word—Her Highness Ludivine Marie-Ange de la Tréfle.

Standing next to her and bearing a sword was another beautiful girl, the proprietor of a wonderfully supple and elastic butt. I couldn't fathom why she was wearing her blade. Did she come to mete out punishment? If so, I was all too aware of my many sins.

"Good day, Ms. Marino, Ms. Hatsumi, and Mr. Kousuke."

Ludie stared at me after giving her greeting. I returned her "good day," using the stiff greeting for the first time in my life. I think my voice cracked, too.

"I believe Ms. Marino has introduced me to you already, but allow me the honor. My name is Ludivine Marie-Ange de la Tréfle. Coincidently, this is my maid. Give them your name."

"I am Claris."

Hold up, "maid"? Decked out in armor and with a blade strapped to her waist? Maybe the concept of a maid in this world significantly departed from what the term meant back in Japan.

"Well, well, that's awfully polite of you. My name is Kousuke Takioto."

After I finished introducing myself, I started to search for my ideal prostration timing when—

"Mr. Kousuke, allow me to take this opportunity and extend to you my humblest thanks."

Ludie was the first to bow her head. As she did, Claris followed suit. Their sudden bows threw me completely off guard, and I sat stunned for a moment.

"Please raise your heads. I didn't do much of anything, really, and honestly, I should be the one apologizing to the both of you."

"Please, you saved our lives. Besides, there's no need to apologize— that was an accident, was it not?"

Ludie dragged out her words with an icy-cold smile, and Claris put her hand on her scabbard for some reason.

Now, why would she do that, I wonder? Was she was saying she was angry, but that they'd overlook my mistake? Regardless, I got the feeling that one wrong move, and I'd be hacked to bits where I sat.

"R-really? Still, allow me to apologize anyway. I'm very sorry for that accident," I entreated with a deep bow of my head.

"Please, no need to bow your head. I have heard and accepted your apology. Let us not speak of this again. More importantly..."

"Is what's next," Marino interjected, cutting into the conversation. Ludie's face made it clear she wanted to me to forget about my little accident immediately. I could never let this slip, but I was confident I'd remember the sensation I'd felt that day for the rest of my life.

"Yes, we have information to share. The people who attacked me… they seem to be connected to a certain band of my countrymen, the Church of the Malevolent Lord."

At the words *Church of the Malevolent Lord*, Hatsumi shuddered. She glanced sidelong toward me.

Ludie continued.

"Once I enroll in the Academy, their attacks against me should quiet down. That being said…"

"We can't be certain she'll be completely safe. Especially since one of them got away," Marino finished Ludie's thought.

The truth was that her prediction was right on the mark. If things played out like they do in the game, then followers of the Church would eventually target Ludie. It serves as an opportunity for the protagonist and Ludie to quickly grow closer with each other.

"We've been able to obtain a certain amount of information related to the Church of the Malevolent Lord from a target captured by our country's spies. Their account contains some truly shocking details."

"Um, is it okay for me to be a part of this conversation? It's getting pretty heavy. I'm just worried it might be a security risk or something."

This stuff was confidential on a national level. That must be why the *MX* protagonist isn't told about any of it until he starts coming into contact with the Church. Should I have been listening to this?

"I am terribly sorry, but…"

The words seemed too difficult for Ludie to get out, so Claris continued on for her.

"The Church's worshippers already had their eyes on the Hanamura family from the start. Now, since you, Kousuke, a member of the Hanamura family, came to my lady's aid, there is a high chance you have been marked as a quarry warranting elimination."

"Really, now…? Wait, what?"

What did she just say? I've "been marked"?

"Thus, as a concerned party, His Majesty has deemed it wise to inform you of everything."

"I—I see."

In *MX*, they're supposed to have their sights set on Ludie and the protagonist. How did this end up with them targeting me?!

"I am terribly sorry…"

Seeing my unrest, Ludie apologized.

"N-now, now, being a part of the Hanamura family meant they had their eyes on you anyway, so we're not particularly concerned, and you shouldn't be, either."

"Excuse me, but going forward, I would say that you *must* be concerned."

Yup. Ludie was absolutely right. If I had a target on my back, that was definitely something to be worried about.

"Good point…"

"I believe you now understand the situation. Now then…Claris?"

"Yes, milady," Claris answered with a salute. No matter how you sliced it, she was clearly a knight, not a maid.

She produced a leather envelope from an ornately decorated bag and placed it in front of Marino. The opening was tied with a navy-blue thread. Marino gathered mana in her hands, and a crest featuring a clover motif rose softly from the envelope.

I'd seen this before in the game. It was the crest of the Tréfle Empire. As Marino passed mana through the wrapping, the thread unraveled smoothly. A single piece of paper flew out from inside.

Sis and I moved around behind Marino and peered down at the piece of paper.

To Whom It May Concern,

I hope you are warming yourself in the early spring air after this recent cold and record-breaking winter.

Our youngest daughter, as though spurred on by the flowers of spring, frolics around our garden, enjoying the plants and animals as energetically as ever.

It appears her infectious smile is not ours alone to enjoy, as it has spread throughout the castle grounds. Thanks to her, the castle has been filled with a vivacious energy the likes of which we have never seen before. Even God himself must be jealous of her adorable charm.

Now to the matter at hand. The most recent incident was truly inconceivable. Oh, for our beloved darling Ludivine to be targeted in such a way. We offer our deepest words of gratitude to you, Master Kousuke. We have permanently dealt with these vile criminals.

In the interim, we have received word that a spy has infiltrated the Academy. However, we have been unable to ascertain the veracity of this information. We ask you to be on your guard.

Speaking of being on guard, recently our youngest daughter as fallen fully under the whims of her bubbling curiosity, showing interest in a great many things. Her most recent favorite is magic. Though she is still far too young to learn magic, she has been grabbing wands and playing with mana. Anxious though we may be, our expectations for her grow further still. Our youngest daughter is extremely adept at manipulating mana. We can see her becoming a powerful mage in her future. Oh how we wish we could show you how she looks holding her wand. She is truly the cutest angel this world has to offer. If only I could marry her.

Now, with spring marching on, we implore you to be well, and we are wishing you all of the best.

Kindest regards.

Now, this was an obnoxiously long-winded and bizarre letter, but there were only a few points being made.

① My youngest daughter is cute.

② Thank you for saving Ludie.

③ There may be a spy hiding out at the Academy. We don't know for sure, but be careful.

④ My youngest daughter is unbelievably cute. I want to marry her.

Where should I even begin with this? For the time being, there was one thing I needed to make sure of:

"Is your homeland okay?" *With His Majesty being like this, I mean.*

"…I would say His Highness is very capable when it comes to governing his people."

Sympathy welled up inside me as I watched Claris wince in reply. Ludie's puzzled look was no doubt a product of her pampered upbringing. When playing through her route, one of the events even has His Majesty show up at the Academy, so clearly, he was quite the doting father.

"A spy at the Academy…"

Marino frowned at the letter. Unfortunately, there was indeed a spy on campus.

"It'd be a good idea to keep note of it for now. Those guys were brazen enough to attack a Hanamura family hotel, after all."

When I responded, Marino mumbled that I had a point.

"With that in mind, my father has a proposal for you. Ms. Marino, I believe you are somewhat aware, but…"

Ludie then looked toward Claris, who gave a small nod before continuing for Ludie.

"The Tréfle Empire estimates that Princess Ludivine and Mr. Kousuke are the two people who will be specifically targeted at the Academy."

Ludie was definitely going to be targeted. In the game, a bunch of small-scale events happen, and as you begin resolving them all, angered Church fanatics start taking increasingly drastic measures.

Looking back, it had been a lot of fun. In the beginning, they take hostages to try and threaten Ludie. Then they use perilous, forbidden summoning magic, and then a dungeon just pops up in the middle of the town. That one is a bit of a pain, since Ludie gets separated from the rest of the party… I needed to remember to prepare for that event down the line. Although, events with the Church of the Malevolent Lord don't get going until after you start school and begin challenging dungeons, so I didn't need to worry about it yet.

"…As such, we have a duty to protect Mr. Kousuke and Princess Ludivine."

Marino nodded in agreement with Claris's statement.

Judging by Marino and Hatsumi's skills as magic-users, they were much less likely to be targeted than I was, and they were honestly far more likely to send any would-be assailants to the grave themselves.

"That explains that issue, then, doesn't it…?"

Marino nodded solemnly as she spoke. However, I had no idea what she was talking about.

"What is this 'issue' you're talking about?"

"Well, I was actually asked if we could take in Ludie and her bodyguards here at our house. Since both Hatsumi and I are here, we could spring into action in case there was an emergency."

It made sense to me that being under the protection of someone as strong as Marino would greatly ease any worries about potential attacks, and by bringing the two of us together, the cost of protecting…… Hmm? Hold on a second. Bringing the two of us together? Take her in? Here?

"Whaaa—?! H-have her live here?!"

W-were they crazy?! What the hell were they thinking? Of course she couldn't live here. For starters, being under the same roof with a pubescent young girl was too absurd of a development, even for an eroge…… Actually, comparatively speaking, it was a fairly classic setup.

N-nope, no way was this happening. This house was already home to a guy at the pinnacle of perversion! We were talking about someone with the soul of a veteran player who'd been blasting through two eroge a month! She might be safe from the Church of the Malevolent Lord, but her chastity would certainly be under threat. Anyway, in the game, the emperor dotes on his daughters, right? His Majesty gets furious when he finds out about Ludie dating the protagonist and sics a whole knight platoon on him. You're telling me this same guy was okay with Ludie living with me? Honestly, that was the real miracle here.

"I'm opposed. I can't agree with having strangers living here long-term."

Suddenly, Hatsumi, who had been keeping silent, spoke up. I honestly wished she'd keep going.

"As such, since you and Claris are already acquainted, Ms. Hatsumi, I was thinking of having her be the one to live here. Father judged that with Ms. Hatsumi and Ms. Marino present, having Claris as the sole bodyguard was more than enough protection. This method would provide a high degree of security without requiring too many people for the job. A win-win, as it were."

Sis and Claris knew each other, huh...? I hoped she would decline the offer, but I wasn't holding my breath.

"In that case...I don't mind."

There it was...but to be perfectly honest, even I wanted to accept the offer. Hell, I would have gotten on my hands and knees for an opportunity to live together. While our marriage hadn't been officially recognized back in Japan for some unfathomable reason, Ludie had been my wife. One of my wives among dozens of others. I wouldn't deny that I longed to have her stay by my side if it was possible. All that said, reputation-wise, this was clearly not a good idea!

"Kousuke."

Hearing my name, I turned to Marino. She pounded her fist into her chest with a serious look and then grinned and winked, as if to tell me she would handle everything.

Of course, Marino would still be here. She was a very respectable adult and a mother who had raised Hatsumi into a brilliant member of society. Unrelated teenage boys and girls living under the same roof—surely she understood that physical dangers and publicity nightmares were bound to happen!

"Don't worry. I know exactly what you're going to say."

See, I knew I could rely on an adult's common decency and sense of restraint. Go on, say it!

"Tee-hee... We need to prep for the welcome party, right? ♪"

Ah yes, of course. Now that there were new people coming to live with us, we needed to have a big welcome party to get know each other! ......Huh? Something wasn't right here.

As I stared blankly at Marino, I felt a tap on my shoulder. I turned around to find Sis looking the same as she always did. However, while she wore her usual deadpan expression, I couldn't help but sense a subtle air of self-confidence about her.

"I understand your concerns, Kousuke. Let your big sister handle it."

Hatsumi then gave me a big thumbs-up.

My savior was here! My affection rank just rose through the roof. She could ask me to marry her right now, and I'd say yes in heartbeat. Though I guess I would've said yes before all of this anyway.

Okay, Sis, it was all up to you. Settle this once and for all!

I gazed at her, and she puffed out her voluptuous chest, saying:

"I know a good place to buy the cake."

That's not what I was worried about...

Chapter 5 | **Yukine Mizumori Is a Goddess** | Magical★Explorer

Reborn as a Side Character in a Fantasy Dating Sim

Truly unbelievable things don't really happen very often. However, they do still happen on occasion. Above all else, this was the world of eroge—a type of exaggerated reality.

Now, I'd seen a number of unbelievable things since arriving in this world. It would be too annoying to count them all, but the most recent one would be Ludie and Claris moving in to my house. Then. On top of that. The situation presently unfolding before me was also unbelievable.

While on my daily run, I happened to glance over to my side.

"Hah...hah...hah...hah..."

A flowing black ponytail swayed back and forth like an excited puppy's tail. Normally, she would keep her hair down, but she must have tied it back for her run. Strapped to her back was what could easily be considered a fundamental part of her identity—a light-pink naginata.

As always, her gorgeous face and figure were worthy of exaltation, almost enough to make me stop running just to appreciate them in full. This was especially true of the two mountains swaying up and down in front of her; there was no more commanding a presence this world could offer, and I had to actively force myself not to leer at them.

Okay, now could someone please tell me—why Yukine Mizumori was running next to me...?!

I had no idea. Had I done something to spur her on or something?

I couldn't deny the fact that, for the past three days or so, I'd been watching her training as way to pump myself up. But wait, that wasn't what it sounded like. I wasn't ogling her or stalking her. Nothing like that. From my perspective, it was simply as though I'd come to the library, and upon seeing someone else studying, found an urge to do the same.

Though I will admit I'd been staring at her boobs. They were shaking and jiggling—how was I supposed to help myself? It wasn't my fault at all. It was my upperclassman's fault for shaking her shapely bosom so much...... Nah, actually, I was clearly the bad guy here.

After finishing my planned running distance, I pondered whether or not I should try talking to Yukine Mizumori. Unable to figure out the best way to strike up a conversation, I decided to turn my attention to my usual training regime.

Starting with offensive drills, I would use my Third and Fourth Hands during a state of post-run exhaustion. From there, I would run defensive drills by thrusting my stole, filling it with mana, and then instantly opening it up and hardening it with an enchantment. Despite being simple and monotonous, these exercises would serve as foundational movements I would be using a lot in the future. That's what I hoped anyway.

Casually shifting my gaze, I saw that Yukine Mizumori was swinging her naginata again.

Finished with my training regime at long last, I adjusted my stole's position before morphing it into the shape of a chair and sitting down. Despite our similar training routines, I was gasping for air and barely able to stand, while Yukine Mizumori was breathing more roughly but otherwise betrayed not a hint of exhaustion.

I didn't expect there'd be such a gap in our physical fitness... I need to practice even more.

Brushing off her sweat-soaked skin, Yukine Mizumori steadied her breath. She sheathed her naginata and walked toward where I sat. Had she noticed me stealing glances at her breasts, her butt, her arms, her nape, etcetera, etcetera while I'd been training?

"...Are you always doing this?"

"...Yes, unless it's raining or something."

"I see..."

Her eyes were focused on my stole. By sectioning off where I gathered my mana, I'd turned it into a comfy seat with strong legs supporting it.

"...Would you like a seat?"

"Oh, no...... Sorry, actually, do you mind?"

After her initial refusal, she accepted my offer. I quickly altered the chair's shape and reformed it to seat another person.

Yukine nervously touched the chair. She felt it up from top to bottom, gingerly rubbing the material... Then, letting her weight go and forcefully pressing into the chair, she slowly dropped into the seat.

That was the very first time in my life I wished I could swap places with a stole.

"Oh yes, that feels wonderful."

Hrnk. Her words were music to my ears.

"Though I still can't really believe it...," Yukine Mizumori noted, still rubbing her hand along the stole.

"Wh-what can't you believe?"

I attempted to act normal as I tried to pull my head out of the clouds.

"...Your mana pool; I've already used all mine up. And that you can be so exhausted and still maintain this enchantment of yours... Are you a new Academy student?"

"Yes. My name's Kousuke Takioto."

"Shoot, I should've introduced myself. I'm a first-year... Oh, no, I'll be a second-year once you start school. I'm Yukine Mizumori, the lieutenant of the Morals Committee. It's like being the committee vice president."

"The Morals Committee's lieutenant?" I asked, feigning surprise. In the game, the Morals Committee operates as a powerful and influential force within the Academy. It was something to be surprised about.

"Yeah, the position isn't all that impressive, though. That, and there's higher heights to climb..."

At that, she looked off into the sky. Based on the vibe I got from her, I assumed she was currently facing the same troubles as her in-game counterpart.

"You should be able to get a position within one of the Academy's Three Committees without any issue."

I shook my head.

"I don't know about that... My special constitution dampens the effects of any emission magic I cast."

Although this was what I told her, in truth, I did intend to immediately join one of the Academy's Three Committees. While it was still incomplete, I'd been formulating a plan to make it happen. To be honest, I'd thought it up to distract myself while I'd been unable to think up a proper excuse to give to Ludie. When I brought up "special constitution," Yukine gave an understanding nod.

"A bit like the Founding Saint, then?"

"Um, similar, but still a bit different. The Saint was blessed with tremendous healing magic instead, right? In my case…"

Yukine's eyes turned to my stole.

"It's enchantment magic. My emission magic doesn't get any better than this."

I aimed a fireball and shot it at a nearby tree. The tree was new-growth, so with the pitiful amount of power I could muster, I wasn't worried about burning it.

"I get it…… You're, well…… Nah, forget it."

Yukine began to say something but cut herself off. That didn't stop me from figuring out what she was trying to say, though.

"As a magic-user, I do think it'll end up being a significant handicap. I'm living with true masters who can easily handle large-scale magic. For one."

She stared hard at me in silence.

"Of course, I think they're amazing, and the difference in our abilities does make me depressed sometimes. But."

"But…?"

I grinned and stared back into Yukine's gemstone eyes.

"But there's a chance I can grow stronger with these limitations. That, and being at a disadvantage? It actually gets me fired up. It's fun to think about how I can use this finicky ability of mine to defeat my opponents… This incantation has a surprising number of applications. Here, like this—"

No sooner had I said this than I changed the shape of my stole bench to give it a backrest. Then I put my weight on it and reclined. After I'd constructed one on Yukine's side as well, she tested it out with her hands before slowly shifting herself backward.

"I see… You seem pretty strong."

Her stiff expression melted away to reveal a compassionate smile.

"Sometimes I think to myself, 'You know, I'm gonna stand at the top of the Academy. Just you wait.'"

"That's the spirit. A good goal to have."

I knew how hard it would be to get to the top of the class. There were powerful challengers to overcome, from the protagonist to the student council president. Still, I had yet to fully reach the limit of my abilities in this world. Besides, there were plenty of ways to take down the protagonist or the student council president.

Just as I was about to address Yukine, a breeze blew in. Passing through my flushed body, it brought the smell of dried earth and just a hint of Yukine's aroma to my nose. It felt lovely. Placing her hands on top of her martial arts hakama robes, she stared blankly in front of her, absorbed in some sort of meditation.

Yukine Mizumori was a character I truly loved. Personality, looks, everything, really—I was smitten with it all. That was exactly why I planned on triggering the awakening event that directly dealt with her current dilemma and would make her grow strong.

Leaving my beloved heroine plagued by her problems and unable to show the world her true potential was absolutely out of the question. On my road to eventually becoming the mightiest of all, I wanted her to become one of my comrades, maybe even a steep height I could aspire toward.

As these thoughts circled about in my mind, Yukine suddenly let out a quiet exclamation, as if remembering something.

"Actually, that reminds me... You know what, Kousuke?"

"What?"

"This is private land. I've been using this place with permission. Knowing her, I don't think she'd mind you being here, but I'll ask if it's okay on your behalf, just to make sure."

"Oh, that's okay. Marino is my mother's cousin, and it's a bit of a long story, but she's looking after me."

She was stunned by my reply, her eyes going wide and her mouth hanging open.

"When you mentioned living with strong magic-users......you meant the Academy director?"

"Yes. Also, Hatsumi is my second cousin."

"You don't say... Sorry. In that case, there shouldn't be a problem."

My answer seemed to have convinced her. She then grabbed her chin, deep in thought.

"Is something wrong?"

She shook her head slightly, as if to tell me not worry about it. Then—

"Going off topic a moment, is it okay for me to be using this place, too?" she asked, scanning the area.

Puzzled, I also looked around. Stretched out before me was a wide-open oval-shaped clearing surrounded by a thick overgrowth of trees. Clover or some other kind of wild grass sprouted up everywhere you stepped. It must have felt great to bask in the sun under the large tree on the far side of the clearing. I don't think it could hold a candle to my classical Japanese literature class back in middle school, but I knew it would send me off to dreamland in no time.

Okay, time to snap back to reality. What was Yukine trying to say here?

This was Marino's privately owned land, but she had already given Yukine permission to be here. If that weren't true, she wouldn't have been training under the waterfall in the first place.

"I'm pretty sure you can?"

"That's not it; I'm asking you. This is your running course, right? I've caught glimpses of you here and there."

I finally figured out what she was trying to say.

"You're not bothering me at all. Please feel free to use it. Besides, when I see someone really giving it their all, it helps motivate me."

"Really? Then I'll keep coming here. Also, say the word, and I'll avoid training under the waterfall. I ruin the view, right?"

How exactly was I supposed to answer? Forget ruining the view—if anything, she harmonized with it perfectly. More than that, she honestly elevated it to another level.

"Oh, come on now, you can't be serious! Sure, the scenery around the waterfall is beautiful, but it's no match for you. Please practice there as much as you like!" I responded, smiling. Yukine replied with a delighted snicker.

"Hee-hee, thank you. I'll take you up on your offer."

It appeared that she'd taken what I'd said as a joke, but it had all been straight from the heart.

From there, we continued conversing about nothing in particular before Yukine eventually got up.

"Well, that was enough of a break and then some. I'll be heading home."

"Okay, then...... Oh, Yukine."

Now standing, Yukine turned around to face me.

"Hmm? What?"

"Um, if I may be so bold, I have a favor to ask you."

"A favor?"

I nodded at the puzzled Yukine's question.

"Yes, I'd like you to train me, whenever you have free time, of course. Until I learn the Mind's Eye skill, if possible."

She stared at me in surprise.

Yukine Mizumori was an undeniable goddess.

To be perfectly honest, I'd expected her to turn me down. It had been our first time speaking together. Outside of that, our relationship had consisted of occasionally glancing at each other while training. She'd agreed to my request, though. She really was divine. If there were indeed a goddess in this world, then she should pack up shop and surrender the position to Yukine Mizumori posthaste. That aside, wasn't this a little *too* intense?

"Y-Y-Y-Yukine, is there r-r-really a m-meaning to all this?"

The waterfall gushed down on my head. While the weather was just starting to get warmer, the water was cold enough to freeze me to the bone. It felt as though I'd dived naked into a snowbank—scratch that, the frigid water pouring over me might have been even colder.

"Kousuke, I can see your distracting thoughts."

That was her way of saying *Shut up and do it.* Taking her at her word, I crossed my legs together in a meditative pose. Next to me, Yukine closed her eyes and made the same pose, the waterfall hammering away at her from above.

"Once you've cleared your mind of distracting thoughts, close your eyes and release your mana. Then imagine that mana being sprinkled all around you."

She made it sound easy, but I was still totally lost. For the time being, I closed my eyes just as she told me to and activated the mana inside me, but that's where I ran into trouble.

"I c-can't s-s-see anything!"

"Do it properly. You should be able to sense where I am. When you get used to it, you can even see your opponent's mana, giving you the upper hand in battle. I've heard you can even gain seethrough vision and future sight, too, but I haven't reached that level yet."

In the game, the Mind's Eye skill greatly increases a character's dodge chance and attack accuracy. It also has a secondary effect where if the character is in a dark environment or temporarily blinded, their accuracy won't be lowered.

The in-game skill description reads something like, *"Using your inner eye, you can locate your opponents and read their movements."* I hoped by learning this skill, I could compensate for losing my forward vision while using my stole wall. There were multiple ways to obtain the skill, but the simplest method involves having Yukine Mizumori teach it to you.

I opened my eyes and glanced over at her.

She was the exact opposite of the timid and trembling weakling beside her. Unbending against the cold pounding of the water, she arched her back skyward. My favorite heroine struck a gallant and beautiful figure.

In the game, she's one of the select few characters who possess Mind's Eye from the start. The skill is so effective that a subset of eroge afficionados considered it one of the most overpowered skills in the game by far, so it was recommended that every player pick it up.

With the Mind's Eye skill alone, you gain increased accuracy, increased affinity, and a 30 percent dodge chance boost against all attacks except for area of effect magic and special skills with boosted accuracy. The dodge chance augment was low-key great, but more than anything else, the increased accuracy was fantastic. In the latter half of the game, there are a lot of enemies with a weirdly high evasion rate, so it's important to make sure you equip the skill to any party members who specialize in large area of effect spells. It was an absolutely essential skill, even to someone like me who was totally inept with area of effect magic. Plus, if I could put Mind's Eye to good use, it could help resolve the biggest drawback of my stole wall. Two birds with one powerful stone.

Kousuke is able to learn the skill in the game, but in actuality…

I shifted my view away from Yukine and settled it on the lush scenery visible from inside the waterfall. Then I focused my attention and closed my eyes. I continued my meditation for about an hour, but despite my best efforts, I didn't acquire the Mind's Eye skill.

"Maybe I'm making a more fundamental mistake here."

Although the *character* of Kousuke Takioto is able to learn the Mind's Eye skill, it was *me* inhabiting him right now. The guy whose excitement soared through the roof on the last Friday of every month. I mean, since eroge companies released their games on the final Friday of the month to line up with their customers' paydays and the weekend, it only made sense to get hyped.

Of course, the fact that I was asking myself this question meant I couldn't expect an answer.

Two days had already passed since I'd asked Yukine Mizumori for her help, but I still showed absolutely no sign of learning the skill. With school starting up soon, there were still many other preparations I needed to make, yet here I was, being pounded by the waterfall.

What distracted me more than anything else, though, was the girl sitting next to me under the falls.

I didn't have a clue where she'd gotten it from, but Yukine was wearing what looked like a shrine maiden costume. The way the white cloth stuck fast to her skin was very sexy. While I wanted to gaze upon her form forever, the continuous stream of cold water hammering me from above immediately banished any lewd thoughts from my mind. Seriously, I'd lost all bodily sensation. Conversely, it was probably because these thoughts disappeared so quickly that this ascetic training made it easier concentrate.

After our waterfall meditation ended, we warmed ourselves with magic. I spoke up while Yukine was pulling down her hair.

"I'm truly grateful for your help here, but are you sure you're okay with this?"

I wasn't the only one just about to start school, of course. Yukine was in the same boat. Despite that, she would immediately join me whenever she saw me at the waterfall.

"Don't worry about me, Takioto. I'm doing this as part of my own training," she replied with a grin, but I still felt incredibly guilty. She was a very considerate and attentive person—something I knew from the game. That was part of why I'd fallen for her.

Nevertheless, I didn't expect that attraction would lead me to be consumed by self-reproach.

"It's all about your ability to concentrate. Focus every nerve in your body, more than you've ever done before, and feel the mana. Don't use your eyes. Feel it with your seventh sense."

Hold on, *seventh* sense…? Anyway, I understood what she was trying to say, but putting it into practice was hard. For starters, I hadn't possessed some kind of mana-detecting seventh sense back in Japan, so trying to be conscious of the magical energy alone was hard enough already.

"From what I've heard, you can perceive exactly what your target's sensing through strengthening Mind's Eye. My father told me he can intuit a monster's weak points that way."

This ability to sense weak points resulted in both increased affinity and heightened skill proficiency. Mind's Eye was essential when it came time to battle monsters, and I definitely wanted it.

But just how long would it take for me to learn this thing?

"…Hey, Takioto, I think you're misunderstanding something here."

Unable to watch me sit in silence, Yukine raised her voice. I turned and found her staring intensely at me, arms crossed in her soaked-through shrine maiden outfit.

"You don't just learn a skill overnight, all right?"

That may indeed have been in line with the conventional wisdom of this world. But I knew the truth. In the game, it takes three turn cycles to learn a skill. If I converted that to days…it should be about three or four? When I thought of it like that, it wasn't *totally* unreasonable that I hadn't learned it yet.

"Be patient. Keep moving, make headway little by little, and you'll get there. Just keep at it."

She spoke as if she was trying to convince herself of the same thing. Considering her current circumstances, her words carried a great deal of weight.

"Yukine…… Never mind, it's nothing."

I choked back my words. I'd started speaking involuntarily but figured it would be best to hold back what I'd wanted to voice in my current state.

"Well, then."

With that, she looked at the river. Its waters, clear enough to see to the bottom, continued to flow on endlessly. From up above, tiny leaves fluttered down and, abandoning themselves to the currents, leisurely floated along. However, when some got caught on a large rock, they remained stuck, utterly stagnant.

The Hanamura household was teeming with moving boxes and beautiful elven women.

Cardboard containers affixed with descriptive labels like *books* and *tea set* piled up from the entryway through the main hall, and a group of elves were divvying them up to remove their contents and carrying them to Ludie's room.

"…Is something wrong?"

A voice called out suddenly. Behind me, the beautiful-buttocked…… um, Claris was staring back at me. Instead of her knightlike equipment from before, she was dressed in a basic green sweater and shorts. She held a small cardboard box in her hands.

"Oh, no, just thinking to myself…"

I couldn't stop my eyes from drifting down to her slender legs. From what I could tell, she was taller than the average elf, about a head taller than the other elven women running about. She was close to eye level with me. Still, she had a pretty face that was small and attractive. Although, if this world was true to the world of the game, every elf had a pretty face when compared to humans.

"Is that so…?"

Claris kept her gaze fixed on me. Seeing this reaction, I got the impression she bore a significant amount of suspicion toward me, but…why?

Intending to ask her what was wrong, I tried taking a step forward, but something blocked my path. Curious, I looked down to see my foot had gotten caught on one of the moving boxes. A label was affixed to the box, on which a couple of words had been scribbled:

Claris Clothes

Now I knew what was going on. Claris had definitely gotten the wrong idea here. True, I was interested in the clothes of beautiful women, particularly of a woman as attractive as her. And yes, I would have agreed to lick her feet right then and there if it meant a getting a peek inside her chest of forbidden treasure. A spectacular treat, for sure.

No, no, no, I needed to cool it with the stupid fantasies. Getting lost in thought in front of a box of her clothes was my fault, but either way, Claris had the wrong impression.

"O-oh, no, that wasn't my intention at all."

"Is that an admission of guilt...?"

"N-no, that's not it. My strength's plateaued recently and I... I was just mulling it over."

"I see..."

She remained dubious as she looked my way.

"I—I know, how do you learn skills, Claris? There's this skill I really want to learn, but it isn't coming to me no matter what I do."

At times like this, it was best to change the subject. Of course, there was a chance it'd end with the classic *Don't try to change the subject*, complete with the thud of hands slamming on a table... Those moments usually ended with a slap.

"Skills?"

Her glare softened somewhat. This was my chance, in more ways than one. On top of changing the subject away from this box, I could get some skill advice from her.

"Yeah, a friend of mine is teaching me the basics, but I haven't shown any signs of learning this skill yet..."

Claris frowned as she considered my plight with a hand on her chin.

"Hmm, let's see... I guess focus single-mindedly on training it?"

I couldn't hold back my sigh.

"That's really the only option after all."

At the end of the day, I guess I just had to buckle down and do it. Still, stumbling along without knowing when the skill would come to me was pretty taxing.

"This is just a theory, but...," Claris began, stretching the palm of her hand out in front of her. "Apparently, skills manifest more readily at times when you most desire them."

Then she created a transparent, board-shaped object in her hand.

"I actually had a skill manifest like that myself. Maybe you should practice with that in mind?"

She seemed to be thinking back fondly on something as she smiled, stroking the plank she had made.

"...Actually, when I was little, I was really terrible at using magic, in spite of having a huge mana pool."

My eyes widened in surprise.

"Really, now?"

"That's right. That's why I learned how to wield a sword and bow. After I gained skills and got a handle on using a certain degree of spellcraft, I shifted my combat style toward using sword and shield incantations."

I sighed in admiration. Much like Yukine Mizumori, Claris also seemed capable of handling long-distance battles, despite leaning toward close-quarters combat.

"I've been informed of your unique constitution. Somewhat similar to my own, isn't it? Learning skills could open up new paths forward for you."

In the game, no matter what the player tries, Kousuke Takioto never develops the ability to use long-range spells. He's not the only one, though—the widely-known Founding Saint is the exact same way. However, it remained unclear if this world matched up exactly to the eroge. It would be a good idea to test things out a little bit more.

"That's a good point... Thank you. I'll stick with it a bit longer, then."

As I replied to her, something crossed my mind.

"Would you like me to help you out?"

Ludie had a number of elves carrying her belongings, but no one was helping her maid (who looked more like a knight), Claris. I guess it made sense that Her Highness would take priority.

"Oh, no, it's fine. Some of these boxes are pretty heavy..."

"All the more reason for me to help. Besides, I might be asking you for more skill advice later, so let me do something in return!"

I filled my stole with mana and had it strike a muscle man pose. At this, Claris nodded with a grin.

"I see. If you want to help, those boxes there are my personal belongings. Can you carry them up the stairs for me?"

"Of course. Leave them to me!"

I leaped into action. The box of clothes was nearby...but I opted to lift up a box labeled *Claris Books* with my Third Hand instead.

"Huh, this pretty light..."

"Aaaaahhhh!"

Taken aback by Claris's sudden, uncharacteristically feminine squeal, I nearly dropped the box entirely.

"Kousuke! Take this one, please!" she shouted, pointing toward the box labeled *Claris Clothes*.

Okay, what exactly was she getting at here?

I'd purposefully avoided her container of clothes, and now she was offering them to me?

"O-okay," I responded, taking it in my Fourth Hand. This container was unbelievably heavy, many times the weight of the carton of books.

"I'll carry this one!"

Snatching the container away from me, she hastily headed for her room.

Now, why was the "books" box so light, when the "clothes" box was so heavy? I couldn't say for sure, but I had a hunch. The contents in the boxes likely didn't match up with their labels.

The swap must have been for security purposes. It was easy to imagine that a depraved pervert lusting after a girl's clothes would try stealing them from the box labeled *Clothes*. By contrast, there weren't any perverts out there trying to steal books. The labels could have been written incorrectly, but I doubted Claris would make as klutzy a mistake as that.

Shifting the box in my Fourth Hand, I followed after Claris.

A little way on, I gazed in awe at her ascending the stairs.

What a marvelous butt. Though thick, it had a tightness to it, and it was perfectly shaped. The mix of her gorgeous derriere accentuated with each step and her milky-white thighs poking out from her shorts combined together to form an image that could only be described as art. She could tell me to kiss her ass, and I'd consider it an honor. If anything, I'd happily oblige.

"Make sure you watch your step down there."

"Naaah, no worries. I may not have lived here that long, either, but I wouldn't trip like that."

"I suppose not… Hee-hee."

She giggled as she continued up the stairs, when suddenly, she shifted.

"Gaaaah!"

Not two seconds after giving her warning, Claris missed the step in front of her.

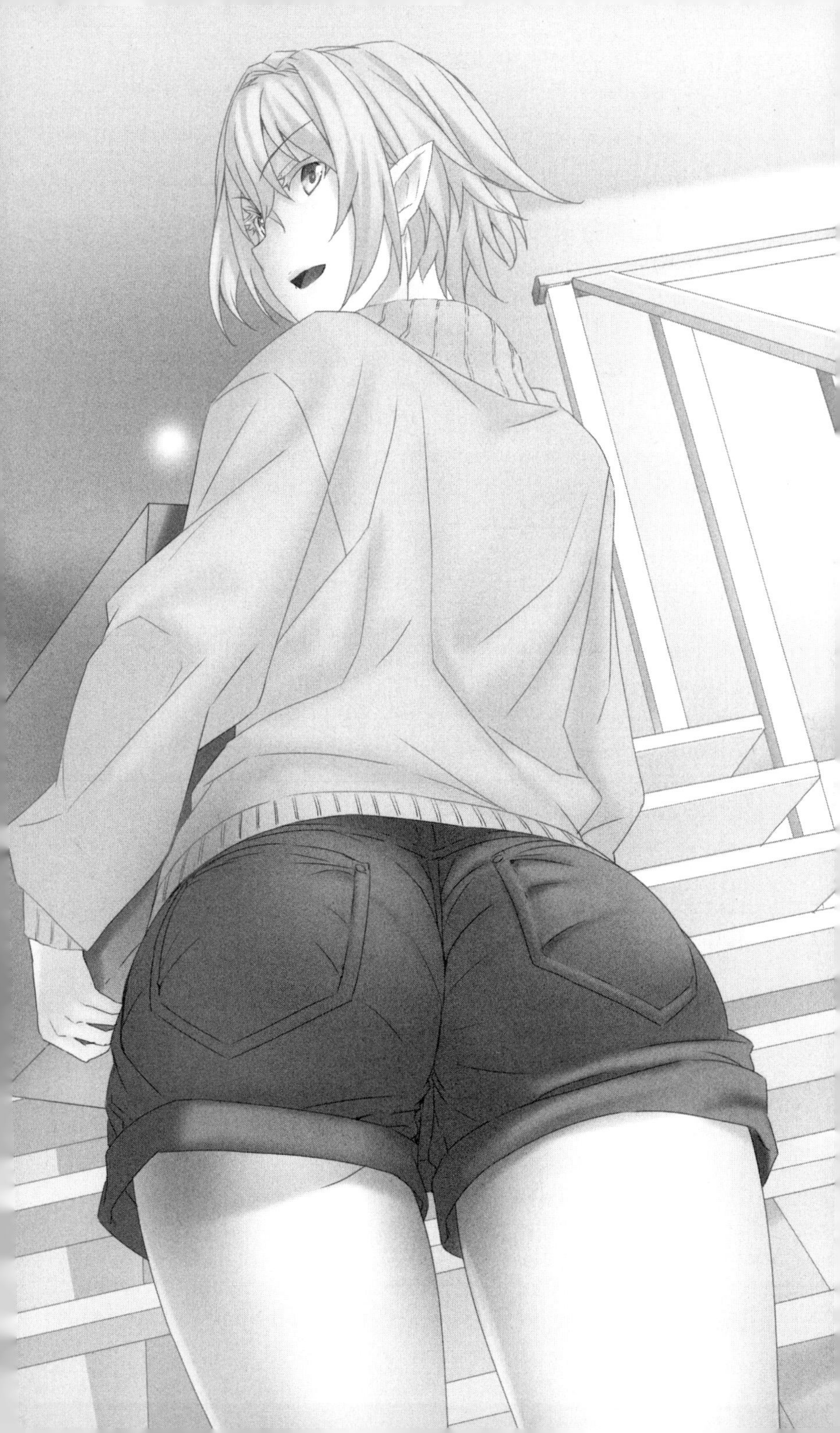

For some unknown reason, she tossed up the cardboard box in her grip as she fell. At this rate, the container in her hands was going to slam on top of my head.

I might have been able to dodge it. Could I have done it in a vacuum? Sure. However, we were standing on a stairwell. Evading the package would have put Claris in danger.

Fully resolved to take the box's incoming blow, I reached out my hands to support Claris. Then, I used my Third Hand to grab the banister.

"Mmph?!"

Not a moment later, my vision went pitch-black. Some sort of fabric covered my head, and it was difficult to breathe. It smelled wonderful, though. Like a sunny spring day.

"Aaaaaaaah! I-I'm so sorry!"

She leaped up, out of my arms, and went to take the container off my head.

"U-um, are you all right?"

"Just fine. No problems at all."

Right as I gave my strained answer, the box came off my head, and with it, the bright light of day rushed into view. I suddenly felt something strange hanging off my head. It seemed to be caught, so I took the unknown object off to scrutinize it.

"A string?"

It definitely looked like one at first glance. Nevertheless, a string it was not. At the end of it was a thin bit of fabric. *That's* what it was.

I instinctively took a big gulp.

This sacred piece of cloth protected a person's most precious areas. They were sexy black panties.

And man, were these really something else. Since the panties were almost totally string, I could only imagine what her butt would end up looking like in them. Not only that, but the front side was almost totally see-through, and...... Wait, why was there a fist coming at me?

"Noooooooooooooooooooooo!"

Once again, my vision went pitch-black.

Now then, if you asked me who was at fault in this most recent incident, Claris was the undeniable perpetrator. I'd simply offered to help her out of the goodness of my heart. Also, I'd fulfilled my duty by supporting her as she fell down the stairs, and in a way, I'd also saved her from harm. Despite all that, Her Highness Ludie continued to glare at me, dubious.

"Seriously?"

It came across not only in her expression but in her speech, too. Her manner of speaking was starting to slowly align with her true nature.

"Absolutely."

At my answer, Ludie turned to Claris, her disbelief palpable. Claris nodded in agreement, of course. It was simple, really.

"Y-yes, um, it's true."

Claris backed up my reply while looking extremely apologetic.

So then why was Ludie still glaring at me like I was a creep? I mean, given that my rap sheet included groping their chest and butt, her reaction made some sense, but I wanted her to have a bit more faith in me. Unfortunately, however, I couldn't deny that I was indeed a debauchee.

"Well, sorry, then. I shouldn't have hit you."

Ludie still seemed unconvinced but bowed her head.

"It's okay. Anyone who saw us back there would've gotten the wrong impression."

Finding a guy in a pile of women's clothing clutching a black pair of panties? Yeah, that's gonna lead to punches. I will admit that I hadn't expected to get hit by both Claris *and* Ludie, though.

"I'm so very, very sorry..."

Claris deeply bowed her head.

"No worries. I don't mind."

When I replied, Ludie whispered something in Claris's ear. She then responded, "No, I don't think so. I think...," in a voice loud enough for me to hear. Ludie continued to press further, and this time, Claris's face went beet red before she answered loudly, "N-no, not something so shameless! Though I did catch him looking..." Just what were they muttering about? Whatever it was, I knew it wasn't good.

Suddenly, there came a knock on the door.

"Miss Ludie, a call from His Majesty..."

An elf dressed as a maid timidly poked her head in. *Now this is what a maid's supposed to look like*, I thought to myself as I compared her with Claris. With her nice figure, Claris would definitely look good in

a maid getup. Her current everyday wear was wonderful, too, empha-
sizing her lascivious...*ahem*, her healthy legs.

After having a word or two with Claris, Ludie kept a watchful eye on
me as she exited the room.

"............"

"............"

The silence was deafening.

Well, what should I say to her? I'd never been in a situation like this
before.

It was Claris who broke the awkward atmosphere first.

"You've saved me multiple times now, and, well, if there's anything I
can do for you, I will. Please just let me know."

I wasn't sure I'd heard her right. Did she just say she'd do *anything*?

Whoa there, what was I thinking...? My mind had gone there on
reflex. She of course meant she'd do anything *within reason*. With that
in mind, did I have anything I could ask for help with?

.........There was a lot, actually.

"In that case, I do have a request!"

My energetic lunge forward spooked her, and she stiffened up a little
before she nodded gravely.

"O-okay, I'm ready."

What exactly had she prepared herself for?

"Um, it might be hard to understand what I'm getting at, but...I'd
like to spar with you."

I'd simply wanted her to help me out with my training. Unfortunately, Ludie's parting remark seemed to have brought a more licen-
tious possibility to the forefront of her mind.

"........."

Claris blinked repeatedly before responding, "So, like, a sparring
partner?

"Yes, that's right..."

Well, great. What was I going to do about this weird tension?

Then, giving a loud "Ah-ha!" Claris stood up, red in the face.

"R-right, yes, sparring, of course. Allow me to help. Let's start with
physical stamina first. Time for a run!"

Whoa, whoa, just hold on a minute, please.

I used my Third Hand to stop her as she headed toward the door.
She was being way too hasty.

"W-wait a second. Um, I didn't mean at this exact moment. Look out the window."

I pointed toward the sunless sky, which was slowly filling with stars. It had grown dark, and dinner would be soon.

"Not a problem, I'll be our light!"

"Um, excuse me?!"

"Leave it to me; I'm very good at it."

"That makes even less sense. Please calm down."

She was so flustered that if she were in a manga, she'd have swirling spirals for eyes. Even in reality, they were darting all over.

"I'm very calm, I assure you. It'll be fine. In Tréfle, they even say I'm the light on when nobody's home—"

Okay, the light isn't the issue. Besides, I'm pretty sure that phrase isn't the compliment you think it is.

"Heeey, Princess Ludivine! Ludie! I need your help!"

I opened up the door to her room and shouted. I couldn't take it anymore.

Unfortunately, the person who soon answered my call wasn't whom I had hoped.

"...Is something wrong?"

Wearing her trademark blank expression, Hatsumi tilted her head slightly. I had no idea what she had been up to, but the white robes she wore had been scribbled over with paint.

"Um, it's Claris. She—"

This was enough to prompt an understanding nod from Sis.

"Don't worry about her. If you leave her alone, she'll be better by tomorrow."

Wait, ignore her? More importantly, though...she was going to be like this for a whole day?

It took about ten minutes before Claris calmed down and returned to her room.

With things finally settled down, I was in the middle of explaining what had happened to Sis when the original person I'd requested arrived.

"Sorry it took me so long. I heard you calling for me, but...it appears as though the problem's been resolved?"

"Yes, everything's fine now."

"I see…"

After she spoke, Ludie's attention fell on Sis's robes. I wasn't the only one curious about all the stains. However, Hatsumi didn't seem to think anything of them.

"Anyway, Sis, as I was saying… After that, Claris's feet slipped, and her…uh, luggage, ended up over my head."

"Along with a pair of women's underwear, too."

Her Highness smoothly interjected with exactly what I'd wanted to leave unsaid. Sis nodded sagaciously.

"Lucky you."

"Indeed, I thought the sam— Um, Ludie?! I'm joking, please stop gathering mana in your hand like that!"

Okay, it wasn't really a joke, but I did let my true feelings slip out for a second there.

"'Ludie'?"

She furrowed her brow. Ah, this was the face she makes in the game so many times. It delighted me whenever she'd browbeat and verbally abuse me while playing, but I never would have thought it would be so terrifying to experience in person. Though a small part of me was still overjoyed.

"Eep, my utmost apologies, Your Highness Princess Ludivine!"

She gave a slight shake of her head.

"Ludie is fine, and you can hold off on the royal honorifics. I plan on speaking casually, too. Oh, and feel free to do the same thing, Hatsumi. Listen here, though—you didn't trip Claris on purpose to try to get at her clothes or anything, did you?"

Uh-oh. One single quip from Sis, and Ludie's previously retracted suspicions had flared up again. Actually, giving my candid feelings on the matter was the bigger factor, probably.

"O-of course not, I would never."

"I suppose so. But remember this: If you ever come at us with some ulterior motive in mind…"

Her smile sent an involuntary chill up my spine. The atmosphere in the room had taken a turn for the worse. I needed to change the subject.

I looked around for a new conversation starter, my eyes landing on Sis's clothes. Now that I thought about it, how did white robes end up looking like a painter's palette anyway?

"U-ulterior motives? Me? Of course not! B-by the way, Sis, what were you doing anyway? You weren't busy or anything, were you?!"

If I wasn't going to get in her way, I'd offer her my help. Then I could just fade out of this whole mess.

"I guess I was busy. The truth is, Mom…was instructing me on how to make dinner."

"Ahhh, I get it. Cooking! Right………"

………Cooking?

I took another look at Sis's robes. The cooking I was familiar with had exactly zero probability of resulting in paint or fluorescent coating all over your clothes.

Actually now, hold on a minute—it could be that preparing food here looked a bit different compared to preparing food back on Earth. Absurd as it might sound, monster meat was actually delicious. Other countries, not just Japan, had their own weird-colored candies, and I even had some whenever I got the chance to vacation abroad. Yeah, right, that had to be it. It may have *looked* bizarre, but surely the food was safe. It would be weird if it wasn't. Definitely safe.

Ludie was right next to me at the moment. I should try asking her about this world's cooking. I assumed she would respond with her usual attitude—*What, you really don't know? Fine, I guess I'll teach you*—and tell me what I wanted to know.

In an attempt to dispel my vague disquiet, I looked toward her. She had forced a smile, and all the color had drained from her face.

Oh boy, we were in trouble.

"I went to ask Mother to taste test it for me, but she had some work come up, I guess… But if you're not busy, Kousuke, then…could you?"

Marino had up and run away. She'd thought it would be too much for her to handle, so she'd booked it.

"Hmm… Ohhh, right! Sorry, Sis, I forgot to get this magic tool I'm gonna need for school, and…I was just about to head out and buy it!"

At this, Hatsumi's blank expression showed the slightest twinge of sadness…or at least, I got the feeling it did.

"Okay… How about you, Ludie?"

Ludie jerked stiffly as the conversation turned to her.

"Yes, well…you see…"

Faltering, she looked at my face and broke into a grin after having some sort of realization. Then she came up right beside me.

"Right, we were both planning on going shopping together!"

What, now?

"I don't remember any—*oomph*!"

Before I could finish my statement, a sharp pain ran up my back. Ludie had used enhance magic and pinched me hard. Was the enhancement really necessary?

"Roll with it!" she whispered in my ear. This was bad. I could see her veins popping out in anger.

"Y-yeah, right, of course! Sorry, Sis. Maybe next time…"

"I see. That's too bad," Sis muttered, still looking somewhat disappointed as she left the room.

After watching her leave, Ludie and I heaved simultaneous sighs of relief.

Now then, why had I used a shopping trip as an excuse?

I mean, for starters—didn't I mention it before when trying to curb Claris's rampage? The sun had set. Admittedly, it wasn't that late yet, and there were still a number of cars in the road and people walking around. Nonetheless, the stars were already shining.

I began walking the moonlit streets with Ludie. She seemed to be enjoying herself, in complete contrast to me. I felt like the day had been one failure after another. For the past few minutes now, she'd been repeatedly pointing to things along the way and asking me to explain what they were. I didn't fully understand why, but I was glad she was enjoying herself.

Once her curiosity had been sated a bit, I decided to ask her about something that had been bothering me.

"Hey, what do you think Hatsumi was making anyway?"

Ludie stopped for a second before regaining her stride.

"…She told us, didn't she? Um, it was…food, right?"

"When you're making food, do you end up with paint or fluorescent coloring on your clothes?"

Ludie was silent. The only thing I heard was the sound of our footsteps.

"…………A biological weapon, perhaps?"

I would have liked to call the idea absurd, but…

"...It's an undeniable possibility."

The atmosphere turned dour. Shifting my position to prevent a drunk passerby from slamming into Ludie, I voiced my hopes aloud.

"Maybe whatever it is will be edible."

"You can eat food that gives off a fluorescent glow?"

Weeeell...

"I don't really want to have that in my mouth."

"Of course you don't."

The heavy atmosphere lingered as we arrived at our destination. A place you could find anywhere nowadays—a twenty-four-hour convenience store. We'd decided to come here together, although we'd settled on it mainly because it was close by and dinner was around the corner.

"Have you ever been to a convenience store, Ludie?"

"Don't be ridiculous, I've been in one, once."

Wait, only *once*? Back in Japan, I'd relied on convenience store hospitality more times than I could count.

After entering the establishment, she looked around with restless curiosity, then started to wander through the aisles. I'd already made up my mind on what I wanted to buy, so I made a beeline straight there.

The instant ramen section.

I haphazardly put whichever ramen looked the tastiest of the vast variety in my shopping basket and looked over at Ludie.

She was flipping through a magazine, the kind popular with modern high school girls. Judging by her cocked head, however, the content didn't seem to be immediately clicking with her. Returning my attention to the ramen section, I put one of the most expensive options in my cart.

When I exited the convenience store, a crisp breeze brushed up against my skin. If this chill were to linger on, it would still be a little while before we would get to see the lovely sakura start to bloom.

After checking out, Ludie exited a few moments later while playing with one of the special cell phones Marino had given us. She'd urged us to always carry them for self-defense.

Seeing me, she raised her head from her phone and stared at my shopping bag.

"You bought a lot, didn't you?"

"Well, it's never bad to have some on hand, really."

I'd bought enough instant ramen to fill up a big shopping bag, but Ludie held just one small bag in her hand. My gaze lingered on it as I asked her:

"What did you buy?"

"There was this strange confection of some kind... I couldn't help myself."

She pulled something out of her bag. On closer inspection, it resembled some kind of cheap children's candy.

"Ah, I used to love that stuff. I was a real addict."

"Really? Does it taste good?"

"As long as it's the same as the one I'm thinking of, yeah. Right, do you not eat too many sweets and stuff, Ludie?"

"Huh? Of course I do. Why?"

"Oh, I just noticed you were really giving the candy aisle a serious examination is all."

Ludie gave a knowing mumble, taking out more candy as she continued:

"Well, I mean, my family's big, and we have a long history, right? That's why I haven't been to those kinds of shops very much, and one of our nutritionists would stop me if I tried to eat candy like this. I had a lot of fun in there, actually. I'm a little excited for what's next."

She beamed as she put the candy back in her bag.

I thought on what she'd just said. I could see how the number of constraints placed upon you could rise with your status. She probably hadn't visited many shops frequented by commoners. Now that she was free of these restrictions while living in the Hanamura house, it was the perfect time to experience these places for herself.

"Well, in that case, I'll take you somewhere really interesting next time."

"Oh, will you, now?" she asked, smiling.

"Yeah, leave it to me. I haven't been in this town long enough to know it super well, but I'm really good at finding cool spots. People tell me I always look like I'm enjoying life, and they mean it, too."

I'm sure half of that was sarcasm, though.

"Heh, what's that even mean? I'm *very* suspicious, but...I'll take you up on your offer. I better enjoy myself."

"Don't worry, you're in good hands," I responded with a grin as we continued walking back toward the house.

We headed a bit farther on, and right as we were around the corner from the house, I casually put my hand in my pocket. I felt a stringlike something wrap itself around my finger. Confused, I gave it a good once-over with my hand.

"Wha—?!"

I couldn't hold back my surprise the instant I realized what I was holding. A cold chill ran down my spine.

"What's wrong?"

"O-oh, uh, nothing. I, uh, remembered something, that's all."

"Really? Remembered what?"

"It's not important or anything. Don't worry about it."

At my reply, Ludie frowned, humming quietly with curiosity.

"Hearing that just makes me even more curious."

"S-seriously, it's no big deal! Besides, shouldn't we be worried about dinner right now?"

The moment I mentioned dinner, her shoulders drooped low.

"Good point…"

Her face was pure despair. Given that I, too, had a chance of falling victim to the horror she imagined was waiting for us, I should have been focused on how to avoid our fate. But now I had a much bigger problem.

After arriving home and parting ways with Ludie, I rushed back to my room.

As soon as I closed the door behind me, I let out deep sigh of relief. Now, how exactly did this end up on my person?

I put my hand inside my right pocket. A stringlike something brushed up against my finger. If what I was imaging was true, it was neither a shoestring, nor an earphone cord, nor a charging cable. It didn't even belong to me. Catching it on my finger, I brought the mystery item into the light.

Before my eyes was a black piece of string connected to a very small piece of fabric… They were Claris's panties.

"Hah, hah…… Uhhhhhhh."

Clutched in my hand was a problem that, in some ways, would be more difficult to solve than even Fermat's Last Theorem.

That night, the Hanamura household was unusually silent.

It was partially due to the crowd of elf maids who had been running around all afternoon. With all of them carrying luggage in and out, the house had been pretty noisy. Compared to that din, anything could sound quiet.

Even so, now it was *too* quiet. All but a single person in the dining room looked as though they were at a funeral.

Now, why was it so hushed? Okay, okay, enough of the charade. Honestly, the answer was painfully obvious. Anyone would clam up in this situation.

I looked up.

Spread out over the table was a multicolored smorgasbord of food that was impossible to stare at for more than five seconds. Each dish bore a hue reminiscent of a nighttime view of an amusement park. No, not the daytime scenery—the nighttime scenery. The one saving grace I found was the seemingly standard bowl of white rice.

I glanced around the table.

"……"

Ludie was deathly pale, completely at a loss for words. As I examined her, she slowly glanced my way. Her lips were trembling. However, all I could do was give her a small shake of my head.

"W-wowee, it's so pretty!"

Marino smiled stiffly as she spoke. Since she'd fled from the scene of these gastronomical weapons' creation, I felt that she bore the most responsibility for the horrible sight before us.

"My finest work," Sis said unceremoniously, puffing her chest out with pride. I would have liked to spend an hour or so interrogating her about where that self-confidence of hers was coming from.

Claris's absence meant she was still recovering. She'd been found collapsed on the kitchen floor about thirty minutes prior. The sparkling emerald-green substance stuck to the corners of her mouth told whole story. It would take some time for her to completely recuperate.

Thanks to her absence, I'd completely missed my opportunity to return her panties. At this stage, the only option left for me was sealing them away as my personal treasure for the rest of time.

"Dig in."

It was strange. Sis's announcement sounded like a death sentence somehow.

I shifted my gaze and noticed Marino and Ludie staring my way. Silently, they entreated me to take the first bite.

I picked up my spoon and scooped up a bite of the mysterious substance in front of me. It had a jellylike consistency. It was puzzling, though—the colors would change depending on which angle I examined it from, like oil floating on the ocean's surface.

"I simmered the meat really well, so it should be good."

Had she sparked some chemical reaction or something?

Prayers for the food to taste delicious rattled around in my head as I brought the spoon up to my mouth.

I didn't know where they were coming from, but I heard voices. Not just one, but many. A number of women were calling me over to join them. They told me there were many beautiful women waiting for me (all of them over the age of eighteen, no matter how young they looked!), and that on top of being woken up by a lovely younger sister in the morning and fed breakfast by a gorgeous mother, I would get to walk to school with my adorable childhood friend. They continued on to say that I'd get to enroll in an all-girls school even though I was a boy. What a wonderful place. That settled it; I would join them posthaste.

The moment I'd made up my mind, pain shot through my left leg.

"Urk!"

Ludie was staring at me, stricken with panic. Her leg pinch appeared to have brought me back to reality.

"How is it?" Sis asked.

"U-uhhh, I think you might need a bit more practice," I replied. I needed more training to face death head-on like this.

"Urgh!"

A sudden cry erupted beside me. Turning to its source, I saw that Marino had eaten a bite of the risk-free white rice and was clutching her throat.

"Hatsumi, I can't believe I'm asking this, but did you wash the rice with soap?"

"Yes, I used some that looked really strong."

"I—I see. Um, actually, Hatsumi, you don't have to use soap. Washing it with water is enough."

A lethal trap had been hidden in the rice.

"I'm sorry, I'll be careful next time. Ludie, go ahead, have anything except the rice."

Ludie had been watching Hatsumi and Marino's back-and-forth in blank amazement before reacting to her name with a jolt.

Her expression read as if she'd lost all her money on the stock market but made it back to reality.

"O-okay."

With a stiff smile, she picked up her spoon.

Unable to take any more, I turned away as she tried to calm her trembling hand and bring the food(?) to her mouth.

I could only describe the dinner as a full-course meal of pain that ran the gamut of spice, acidity, and bitterness. With each bite, the juicy, popping mouthfeel, similar to salmon roe, was too disgusting to bear. On top of that, each pop filled the mouth with a bitter and sour flavor. The food's tepid temperature added another layer to the gross cornucopia.

Its horrid flavor gushed in the moment you took a bite, yet it still lingered on after you gulped it down. Just how damn stubborn did it have to be?

"Auuugggh… ○×■#★〒▼※!"

A scream rang out next to me. It was Ludie's.

She followed up her unbecoming squeal (most likely a shriek that rose from deep inside her body) by jumping out of her seat and fleeing the room.

Hatsumi hung her head low in disappointment. Marino frantically spoke up upon seeing her reaction.

"O-oh my, I wonder what's wrong with little Ludivine, hmm? M-maybe she's pregnant?"

Marino's joke suggested she was losing it as well, but I didn't have the energy to follow it up. All I could do was desperately stuff my face with the food as I tried to bring a smile back to Sis's face.

How did I end up here?

When I came to, I was in my own room, in front of my desk. Written in the notebook on top of my desk was the phrase *form is emptiness, emptiness is form*. Whatever ultimate truth I may have grasped, I hadn't remembered any of it, nor did I know whether I should consider my lapse in memory a blessing or a curse.

There was a knock at my door. It wasn't Marino or Sis. They always called to me through the door. That meant it was one of the other two. I called out, bidding them to come in.

Ludie slowly opened the door and poked her head inside. Her perky elf ears were drooping low, and the color in her face hadn't returned. She'd clearly not fully recovered from her recent misfortune.

She came into my room without a word and sat with her legs under her on the carpet. Then she seemed to drum up the energy to speak.

"…Hey, what's the point in living?"

Her condition was critical. I'd probably been the same way up until a few minutes ago.

"…Gotta be happiness, right?"

"Happiness…what's that?"

As if on cue, an adorable little growl escaped from her stomach. However, she didn't seem to notice. The Ludie I knew from the eroge would've turned bright red and insisted, *No, I'm not hungry or anything, I swear!* Instead, she meekly placed her hand over her bowels.

I sat Ludie down in a chair and offered her one of my instant ramen packages. It was the most expensive one I'd bought.

Yet after accepting it, she remained motionless. She didn't appear to know what to do with it. Taking it back from her, I filled the kettle in my room with mineral water. Next, I walked her through the steps of making instant ramen before handing the finished product back to her. After I'd passed her a pair of disposable chopsticks, she slowly began to eat.

Sentimental tears welled up in her eyes and dripped down her cheeks.

"*Hngh…* It's good… It's so good…"

She was crying her eyes out. I knew all too well what she was feeling. However, her tear-strewn face shook me in a number of ways, sending even more flutters through my heart.

Ludie wasn't the type to cry in the first place. She often looked on the *verge* of tears, and I'd already seen her like that during the incident at the hotel. That was it, though. The only time you see her actually cry in the game is during a crucial battle against the Church of the Malevolent Lord. Nevertheless, here she was, weeping.

I never would have expected to see her tearstained face, reserved for the decisive final battle with the Church, while she chowed down on a cup of instant ramen…

Chapter 7 | Acquiring Skills the Eroge Way | Magical★Explorer

"What happened to you?"

Those were the first words out of Yukine's mouth after meeting me under the waterfall. She was very concerned.

"If you saw a plate of food brightly decked out in what seemed like fluorescent paint...what would you think?"

She cocked her head to the side.

"You sure that's food?"

"It was a weapon powerful enough to drive the mind toward the brink of madness..."

"...I still don't really understand, but how about we call it here for today?"

I considered her offer for a moment. I felt like I'd crumple under the pressure if I sat under the waterfall right now. Today was a good day to skip it.

"That's a good idea... Why don't we stick to running? I'm sorry for making you come all the way out here. See you."

Apologizing, I went over to my usual running route when I felt a tug on my shoulder.

"Takioto. That's not what I was trying to say. I meant you should take a break from *all* your training today."

"What? Don't you find yourself falling asleep, getting muscle spasms, or starting to hallucinate when you don't train?"

"You go through withdrawal when you don't train?!"

Now that I thought about it, what I'd just described did line up with general withdrawal symptoms.

"I don't know, I just feel anxious if I don't move my body a bit..."

"Anxious, huh...? I can get nervous before a big match, too. But I feel like you're going a bit too far... I've got an idea. Go change out of your training gear. I know just the place to take you."

After we'd changed, she took me to a shopping district not far from the Academy.

"You like sweet foods?"

I nodded to Yukine beside me. This question gave me a good idea about where we were heading.

"That's good. You'll like where we're going."

I was mentally sifting through all the places I went in-game during dating events when Yukine suddenly ground to a halt.

"Yukine, what's wro.........? Suspicious, isn't she?"

It was a blond-haired girl wearing a hat low on her head. She wore dark-green sunglasses and had a mask over her mouth. She wasn't as tall as Yukine but was still tall for a girl. Given her dainty face and long, slender legs peeking out from her skirt, she could have easily been a model.

"You think so, too?"

Was she a celebrity of some kind? However, her outfit was so suspicious that it made her even more conspicuous. Her tropey manga disguise was so poorly arranged that it was as if she was asking to be picked out of a crowd.

The girl was milling about between a restaurant and a ramen stall. It seemed something was either on her mind, or she was conflicted.

"What should we do?"

"She's too suspicious. Sticks out like a sore thumb, too. Let's try talking to her," Yukine announced before she started walking. I quickly rushed in front of her, sending mana through my stole and preparing to morph it into any shape at a moment's notice.

"Excuse me, is something wrong?" Yukine called out to the woman. The second she looked at us—and me, in particular—she jumped with a yelp.

"N-nothing of the sort!"

I felt like I'd heard this voice before. Not only that, but it was one I'd been hearing a lot recently. When I looked closer...

"...Wait, is that you—?"

The second I went to say her name, she turned around and tried to flee the scene. However, I'd been prepared, and I immediately used my Third Hand to capture the girl. She kicked and struggled in my stole's grip. As she did, her sunglasses fell off, revealing an unsurprising face.

"...What are you doing, Ludie?"

The suspicious loiterer wrapped up in my stole was Her Highness Ludivine Marie-Ange de la Tréfle.

"Please take your time," the waiter said before leaving us. In front of me was Yukine Mizumori, and in front of her was a matcha tiramisu served in a small *masu* cup along with a glass of green tea. Sitting next to me was Ludie, who had ordered a matcha parfait. A heaping serving of strawberries and whipped cream sat atop her green-tea-flavored ice cream, stuffed inside a layer of corn flakes. It looked delicious. I honestly wanted to devour everything.

Maybe I should have ordered something on top of my matcha chocolate fondue plate.

"Princess Tréfle, I had no idea...," Yukine muttered. Ludie was busy chewing something as she shook her head.

"You're Kousuke's mentor, right? Just Ludie is fine. I'm not fond of stiff formalities."

Ludie appeared to have gotten over being seen in her embarrassing getup and skipped putting on any royal airs before speaking as she normally did. Honestly, that outfit of hers had been a little out there.

Yukine gave a small sigh. She felt humbled in the presence of royalty, much as I had been at first.

"Still, though, what exactly were you do—hngh!"

Before I could finish asking, Ludie pinched my leg. She clearly didn't want me talking about it.

"Th-that's right. I was about to ask about Tsukuyomi Magic Academy. I'd like you to tell me what you know, if possible," Ludie interjected, forcibly changing the subject. Though confused by the awkward conversation change, Yukine began answering her questions. A few of her answers even provided me with some useful information of my own.

"I see, so we need to wait a while after starting school before we're allowed to enter the dungeon."

"The teachers are adamant about 'safety first.' Also, you're required to bring an upperclassman along on your first expedition."

Ludie and I nodded in understanding. Things seemed to be set up the same way they were in the game.

Assuming I'd have the same party members for my first trip as you have in the game, I'd be dungeon diving alongside the main character.

The other members change depending on the whims of the protagonist. Depending on what choices he makes, the party members besides ourselves could end up anywhere from being all beastfolk to including Ludie and Yukine as well. I hoped I would be with at least either Ludie or Yukine, since I would be able to speak more openly with them as opposed to a stranger.

"Would you be willing to go into the dungeon with us, Yukine? It'd be very reassuring having you there."

She chuckled at my request.

"If they're using the same randomized selection from last year, the chances'll be pretty slim. I'll try asking one of the teachers I know, but don't get your hopes up."

I had mainly asked as a joke, but it sounded like she would put a word in for us, at least. Now that I thought about it, I had a feeling Marino would adjust things for us if I asked.

"Thank you."

Yukine smiled and nodded.

"I've got one other thing to ask you. I've heard there are a number of dungeons around here, but can we go explore them if we feel like it?"

"No. If things go smoothly, you'll be able enter them all eventually, but you're only allowed in a few to begin with. You'll need to wait a bit after school starts for those as well…as I said before."

"I see," I said, nodding. This was almost exactly the same process as in the original game.

What I was a little curious about was whether the dungeon added in the expansion existed here or not. That had to be around, too, right? A lot of things would get harder without it. That reminded me…was the April Fools' Dungeon here as well? That was really out there, in a lot of ways. The person who thought up that event had reached a plane of existence no mortal could ever tread.

Thinking back, it had been a lot of fun. I'd really worked hard to unlock all the available dungeons. Especially since the five different bonus dungeons had been split up across five different retailers, so they made you buy five damn copies of the game to get them all. I remember splitting the purchases up with a friend. However, I'd wanted body pillows of Ludie, Yukine, and the prez, so despite owning the game, I ended up schlepping over to Mango Books and ComfyMap to get them.

I reached over to my matcha chocolate fondue. Casually glancing

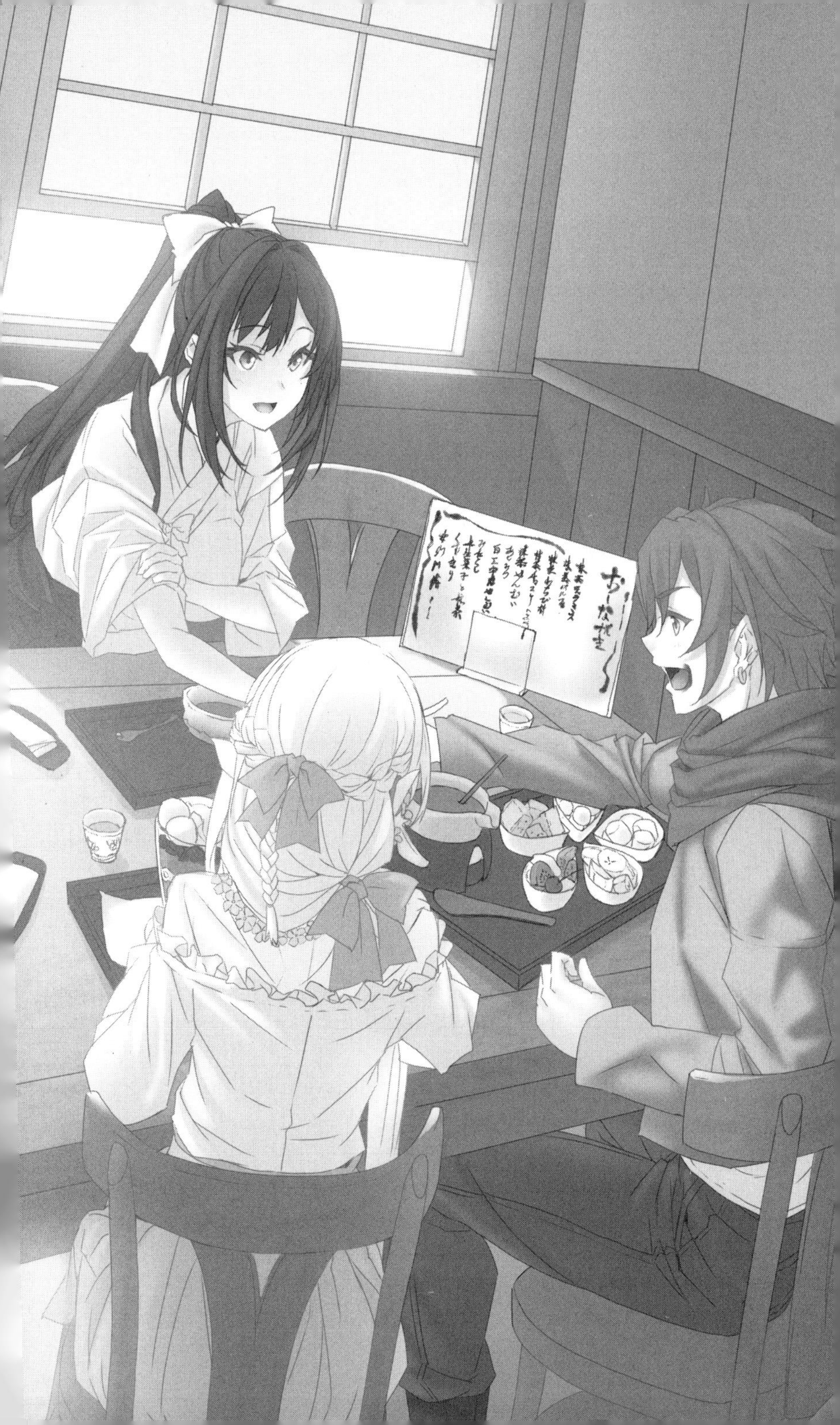
おしながき

beside me, I caught Ludie right as she was bringing a spoon full of strawberries and matcha ice cream up to her mouth.

"What?"

"Oh, I just thought your food looked good is all…"

After saying this, I opened my mouth. I thought that by some miracle, she'd feed me some of her ice cream, but of course, nothing of the
sort happened.

"Seriously? What…do you like parfaits or something?"

"I love anything and everything sweet. I have a particular weakness
for matcha, too."

Naturally, I loved the *other Parfait*, too. Ever since playing that game,
I've developed a label for a common eroge phenomenon by tacking
syndrome after one of its heroine's names. I am of course referring to
the phenomenon where you get second thoughts in the middle of clearing a heroine's route whenever another one shows up. Though Key
fans would probably use a different heroine's name for that particular
syndrome.

"Oh, what a coincidence. I'm a sucker for matcha, too. You want a bite
of mine, then? I've already had some, though."

Yukine then turned her box cup and faced it toward me. Ah, right, by
using a new spoon and eating an area she hadn't gotten to yet, we could
avoid having an indirect kiss. My disappointment was immeasurable.

"Thank you."

I pushed my matcha chocolate fondue toward Yukine as I thanked
her. She'd gotten the message and reached toward it.

I took the spoon provided to me and sank it into the matcha tiramisu.

"Oooh, this is delicious."

I couldn't help but grin. The matcha chocolate fondue was good, but
the tiramisu was also yummy. Excellent, in fact. I would definitely
order it next time.

"…Seeing you enjoy it so much makes me want some, too… You
really make anything look good, don't you?"

As she spoke, Ludie passed her parfait toward Yukine.

After that, we all split the sweets among one another.

"What if you used your whole body instead?"

"My whole body?"

"Yes. What if you did it like a roundhouse kick and turned your whole body around when throwing a punch?" Claris suggested, showing me an example of a roundhouse kick.

"...I'll give it a try."

After she readied her shield, I aimed for it as I spun around and threw my punch.

"Depending on the situation, it might be a good idea to use Third Hand and Fourth Hand in tandem."

At her proposal, I tried it again using both Hands, slamming them into her shield like a hammer. I indeed felt an explosive increase in power. However, using both ends of my stole also meant I was less stable defensively, so it felt like I was leaving myself wide open. If I chose my timing carefully, though, the move was definitely promising.

After repeating the move a number of times and getting accustomed to it, we moved on to a mock duel. Obviously, I made sure to try out this new move as well.

"...Not bad at all. Let's call it a day here. I think it'd be best to keep using it repeatedly to raise your proficiency with it. It's sure to come in handy."

"Ha-ha-ha...... Thank you, Claris."

"Please, I'm always available to help with this sort of training," she responded, smiling as she wiped away her sweat. Here I was, panting my lungs out, but she didn't show nearly any signs of fatigue. On top of that...

"I've still got a long way to go..."

Her coaching sessions had really driven home the fact that I still needed a lot of training.

"That looked plenty remarkable to me. Why, I can't even put up a decent fight."

A towel came flying at me with her reply. Catching it, I thanked Ludie and began wiping down my face.

"Please, Princess Ludivine, you're very strong for your age."

Claris tried to reassure Ludie, but it didn't seem to get through to her. She glumly looked back at her maid.

How to make Ludie stronger...?

"Ludie...shouldn't you start by learning Shortened Incantation?"

Since she was one of the main heroines, it didn't take much to turn Ludie into a powerhouse. Plus, in the game, she learns one long-ranged attack enhancement skill after another. That's why no skill was more beneficial to her than Shortened Incantation.

Her abilities were the exact opposite of Kousuke Takioto's, thinking about it now. He could throw things, but that was pretty much it. In close-quarters combat, though, he had quite a lot of brawn at his disposal.

We might have been the perfect duo, combining our strengths to cover each other's weaknesses.

"Well, I do want to learn it, but...do you think I would be able to right now? And who exactly am I supposed to learn it from in the first place?"

Ludie cocked her head. For characters like her, who could fire off long-ranged magic willy-nilly, learning skills like Shortened Incantation or Void Incantation is practically a requirement. Characters can learn Void Incantation by collecting an item from a high-level dungeon or from an endgame event, regardless of level. Before that comes Shortened Incantation, though. This is also granted to you regardless of character strength in the game, but...given that I had yet to master Mind's Eye, it seemed nothing was a guarantee. However...

"I know a person nearby who should know it and who would likely be willing to teach you. Two people, actually."

"Huh?"

Ludie was completely in the dark about who I was gesturing toward. As such—

"Please teach her, Sis!"

I bowed in front of Hatsumi while she sipped her coffee and looked over some documents. Ludie bowed next to me. I'd thought it best to avoid having Her Highness prostrate herself, but on second thought, she must have been allowed to bow toward teachers and mentors, right? Right?

"I'll be busy once school starts... Now's fine. But don't ask Mom. She should be busy."

Leaving everything in Sis's hands, I headed to the library by myself... at least, until Claris showed up out of the blue.

"You're fine not learning Shortened Incantation?"

I nodded in answer to her question while she followed me to the library. Was it okay for her to leave Ludie? Well, I guess Sis was there to protect her.

"I generally only fight by sending mana through my stole anyway."

Since I had been keeping my mana activated all day lately, my magic had an almost 100 percent uptime, without the assistance of any incantations. Come to think of it, I'd been continuously using magic for almost a full day, but...what exactly was happening to my mana pool...? I felt like I'd already developed it past my limits.

"What, then, are you going to do at the library?"

There was some time to kill before my meditation session with Yukine. I could have relaxed in my room, but since there was a library here...

"Oh, I don't know, I just thought I'd come check if there were any useful books in here."

I might as well kill time in a way that had practical benefits.

"I see."

When I opened the door to the library, a breeze carrying the smell of ink and paper blew past us. Claris gave the library an initial survey before searching for something in particular from a specific section.

The Physical Strengthening and Recovery Magic area seemed to hold a lot of skills that I could find useful, and after rummaging around for a bit, I was able to pick out a promising book.

I removed it from the shelf and brought it with me to the sofa. Then, taking an iced coffee out of the stocked refrigerator, I sat down and opened the tome.

"Donation Magic, huh?"

Hearing a voice in my ear, I instinctively slammed the book shut. Claris was hovering right next to me.

"You surprised me. When did you come over here? I didn't sense you at all."

"That was because of my Stealth skill," she replied, smiling and looking a little proud of herself. Perhaps her typically stoic demeanor gave me this impression, but this abrupt smile of hers was absolutely adorable.

"...I would very much like to learn that skill at some point."

"Of course. I can teach you during our training together. Anyway, Donation Magic?"

"That's right," I affirmed. This spell allowed you to give your mana to someone else.

"You already know this, Claris, but I have an unusual amount of mana."

Not all the eccentric gentlemen who used Kousuke Takioto had him specialize in defense. After dialing up his MP as much as possible, some of them had him learn Donation Magic to turn him into an MP replenishment battery. This role is perfectly suited for Kousuke Takioto, who has the largest MP pool out of everyone in *MX*. At least, that was what had been believed around a certain time. Ultimately, this build had only been utilized for the first couple weeks after release, or by people who were playing under a self-imposed challenge.

This strategy had quickly fallen out of favor because of New Game+; after defeating the last boss, the mode allows you to carry over your stats, recovery items, and money to a new playthrough. On top of everything else, it also gives you access to the item shop from the very beginning. These holdovers from your prior playthrough let you use MP recovery items like they grow on trees, so soon, players were questioning why they needed to keep including Kousuke Takioto in their party.

I, too, had filled up all the slots in my party outside the protagonist with beautiful women. Naturally.

"I get it. You could probably make really effective use of it with your special constitution," Claris agreed.

If I were on a second playthrough, I might not have thought about this skill. On a first playthrough, though, it wouldn't be a waste of time to learn it.

"Ludie burns through her mana nonstop, so I thought if I could give her some of mine, she wouldn't have to worry about running out."

It was fair to say that Ludie needed some mana supplement to keep up with all the long-range magic she threw around. There isn't an item usage limit in the game, so as long as you have the money, it's a magical smorgasbord.

When I turned to Claris, she appeared to be having difficulty deciding on how she wanted to respond. This baffled me for a moment, but the answer soon became clear.

"Um, Princess Ludivine doesn't know any magic that would consume mana that quickly."

...I screwed up. I'd forgotten that Ludie is designed to only know beginner-level magic when she first arrives at the Academy.

"Oh, uh, I—I was just talking about the future! Yeah!"

"R-right, of course. Indeed, that kind of magic does seem like it would suit her rather well."

Trying to escape the peculiar mood that had overtaken the room, I went back to my book. Out of nowhere, inspiration struck, and I turned to Claris.

"Can you use this magic, by any chance?"

"Yeah, should I teach you?"

I couldn't hold back my dry laugh.

I might have already been blessed with an overpowered skill of my own. Not only that, but a skill that hadn't been in the original game at all.

"Aw, man."

With Donation Magic training over, I came to the living room to see rain outside the window. It had looked like it was going to rain when I'd been out earlier, but luckily, it had held off until after our spar had drawn to a close.

"It's really coming down."

It had been nothing but dry weather recently, so the plants must have considered it a godsend. I, on the other hand, was none too thrilled about Mother Nature's blessing. If it kept pouring until tomorrow, I wouldn't be able to go running, or see Yukine's face, or hear her voice, or breathe in the tranquil air surrounding her, but most devastatingly of all, I would miss out on the sight of her voluptuous body soaked through under the waterfall.

"Kousuke."

Hearing my name, I broke out of my trance. Hatsumi was staring at me, wand in hand. Ludie was trailing behind her, exhausted. She must have just finished up her lesson on Shortened Incantation. From what I'd heard, Hatsumi was extremely strict about magical instruction and left no room for compromise.

Ludie still had to worry about the organization targeting her, so she was definitely motivated. Still, being worked until you ran out of mana made even walking difficult. I grumbled to myself about Sis going so rough on her.

I could tell Ludie was having a rough time, but I still wanted her to train with Sis. The more you emptied your mana pool, the easier it was for it to grow.

"Kousuke, are you ready?"

I cocked my head. Ready for what, exactly?

"School's starting soon."

I nodded. Indeed, the entrance ceremony was just around the corner. I had all my preparations in order, of course.

"I'm all set. Besides, I don't need that much to begin with."

Sis dropped her eyebrows half an inch and squirmed the corners of her lips slightly. It must have been her attempt at a smile. She made an okay sign with her right hand.

"Okay. Don't forget anything."

She then turned toward the stairs and walked off. I tried speaking to Ludie, who looked ready to pass out on the sofa.

"Still alive?"

"…I can't go on. Before I die, I want to eat ra……um, ice cream."

She stretched out her hand. Her Highness Ludivine was ordering me to bring her some.

"All right, fine…"

I opened up the freezer to look for ice cream. Unsurprisingly—or rather, as to be expected of the Hanamura house—it was filled with premium-quality frozen treats. I picked up two cups of Ludie's favorite chocolate-strawberry flavor and brought them over.

"Thanks…"

I handed one to her and peeled off the lid on the one I'd gotten for myself… It was hard to explain, but it felt like I was getting less reserved around Ludie recently, that we had begun feeling like family. It certainly beat being awkward around each other.

On second thought…Ludie should only be showing her true self to the protagonist and the other female characters. Should I be seeing her like this?

"Oh, did I already tell you what my favorite flavor was?"

She probably hadn't. I'd heard it plenty of times in the game, though.

"C'mon now, we talked about it together with Yukine, right?"

These situations were all about speaking with all the confidence you could muster. That was usually enough to fool someone.

"Did we, now?" Ludie replied, lazily scooping up her ice cream. With her mana drained, each move she made was languorous. Seeing her struggle, I had an idea.

"…Hey, Ludie, will you let me practice my magic on you?"

"Excuse me?"

Incredulous, she waved her spoon at me with a scowl.

"Oh, see, Claris is teaching me how to use Donation Magic, but I haven't tried using it on someone else yet. If you're up for it, I'd like to try it on you."

She nodded vigorously, still biting down on her spoon. Where did she learn to act all cute like that? Perhaps she was a touch unrefined for an imperial scion, though.

"Wow, that's some rare magic you're learning. Isn't that stuff not very efficient?"

She did have a point. However, its cost goes down quite a bit if you max out its skill level. That was the whole reason I wanted to level it up as soon as possible.

"It's not great, but I've got an abnormal amount of mana already. There's a pretty wide margin of error."

"I suppose so."

"I'll get some practice in, and it'll help cut down on your fatigue from being out of mana, right? How about it?"

Ludie gave her affirmation.

"Fine by me. Make it quick, then."

I stuck my hand out toward her. However, she cocked her head in confusion.

"What's the hand for?"

"Oh, sorry. I still can't sense any mana without touching my target's hand... Besides, you know about my finicky constitution."

She nodded.

"R-right, of course."

Setting her ice cream down on the table, she wiped her hand with her handkerchief. Then she approached me and held my hand.

"You don't need to be nervous."

"I am nothing of the sort."

Even after wiping it with her handkerchief, her hand was still a little sweaty.

"Your hand's nice and warm."

"Save the creepy commentary and get this over with, idiot."

I didn't recall making any weird comments, myself. Oh well, I'd heed her request and hurry things along.

"Mnh... I can feel it......"

Sensing what little remained of Ludie's mana, I focused on the sensation and sent out my own mana toward it.

"How's that? If you can feel it just fine, I'd like to slowly up the amount... Is that okay?"

"Yes, it's flowing into me. Go ahead... Send...more...mnh......... Gngh?"

I started outputting more and more mana. However, the more I increased the rate of transfer, the higher a proportion of mana escaped into the air. I still needed more practice.

"Hnnggh! H-hey!"

"What, is something wrong?"

When I turned to Ludie, she was red in the face.

"A-are you doing it right? I feel really ticklish."

"Yeah, that's okay. Claris's face got a little red, too."

In retrospect, when I'd transferred mana to Claris, she'd also muttered something really weird. "Hnnngh, stay strong, don't give in," or something like that... What had that been about?

Oh well. I should just increase the output for now.

"Unh, hnnggh, aaaaahn!"

"H-hey now, don't make any weird noises."

Ludie's expression was difficult to describe, both one of pain and pleasure. Her whole face was still scarlet, including her pointed elven ears.

"N-no! Th-this is bad. Stooooop!"

"Oh, sorry. I'm still a bit new at this, so I can't really lower my output at the drop of a hat..."

You know, like those old-school faucets—once they're open, it takes some effort to close them, right? I always had a really hard time turning them.

"Y-you dummmmy!"

I knew I was done for when I saw Ludie trembling wildly, but unfortunately, I had to stop the flow slowly. Maybe I could just suddenly let go of her hand. Or so I assumed, but Ludie's grip had gone straight from tight to vicelike and ensnared my hand. Far worse than that...

"Eeep!"

After I'd failed to remove my hand from her grip, she pulled my whole body toward her in turn. At that moment, her face was right in front of my eyes, and our bodies were pressed together.

Now then, something I hadn't realized up until that moment was, with Donation Magic, the larger the area of skin you were touching, the more efficiently you would transfer mana to your target.

"Wah, wah, bwaaaaah!"

Mana began gushing out from where our skin met. Letting out the kind of scream you'd see in manga from days gone by, Ludie leaned back on me.

"Hwaaah...hwaaah...help me..."

She was breathing irregularly on me. Her uniquely feminine, saccharine smell mixed with a hint of sweat and sent my brain into overdrive. However, that wasn't the only thing that proved titillating. The damp sensation of her soft, warm skin, her weight as she lay on me, the perspiration on her slender, fair neck—all of it sent stimuli racing through my body.

I couldn't handle any more...

"L-Ludie, are you okay?! First, let's separate, okay?!"

She gave me a vaguely wanting look, eyes hazy with tears. Then she clung desperately to my hand, refusing to let go. To be honest, I didn't want to let go, either. But this was dangerous. Dangerous in more ways than one. It was time to separate, and I needed to put space between us. But I didn't want to let go, nor was she loosening her grip.

Ultimately, Ludie finally released my hand shortly after my donation incantation had ended.

Sitting apart from each other, we first adjusted our clothes. A section of her hair was stuck fast to her skin, drenched in sweat, and she fanned herself with her clothes to let air in.

From looking at Ludie, it was clear the Donation Magic had been a sexcess...er, a *success*. Now she was overflowing with mana, and her face was flush with color. Nevertheless...

"............"

"............"

While her body was in good health, the same could not be said for the mood in the room. The silence was heavy.

Ludie abruptly got up. Without another word, she turned around and walked toward the door. Her back was so sweaty that her clothes were clinging right up against it.

I headed over to the Hanamuras' magic practice area for a change of pace. I practiced my magic there for a little while, but I couldn't concentrate.

I guess I'd give up for now and take a shower...

I wanted a cold shower, if possible. My body was still flushed from the earlier incident, and my head felt ready to burst, so I wanted to lower my body temperature as much as I could. If it weren't for the rain, it would have been the perfect time to sit under a waterfall and focus on my mental concentration.

Heaving a huge sigh, I removed my stole. Though I had sweated quite a bit, it was still nothing compared to what Ludie had gone through. Wiping the perspiration running down my forehead, I headed for the bath. The moment I entered the changing area, the door to the bathroom opened up.

Steamy hot vapor buffeted my face. Cloaked in the steamy mist was a blond-haired girl with pointed ears sticking out from her head. Clearly, it was Ludie.

"…………"

"…………"

Silence. Along with a petrified Ludie glaring my way.

I wonder if she would have forgiven me if I gave a *whoopsie* and stuck out my tongue a little bit. No, that would probably just have been pouring oil on the fire.

"…………"

"……Eeeeeeeeeeeeeeeek!"

It was a strange feeling. I didn't know how to describe it. It felt like a localized omnipotence. Time had slowed to a crawl around me, yet somehow, the thoughts racing through my head had burst into over-drive. That sort of feeling.

A warm rush of blood gathered in my head and crotch.

As she screamed, she threw her mana-filled hands up in the air. I was about to eat a direct hit. Still, if I was going to get hit, I at least wanted to get a glimpse of her naked body through the steam before falling over. Unfortunately, while the steam from the open bath door had cleared somewhat, I could only make out her head and part of her legs.

No? Was it really no use? I wasn't gonna get a glimpse? Really? I wanted to see it no matter what. I pleaded in my mind:

Please show me.

My deepest wish seemed to have reached the heavens, since the vapor slowly began to clear. No, it wasn't getting clearer. It wasn't getting clearer, but for some reason, her silhouette was slowly coming into view. It continued to sharpen in focus, as if I were watching through a camera viewfinder. Finally, gazing at Ludie's body in full view, I stood dumbfounded.

Sh-she was wrapped in a towel...

I mentally cursed the towel. First, in confusion—*what's that towel doing there, c'mon?* Next, in anger—*why the hell does she have to be wrapped in a towel?!* Finally, in pure madness—*why do stupid towels even need to exist?!*

In the world of 2D, I had gazed upon her au naturel figure countless times before. Unfortunately, though, the world of eroge was permeated by the worst invention known to man—the censorship mosaic.

I'd just wanted to see it in the 3D world. That was all.

Why was it hidden from me? I wanted to see it. Please.

As I was staring at her towel, I realized something. Something about it looked strange.

I had no idea why, but the towel was gradually becoming see-through. With this opportunity......I could see them. I could see them! The little tips at the end of that huge chest.........?!

"Just what to do you think you're staring at?! *Gaaaaaaaah!!*"

"*Eep!* F-forgive meeeeeeeee!"

The slowly advancing orb of light hit me directly in the head, and everything in front of me turned pure white.

Just how much time had passed while I withered under this sub-zero glare?

She'd barged into my room without a knock, and after I'd quickly offered her a chair, she silently took a seat.

While I'd offended Ludie during our chance encounter in the bath, I'd ended up acquiring the Mind's Eye skill. Additionally, I'd been able to bask in a grand sight, one unparalleled with any other scenery this planet had to offer.

I currently had my knees and forehead pressed firmly on the floor due to my lecherous actions, but I wasn't surprised. I'd asked for it.

I should be good now, right? I raised my head up just a little bit and peeked at Ludie's face. She sat completely still, glaring at me with narrowed eyes. Her mouth was pursed so tightly closed that it seemed as if her lips were glued shut. Glimpsing her slender legs stretching out from the almost-visible underside of her skirt, I desperately fought back the urge to stuff my cheeks between them and kept my head pressed down to the ground.

The next moment, Ludie got up and reached her hand out toward my head. She pinched my right cheek with all her might, then immediately brought her other hand up to pinch my left cheek before pulling them apart as hard as she could.

"Dat haats. Ow, ow, ow."

Ludie heaved a big sigh before finally releasing me from her vice grip. Rubbing my cheeks, I gazed up at her as she stood in front of me with her arms crossed.

"Fine…I suppose I'll let you off the hook. I was wearing a towel anyway," she spat with an exasperated smile. Sorry, but about that towel…

"Th-thank you very much, Mistress Ludie!"

Of course, that was strictly confidential.

"Yes, but! I will only forgive you under one condition…… I want you to make my wish come true."

At this, she averted her eyes from me.

"Your wish?"

What sort of request did she have in mind? Was it even something I could do? If she asked me to be her chair, or to lick her feet clean, I would have happily obliged for as long she'd like. Yeah, no, she *definitely* wasn't talking about something like that.

"……Um, I just…I want you to take responsibility, okay?"

Yeah, take responsibility. What, was that all? *Ha*, responsibility…

"………Ubuh?"

Okay, just hold on a minute. By responsibility, did she mean *that* responsibility?! The kind you see popping up in manga all the time?!

"I get that it may be weird to say this about myself, but I'm a member of the nobility, right? Well, it's just, there are sides of me I don't want people to see."

Whoa, whoa, this can't be happening. The phrases *member of the nobility, sides of me I don't want to people to see*, and *responsibility* gave off a *very* dangerous vibe.

S-still, was I good enough for her? Ludie was confessing to a guy who had several eroge heroines all taking up space in his heart. Though, to be fair, she was counted among them.

"Th-that's why, you know… Based on your expression, you know what I'm getting at, right? It's captivated my mind ever since I first experienced it. I love it. But it's too embarrassing… I couldn't tell anyone. I wish I could experience it every day. If Father ever found out, he would definitely tell me to stop. Yet my body still yearns for it."

I put on a serious expression and adjusted my posture. These moments called for the handsomest look I could manage.

"K-Kousuke Takioto!"

Mustering up her courage, she lifted my lowered head and grabbed my right hand. Her lips trembled as warm pants escaped through them. Her watery eyes looked fit to burst at any moment, which made her green pupils sparkle.

Ludie opened her mouth to speak, but before she could get any words out, she bit her lip and cast her head down. After muttering some magic words of encouragement to herself, she vigorously lifted her head back up again. Her lips, shiny and luscious like strawberries engorged with water, trembled as she took a deep breath.

"I—I…want to eat ramen!"

………………………What?

Time came to a crashing halt.

▲ ⋀ ⋁ CONFIG

Chapter 8 Disaster

Magical★Explorer

Reborn as a Side Character in a Fantasy Dating Sim

"Wow, learning a skill that fast? Impressive! How did you do it?!"

After she'd helped me so much, it was a given I'd report back to Yukine Mizumori about gaining the Mind's Eye skill. She'd done so much for me. That being said—

While her eyes sparkled with joy, as though she'd accomplished the feat herself, I couldn't help but avert my gaze. How exactly had I learned it?

Why, by praying I'd be able to see a beautiful girl's naked body.

...Could I even tell her that? I imagined the moment I told her and saw her smile, which was pretty enough to make the angels jealous, dissolve into a terrifying visage that could send a demon running to the hills. Given my slight masochistic streak, I did almost want to see that play out.

"It was all thanks to you, Yukine."

To ensure she couldn't read into my expression, I quickly bowed my head, using the movement to get my facial muscles under control.

"Ha-ha, that so, huh? Makes me glad to hear it," Yukine said, trying to get me to lift my head up.

"Thank you so much for taking the time to help me out, even with school right around the corner. Please let me know if anything comes up. I know I'm an underclassman, but I'll do anything I can."

I rapidly piled on stock pleasantries that popped into my head. It was best to get the conversation away from my skill acquisition as fast as possible.

Yukine chuckled.

"C'mon, guiding underclassmen is an important part of being an upperclassman. You were trying so hard that it made me want to help you out."

"Really? I wasn't putting in *that* much effort… Oh, right, that reminds me, you ready for the new school year? Doesn't the Morals Committee stuff keep you busy?"

"Ha, it's fine. The student council's pretty busy, but we just show the new students around the campus. If you ever get lost at school, go ahead and ask any of the Morals Committee members for directions, me included."

Mission accomplished. With all these distractions, she shouldn't remember a thing about our skill conversation. If she'd kept prying, the guilt would have probably made me run away.

"I'll be counting on you for that, then. I'm a little worried since they say the campus is huge."

"Heh, it's so big that I got lost pretty soon after my first day. From what I've heard, there's always one new student who uses getting lost as an excuse for being late."

In the game, the protagonist and his friends use spatial magic circles to warp from class to class. Apparently, campus was so big that walking to class was too much of a bother. One of the sub-heroines was always getting lost on campus, so I was scared I'd end up in the same boat. If only there was a GPS map of the campus I could use.

"By the way, are you all set to start school?"

"Of course. Though, there's not much we really need to bring with us."

The school handed out all the necessary textbooks, so all I really needed to bring was a writing implement and my stole. My uniform was ironed and hanging in my closet, ready to go.

"There's a lot I'm looking forward to this year," Yukine noted, looking toward me.

"Me too."

Swords, magic, the Academy, dungeons, and pervy escapades. It was a world filled with enough elements to enthrall boys and eroge players alike. It would be impossible not to be excited.

"I'm going to get strong fast and catch up to you. Don't let yourself fall behind."

"Heh, I won't let you pass me by that easily."

We both stared off into the waterfall. The pounding falls and gently rippling surface reflected the sun high up in the sky, flashing repeatedly on the water.

"Oh yeah, by the way…"

Yukine clapped her hands together, appearing to have remembered something.

"What is it?"

"Aren't you going to tell me how you learned Mind's Eye?"

I got up, turned my back to Yukine, and kicked off the ground with all the force I could muster.

It didn't take long for Yukine to catch up to me. By the time I'd gotten back into town, she was jogging beside me.

"I promised Ludie I'd go eat ramen together with her! I just remembered all of a sudden!"

"What does that have to do with taking off like that, though?"

She was dead-on.

"C'mon, doesn't the setting sun just make you want to go for a run?"

"Not at all. Besides, the sunset's still a way off."

Absolutely correct on all counts. Still, I was in trouble. Normally, I could think up excuses like it was nothing, but today, my mind was drawing blanks.

"Oh, right. Do you want to join us for ramen? The place we're going is supposed to be very good."

I'd only planned on treating Ludie, but why not treat my upperclassman after everything she'd done for me? It was all allowance from Marino anyway.

"I don't see why not, but…are you trying to change the subject?"

I would steer us away from the skills topic like my life depended on it.

"Was I? What were we talking about, again…? Huh?"

It happened right as I tried playing dumb at Yukine's question.

The ground made a loud rumble.

Screams resounded from every which way. Fortunately, there weren't any explosions or collapsing buildings. However…

"What's this?"

A thick line began to form at our feet. It fanned out as though it was being drawn with a compass, and it ultimately stretched out farther than my eye alone could follow.

"…It looks almost like a magic circle."

Yukine's observation made something click.

Fearing the worst, I immediately dashed off.

Passing by the bewildered residents, I made toward the center of the magic circle. The more I carried on, the more convinced I grew that this was one of the in-game events. However…

"C'mon, this is all wrong!"

I didn't understand. This event…shouldn't have been happening yet.

Why was the scene where the Church of the Malevolent Lord revives a dungeon happening now? This was supposed to come after school started… At this point, the game hadn't even technically started yet.

"Yukine!"

When I saw her rushing toward me, I inwardly sighed with relief. She'd chased me down after I'd dashed off.

Under normal circumstances, this Church of the Malevolent Lord event triggers after school starts, once you advance a bit down Ludie's route. The Church tries kidnapping Ludie every now and again, and after losing their patience from constantly being beaten back, they use a certain kind of magic to trigger this event. It definitely shouldn't have been happening now.

Why was the timing so off?

When I examined the possibilities…only one answer came to mind:

"This is 'cause I'm here, isn't it?"

The Church is supposed to slowly take their time in plotting against the main characters. It plays out with the sort of carelessness toward the protagonist you see all the time in video games or superhero TV shows. The villains would assume the heroes were weak and treat them with kid gloves by sending their underlings do the dirty work, only to be wiped out. This happened so often, you had wonder if they weren't actually working to help make the protagonist stronger in the first place.

"Could this be because of that guy I let get away?"

Did the incident at the Hanamura Hotel have something to do with this? It was highly likely. However, investigating into why would have to wait until later. This wasn't the time for that. What I needed to do right now was get an understanding of the situation.

Immediately thinking to get in touch with Ludie, I took out my phone and tapped her name. However, my efforts proved fruitless. When

Marino had given us these unique self-defense phones, she'd emphasized that we would be able to reach each other as long as we were in town, dungeons not included. I also recalled her having a good laugh about reinforcing my phone to prevent it from breaking like last time. That's why I doubted Ludie's phone would be broken. Yet she was listed as being offline. In other words, she was somewhere without service.

I instantly sent a message to Marino asking her to tell me where Ludie was.

"What exactly is going on here?!"

"Yukine, let's head toward the center of this magic circle. Something must be happening there."

At this, we headed for the heart of the incantation.

I didn't know whether it was mere coincidence or if I should have expected as much, but the middle of the circle was close to where Ludie and I had planned to meet up.

At this location, a number of the symbols big enough to fit several people inside them had been generated, and pale-blue particles danced through the air.

I was positive—this was the entrance to the dungeon. Monsters were spilling out from the circles.

Looking around, the people engaged in fighting... Huh?

"...Wait, you gotta be kidding me."

I couldn't contain my surprise upon discovering who was fighting in front of the dungeon.

"That girl shooting magic...is that Student Council President Monica Mercedes Von Mobius?! And the woman dressed in a kimono and using fans as a weapon...Ceremonial Vice-Minister Shion Himemiya?!"

What were two members of the Three Committees, one of the most powerful groups in the whole Academy, doing here?! Had there been some route that had forced them to appear in this event?

No, none of that mattered. If President Monica was here, then I knew I could leave her to clean up the monsters bursting out of the dungeon. I could safely keep moving.

"...Takioto, you know those two?"

Yukine stared at me in earnest. *Shit*, I thought to myself, but it was too late for that. I'd spilled the beans. That conversation would have to wait, though.

"Yes I do. But I'll tell you about it later…"

I glanced over at the two women embroiled in combat. I guess even dark clouds had silver linings. Who knew why they were here, but with one of the Big Three, not to mention the strongest student currently on campus—Student Council President Monica—on the scene, I could rest assured everything would be taken care of.

There were so many foes that I would have a hard time dealing with them to begin with.

When I turned to Yukine, I saw her observing the battle with a grave expression. It looked like she would rush over at any moment, joining the fray, and shout at me to escape to safety.

She, too, wanted to protect the residents of the city from the beasts overflowing from the mouth of the dungeon.

On the other hand, I wanted to storm into that nest of monsters without a moment's delay. If this event were still adhering to the same outline as it does in the game…

…Ludie should be inside right now.

"Quickly, Takioto, you need to… Hey, what are you doing?"

I grabbed Yukine's hand right as she was about to take off. I bowed straightaway.

"I'm sorry, I know this sounds crazy, but I need you to trust me. Will you charge into that dungeon with me?"

"What in the…what are you talking about? And what dungeon…?"

"I can't get in touch with Ludie. Our cell phones should be able to get in touch with each other—unless we're in a dungeon. Marino personally gave them to us, so they shouldn't have failed, either."

I could tell how flabbergasted she was just by looking at her. Despite her exasperation, the latest message on my phone cemented my theory. Marino had already gotten wind of the uproar. She knew my location, too.

"Yukine, I have a message from Marino."

Hatsumi is on her way. You need to get out of there and get back home.

"Now, why didn't she tell me where Ludie was? Marino should be able to confirm her last known location."

That information should have been enough for the quick-witted Yukine to understand what was going on.

"She's thinking, *If Kousuke hears Ludie is in danger, he'll definitely rush there to save her.*"

And Marino was spot-on. If Ludie was in a pinch, I'd jump in to save her by any means necessary. I'd already done as much back at the Hanamura Hotel. That was why she hadn't mentioned Ludie at all before commanding me to get out of there. Unfortunately, her warning had the opposite effect.

Yukine stared at me with hesitation, but I had to do whatever it took to ensure I had at least one strong ally with me in the dungeon.

"I just...I have a bad feeling. Please."

Squeezing down on Yukine's hand, I stared at her resolutely. Her trepidation gradually gave way to determination.

Now it was her turn to size me up with a discerning glare. I met her terrifying yet gorgeous gaze with an equally serious stare of my own.

"...I understand. Let's leave this place up to Shion and President Monica."

Yukine was the one to give in. The rage in her eyes disappearing, she returned to the dignified yet gentle woman I was used to. The Yukine I loved most of all.

"If I try to stop you, you'll just run in there anyway, right? At least it'll be better if I'm with you."

"Thank you so much."

With that settled, we just needed to storm the dungeon. I had the bare minimum I needed to save Ludie... In fact, I could say I had the best person for the job right beside me.

"That being said..."

Yukine turned away, looking a bit embarrassed.

"What's wrong?"

"I—I don't really mind, but, well, you know. I'd appreciate if you'd let go of my hands now."

I glanced down. Both my hands were firmly squeezing hers.

"M-my bad."

Rushing past President Monica as she laid waste to her foes uncontested, we dashed toward one of the magic circles.

All of the magic circles except for one were connected on the other side to rooms known as monster houses, where a large number of enemies were lying in wait. However, the beasts didn't originate from these rooms; even if you reduced their numbers temporarily in a monster house, their source would still be unaffected, allowing them to keep pouring through the circles.

To cut off their source, you needed to charge into the correct magical ring. For someone like me, who'd beaten *MX* more times than I could count, it was an easy target to spot.

Right before we traveled through the portal, President Monica started to chew Yukine out about something, but I imagined she could smooth it over later. We had far bigger fish to fry.

The interior of the Palace of Worldly Impermanence resembled a desolate European mansion.

The dungeon was blanketed in dust, and a breeze along the walls was kicking up clouds of grime. The frescoes covering the ceiling and walls were slightly dirty as well, and some had large swaths that had been gouged out. Along the way, we came across a once-valuable urn that was now so filled with cracks that it could no longer serve its original purpose; yet it hardly qualified as decor.

On top of all that, the scratches on the pictures hanging throughout the previous hallway had clearly not been left by a human.

"Hmm. This dungeon looks like it's already been hit by a group of monsters."

Yukine had pretty much said it all. As its name implied, the area was supposed to resemble a mansion that had been attacked by monsters and was withering away with time.

"Looks like the path branches off here… Let's go to the right."

Yukine preemptively chose which path to take, and I started to jog ahead.

If this Palace of Worldly Impermanence was the same as its in-game counterpart, it had a bit of a unique layout. RPG fans probably would have thought as much straight from the entrance.

If you chose the wrong fork in the path, you would be treated to a monster ambush, with nothing waiting for you once you advanced all the way inside.

The entrance wasn't the dungeon's only quirk—its subsections were equally baffling. Normally, most dungeons would have anywhere from ten to one hundred subsections, with some having even more, but this one only had a single subsection. Compared to other video game labyrinths, however, this sole section was a lot larger than usual.

By far the most unique aspect of the manor, though, was its complete lack of wandering enemy encounters.

Instead, there were monsters in certain areas lying in wait. Thus, if you continued down the right route, it was possible to reach the end without fighting at all. However, that neither applied to monsters that appeared from traps nor the manor boss.

Why wasn't that true for the boss? That was because he actually wandered around.

Generally speaking, video game dungeons have normal enemies wandering around, while the boss is sequestered in the deepest part of the dungeon. That was why I'd thought the design of the Palace of Worldly Impermanence was both innovative and compelling. There's only a set type of monster that shows up, too, which makes it the perfect place for leveling up.

Nevertheless, this was definitely not somewhere you wanted to visit early in the game.

Watching Monica fight had made me realize something. The monsters that appeared here were more than I would be able to handle. If I fought one at a time, I could probably manage. Fighting multiple at once, though, was a different story. Of course, if I'd gathered experience points and powered myself up beforehand, things might have been different. And yeah, I'd been training a lot recently, but that wasn't the same as fighting...

However, by a stroke of pure luck, this dungeon's unique design would allow me to avoid combat almost entirely.

"Left at the next one."

With the manor layout matching the in-game map, it would be smooth sailing from here. Nevertheless, when it came time to square off with the boss, it would certainly be a strenuous battle. Scratch that, it would take nothing short of a miracle to defeat him in my current state.

This was precisely why I'd wanted Yukine to tag along. She wasn't one of the Big Three for nothing. Though I hadn't triggered her awakening event, and she wasn't fully developed, her strength was still nothing to sneeze at. She could take the boss down.

Nevertheless, this fact did nothing to relieve my unease. If anything, I was growing more anxious by the minute.

"Dammit...where are you, Ludie?"

At this point in the game's narrative, Ludie gets dragged into the Church followers' self-destructive plan to summon their Malevolent Lord. However, they actually end up using the incorrect incantation in the summoning process—dungeon restoration magic instead of a Malevolent Lord summoning spell. I guess they don't realize their mistake.

Then, once the dungeon is revived, Ludie gets captured and ends up inside.

Where she starts off in the dungeon changes depending on her character progress and the choices made previously during her route. However, one thing I knew for certain was that her starting location ultimately didn't matter. If she got into combat with any monsters in her current state, Ludie would have a hard time overcoming them.

Especially the boss—given her poor matchup, she would definitely lose that fight. And worst of all, the boss here wandered around. If she happened to run into him, then...

"Calm down, Takioto."

"Sorry..."

The same game knowledge that should have given me an advantage had now become a source of endless anxiety.

We'd already cleared the first possible starting area for Ludie. However, there had been nothing but dust, with only the footprints we'd left behind in the grime to show for it.

Dammit.

If the story progression and Ludie's character growth had been slower, we would have been able to discover her quickly. Going off her current abilities, we should have met up with her already. No, that wasn't right, either—this whole event shouldn't have happened anyway. The kicker was that were we in the game, I could have swapped over to Ludie's perspective and immediately booked it over there to find her.

"Tch."

Ludie wasn't at the second location, either. I couldn't help by click my tongue in frustration.

"What's wrong, Takioto?"

"Nothing. Let's go down the left path."

I needed to pick up the pace. For Ludie, a run-in with the wandering boss could spell certain doom. The thing moved fast, too.

Currently, the only people who stood a chance against him were

Yukine and Monica, the latter of whom was fighting at the entrance. However, we hadn't managed to join up with Monica and Shion beforehand. As such, Yukine and I needed to locate Ludie.

I glanced behind me. Yukine was silently following after me. To be honest, I was really grateful she was here.

Normally, she should have been the one to take charge with her wealth of experience in these situations, not me. Nevertheless, she'd put everything in my hands.

"Not here, either?"

I couldn't help but heave a deep sigh. The next location was the last possible starting point.

"…Takioto, listen…why don't you rest a bit? Coming this far without seeing any trace of her means there's a chance she's not here at all."

She stared at me, worried. I must have seemed really desperate.

"I'm sorry, Yukine. Can you follow me on my wild ride a bit longer?"

I'd begun considering the possibility that she might not be here a while ago, and that doubt only grew larger as we continued to explore the manor.

However, I had no intention of stopping.

"But…"

I interjected before she could finish.

"What if Ludie actually *is* here, then?"

I shut my eyes. Images of Ludie came to me. Always trying act the noble princess but abandoning the facade at the drop of a hat. Looking around a convenience store full of curiosity before gleefully buying children's candy. At a loss for words when faced with a dinner spread lit up like a nighttime cityscape. Wandering around town in the most obvious disguise I had ever seen. Bashfully professing her desire to eat ramen.

If I lost all that, I didn't think I could ever forgive myself.

I would never let it happen.

Opening my eyes, I locked on to Yukine's intense gaze.

"If she's not here, then that's a good thing."

Nothing would have made me happier. Ludie wouldn't be in danger. Even if she wasn't here at all, I still wouldn't have regretted charging in. After all…

"Regardless of whether Ludie is here or not, our efforts wouldn't be in vain. Because if she isn't…"

I exaggeratedly shrugged like I was in a foreign TV show and smiled.

"We could just turn it into a funny story. Laugh it off and say, *Aw, man, I'm so dumb. I searched high and low, and she wasn't even there.* Now, suppose we were still able to stop these monsters from showing up? We'd be heroes."

It was simply the best way to look at it.

"If she's not here, that's good. I don't want her to be here. I want her to be somewhere safe. I want to laugh about it together. But if she is here…what if some fiend is attacking her right now?"

That mere possibility kept me going.

"If she's not here…I'll feel guilty for forcing you to come with me, absolutely, but…until I know for sure…"

"Never mind. I'm sorry."

Yukine turned to me and bowed.

"Y-Yukine?"

"You're right… Pfft, ha-ha-ha! You've got a heart of gold, you know that?"

Why was she laughing so hard?

"Sorry for slowing you down. Let's get back to it."

She slapped me on the back, and I simply nodded in response.

We quickly trekked farther and farther through the dungeon. However, we still had yet to find Ludie. Up ahead was the last possible location she could have started from.

Stepping into the area that held our destination, I couldn't believe my eyes.

"No way. This can't be happening…… Why……?" I unconsciously mumbled to myself.

In the Palace of Worldly Impermanence, monsters sit on standby at fixed points of the map, so they shouldn't appear anywhere else. Really shouldn't.

Then why? Why were they here now?!

Not only that, but there were clearly far too many of them, as well. Had some trap been sprung and summoned them all here…?

A feeling of dread consumed me. The more I ruminated on the situation, the more my mind roiled, and the more my body started to burn.

I couldn't stand it anymore. Unable to hold myself back, I rushed toward a goat monster in front of me.

The goatlike Baphomus monster hadn't noticed me yet. By the time it did, it was too late. Spinning my body around and building momentum, I put my Third Hand and Fourth Hand together and slammed them down on the monster like a cudgel.

Its spiral horns shattered with a *crack*.

I'd practiced the move many times before with Claris. By bringing my stole arms together and adding centrifugal force, I could successfully strike with more power overall than a simple punch. However, since the attack used both my arms at once, it also left my defenses open.

"*Hng————!*"

The goat let out a shrill cry as it went flying, and I saw it start to dissolve into magic particles. I hadn't been able to watch for long, though. Deploying my Third Hand to defend myself from a Hellhound, a wolf-type monster that had been attracted by the other's dying wails, I then used my Fourth Hand to forcefully bash its head. However, my attack evidently lacked power, as the Hellhound immediately recovered. I kicked it with my enhanced right leg to finish it off.

"T-Takioto, what the...? Where'd that strength come from...?"

When I turned toward Yukine, she was staring at me wide-eyed in utter amazement. In her bewilderment, she'd relaxed her shoulders, so it looked like a strong slap on her naginata would be enough to force it out of her hands.

Normally, I would've proudly shot back at her, but right now, I didn't have time to brag. Casting a backward glance at the monster to confirm it had turned into magic particles, I replied:

"Sorry. I'll leave this area to you."

After punching the snake monster beside the Hellhound, I broke into a run without checking to see if I'd finished it off or not this time.

I couldn't shake my feeling of dread. I had to do something. I pushed forward, dodging attacks from enemies as I went.

"T-Takioto, what are you doing?! Come back; it's dangerous!"

Yukine begged me to turn back, but I couldn't answer her plea, not while I was sick with worry from all the terrible thoughts swirling inside me.

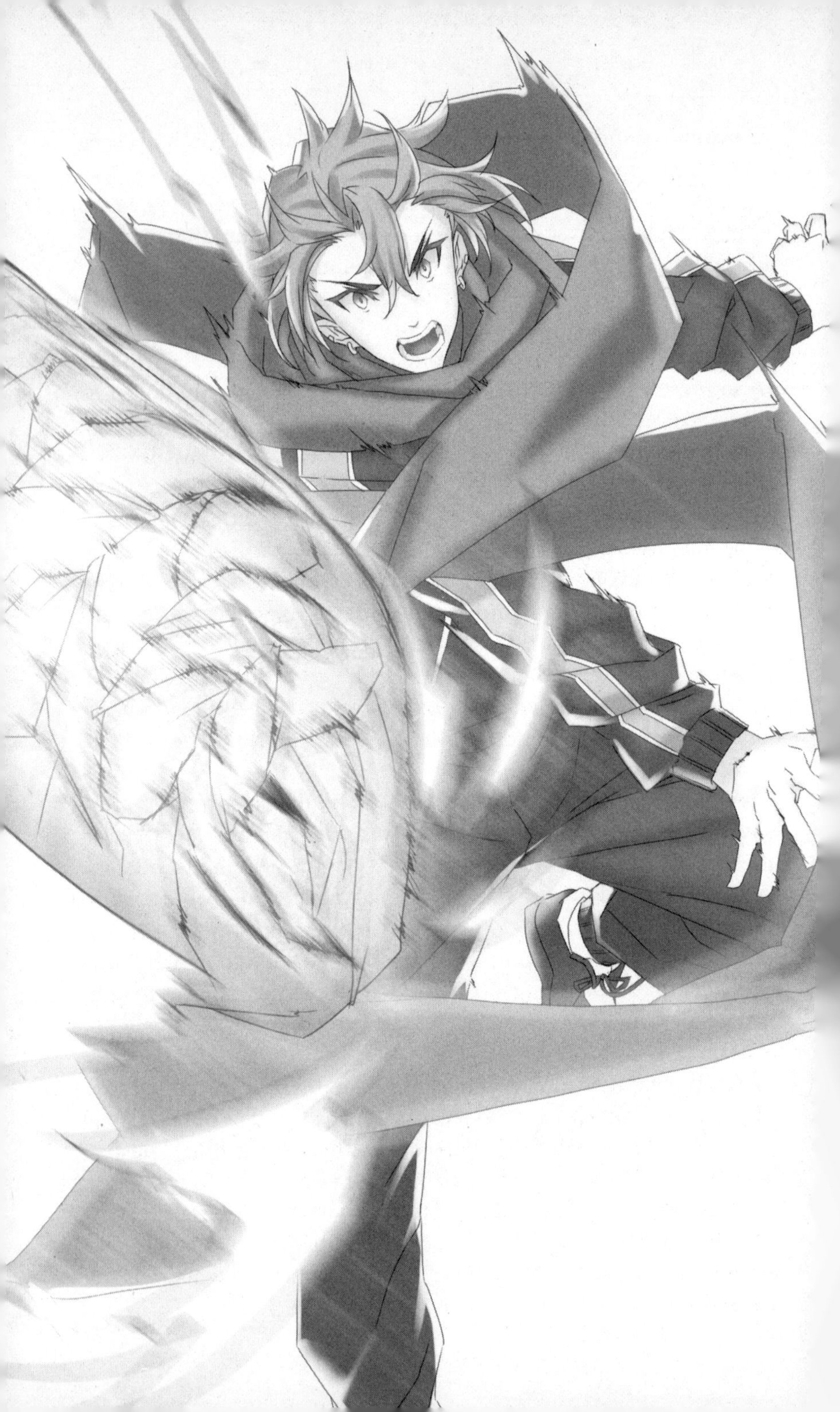

An apelike monster emerged before me. It was already brandishing its club, and seeing an opening, it swung it down on top of me.

"Outta my waaaaay!"

I brought my Third Hand cloaked with mana up to meet it. Its bash did nothing to impede me.

Crushing the ape and sending its obstructive body flying with a roundhouse kick, I pressed on, parrying incoming monster attacks with my Third and Fourth Hands. Strangely, however, the further I advanced, the fewer attacks came my way. I'd assailed so many monsters, yet I was getting attacked *less*—what was going on? I'd expected a much harder time fighting so many opponents at once.

"Fool! I wanted to save Ludie, but now I have to protect you, too!"

When I turned to find the source of the voice, everything clicked.

A blade of water had been dispelling the monsters running after me. It appeared that Yukine had prioritized dealing with the foes coming my way. She had always had my back.

Thank you. And sorry. I'd found a lead, and Ludie was probably in danger, so I had to get to her.

The farther I plunged down the corridor, the more I was convinced my intuition had been spot-on.

"I knew it. Someone is here."

The dust on the walls had been oddly brushed away, and there were footprints where it had most accumulated. Following them, I hunted for Ludie. My heart was going to split in two before long. I needed to find her as soon as possible.

"Dammit. What's this other pair of footprints doing here?!"

I didn't know what had made them, but there were round tracks mixed in with the footprints. Though I grew frantic, my legs couldn't keep up with my restless fervor. In fact, I was close to keeling over in panic.

At the same time my emotions were commanding me to hurry up, a voice in my head urged me to calm down.

Before I could settle my nerves, though, I found her.

"Ludieeeee!"

A black wolf was barring her path. It looked close to five feet long. With each breath, flames spilled from the sides of its mouth.

I noticed that Ludie had a few wounds from something sharp and that her skin was exposed in various places.

"Out of my way!"

Reacting to my voice, the Hellhound turned toward me. Then it opened its mouth as if to bare its sharp fangs and started spewing out fire.

"Kousuke?!"

My Third Hand had been ready to shield me from the assault. However, since I hadn't prepared a water enchantment, the painful heat seared through a spot in the stole I hadn't been able to cover. Immediately enchanting my stole with water, I warded off the beast's flame breath while sending my Fourth Hand barreling into its flank.

Keeping an eye on the Hellhound I'd blown away, I caught Ludie in my arms as she ran over, then used both my stole arms to surround her with a protective barrier. However, the beast remained motionless.

Ludie appeared to have already weakened it. Blood gushed out from the many cuts and wounds that lined its form.

"Kousukeee."

"Thank goodness... I'm so glad you're safe."

I looked toward the Hellhound as I hugged Ludie. Enchanted particles resembling black smoke rose from its body and flew into our own. Then its corpse disappeared from its resting place, leaving a single magic stone behind.

After making sure it was gone, I turned to Ludie.

Her clothes had been torn in a number of places, and several cuts marred her beautiful, fair skin. Her once-radiant blond hair was disheveled and covered in dust. She looked as though she'd gotten stuck in a typhoon. Brushing the dust and dirt off her, I patted her on the head.

I'd made it in time.

She was alive. I could hear her voice. I felt her warmth and her breath on my skin. However, I couldn't stay wrapped up with her like this.

"Ludie, we need to get back to Yukine."

"Yukine's here, too? But why isn't she with you?"

A reflexive "whoops" escaped from my mouth.

"Um, we encountered a group of monsters, and...I just got really worried about you, and I felt like I had to do something. So yeah, I left her behind and rushed over here by myself."

"Sheesh, what were you thinking? Dummy."

Despite her words, Ludie didn't look angry. Instead, she smiled.

"Sure, but... Look..."

"I'm glad, though," she interrupted. Smiling back at her, I immediately turned my thoughts elsewhere.

I had to consider our next move. At the moment, I wanted to join up with Yukine as quickly as possible and put this dungeon behind us. Afterward, I wanted to shut this place down for good. Then I wanted us to get together and celebrate all the joys life had to offer.

However, it seemed that wouldn't be possible under our current circumstances.

Noticing its presence, I detached myself from Ludie.

"Kousuke...!"

Ludie had noticed it, too, and solemnly glared down the gloomy corridor.

"Yeah, I hear it."

It sounded like something massive was being dragged along the ground. On this floor, you basically only encountered monsters that were waiting to ambush you. Furthermore, they were generally all gone by the time you advanced this far into the dungeon. With one exception.

I couldn't tell without properly asking her, but where exactly had Ludie caught the attention of that Hellhound before she led it here? I suppose the most likely answer was that area filled with monsters.

As I moved to shield her again, I instantly ramped up the mana I was sending to my stole and prepared myself.

"Ludie, get ready to run."

If I was right about what was coming our way, we would never have stood a chance in the first place. We'd need to be under some very advantageous conditions to put up a fight.

The dragging sound slowly grew more intense.

Desperately trying to not make too much noise, we began moving away. Then, right as we had almost made it into to the corridor, his face came into view.

He was massive. Large and rugged, with two black horns jutting out from his brow. A mask carved from a skull of some kind cloaked his features, and two keen eyes peeked out from its openings.

The boss seemed to be readying some kind of magic. His sharp eyes were bloodred, and each turn of his head left a crimson afterglow, as if lines were being drawn in the air.

His head wasn't the only thing about him that was huge.

Easily over six and a half feet tall, his gigantic form rippled with muscles that could have easily been mistaken for rocks. Finally, in his tree-trunk-sized arms, he dragged an enormous club made of bone across the ground. Nearly the size of a full-grown man, the club looked like it could instantly pulverize anything with a direct hit.

"All right, c'mon now. This is waaaay too scary…"

The whimper escaped from my mouth involuntarily.

Discovering us, the monster scowled, and his breathing grew heavy. Then he opened his mouth wide.

"_____!"

His roar bellowed all around us.

"Run."

We immediately turned tail and dashed down the corridor.

How unlucky could one guy be? I'd managed to save Ludie without crossing paths with him, and then we immediately bumped into him anyway. Or maybe I should count this as a small blessing. I'd been able to meet up with Ludie before she had a brush with the Heartless Ogre by herself.

The dungeon boss, Heartless Ogre, is a unique monster who generally wanders around the deepest section of the dungeon and initiates the boss battle the moment he spots you. Since you typically run into him around the game's halfway point, Ludie and I wouldn't be able to take him, what with our early-game abilities.

Exiting the corridor into the area ahead of us, we happened upon a treasure chest. When it captured her attention, Ludie's pace slowed before I gave her a light tap on the back.

"Ignore it and run!"

The all-too-suspicious treasure, placed alone in the middle of the floor, was clearly a trap. If we had a character who knew Find Traps with us, they'd be able to tell how dangerous this one was. In the game, this would be the type of chest a player would open with no questions asked. However, that didn't matter right now. We couldn't afford to worry about it.

"_____!"

A roar echoed behind us. His body looked heavy, so why the hell was he so damn fast?

I had thought we would have a remote chance of running away, but it didn't look promising.

I turned toward Ludie, who was out of breath beside me. Anything more than this, and neither Ludie nor I would last much longer. Taking the boss on was our only option.

After I told Ludie to stop running, she breathed heavily, her whole body shaking as she panted. She was covered in sweat, and if we didn't squeeze in breaks like this, she wouldn't be able to move anymore. Still struggling to catch her breath, she grabbed on to my outfit, her legs quivering as she stood like a newborn fawn.

Pulling at my clothes, she looked at me with tears in her eyes and whispered:

"Leave me and run."

What the hell is she saying? I thought.
Sheesh, she doesn't get it at all.

She didn't understand. Hearing that from my beloved heroine was only going to make the opposite feelings come bubbling up inside. That had been true right from the start. Once I knew Ludie was in here, I'd rushed straight into this dungeon knowing full well there was a chance I wouldn't make it out alive.

"There's no way......I could leave you behind...!"

With these words, I resolved that we were absolutely going to survive this together.

I gently undid her hand from my clothes and slowly faced forward as the ogre came into view. Taking one labored step at a time, I began increasing the mana surging through my stole.

I was prepared. It felt almost as though I'd become the hero of a story. Enveloped in this bizarre elation, I felt like I could do anything in this moment.

The ogre had already caught up to our area. However, he simply kept scowling at us and refrained from attacking. I wondered if he'd read the room a little. I wished he'd take the hint and leave us alone, but I wasn't holding my breath.

As I glared back at him, the Heartless Ogre shambled into motion, closing in on us. Dragging his club with a loud scratching noise, he homed in.

Then, twisting his face into a monstrous snarl unlike anything I'd ever seen before, he began running toward us.

A bodybuilder was little more than a stick next to the ogre's form. Compared to this thing's face, a crocodile may as well have been a salamander. And next to his intensity and power, a lion was little more than a house cat.

He was like heavy machinery. You couldn't compare him to animals. If you were going to compare him to anything, you had to start with road rollers, dump trucks, or bucket loaders—that sort of stuff.

I let out a dry laugh. At this point, it felt like I was watching a sitcom.

A *crash* accompanied each of the ogre's steps. Where exactly was it coming from? If someone had told me his body was made of metal, I would've believed them.

To try and stop this superheavyweight-class monster, I prepped an enhancement incantation and started to intensify the mana I sent into my stole.

"_____!"

"Haaaaaaaaaaaaauuugghhh!"

The scream came out completely on its own.

Immediately directing mana into my stole, I lined it up with the ogre's swinging club and opened it up wide.

The area in front of me flashed like a chain of camera shutters.

I thought the sound would blow out my eardrums and the force would shatter my body into pieces. When I came to, I saw my hands bracing me up off the ground.

"Kousuke!" I heard Ludie shout.

"I'm okay!"

It was by a stroke of luck I didn't lose consciousness. If I had, I would be dead. Next to me, I saw that the ogre's club had fallen to the floor.

I had been right to open up my stole in the shape of a triangle. It seemed I had skillfully diverted the force of the club, and it had slammed into the ground as a result.

Then I saw the beast cradle his arms and instantly put space between us.

As I did, a blade of wind came flying past me, hitting the monster. Backup from Ludie.

I could hear her shout "All right!" but I didn't feel any of the same optimism.

The blade had left a gash on the creature, to be fair. Blood was trickling out of him, too. However, when it came to *Magical★Explorer*'s Heartless Ogre...

"———!" he roared.

The area quaked at the sound, and something began flying past the sides of his body. It wasn't something physical. Whether it was his mana, his thirst for blood, his ambitious spirit, or what, I couldn't tell. I brought my quivering body under control and shot more mana into my stole.

Taking labored breaths, the ogre scowled at Ludie. Then the single wound from Ludie's magic started to slowly close back up.

I couldn't see Ludie's face, but I imagined she had despaired. I wanted to rush to her side and cheer her up. However, the instant he started running straight for her, I knew I needed to both protect her and keep my eyes on the creature.

Mere seconds later, the gash had healed so cleanly that it was impossible to tell it had been there in the first place.

Unfortunately, ogres in *Magical★Explorer* have regenerative abilities. Given my wealth of RPG experience, I wanted to chastise the developers that it was *trolls* that regenerated themselves, not ogres, but now wasn't the time for that.

Regardless, in-game, this monster can use mana, regenerate his body, and enhance himself. Without any attacks able to surpass his self-regenerative abilities, Ludie would probably never be able to defeat him. What could we do against an opponent like that?

As the ogre ran toward her, I threw my Third Hand right into his gut.

My blow appeared to have damaged him. Bending slightly backward, he clasped his stomach in pain, but that was the extent of it.

This thing could recover very quickly. I had to do something to stop that.

"Hoo boy, that was close!"

I'd turned the retaliatory downswing of his club away from my stole by spreading it out in an oval. At Marino's advice, I'd practiced transforming it into various shapes, and clearly, my training had paid off. I couldn't let his strikes hit my stole square-on. They had such ridiculous power that I'd just get sent flying.

I put everything I could muster into our defense while Ludie's occasional blades of wind chipped away at the ogre. Unfortunately, it was unclear how long we could keep this up.

We needed to do something to break through the deadlock, or our difference in stamina would finish it for us. That's the impression I had—but how were we supposed to turn the tides?

If Yukine were here, it would be a different story. She could have repeatedly hit the ogre with moves that would have overpowered its regeneration. Even accounting for the beast's monstrously muscular physique, she was probably even stronger.

But would Yukine be able to get here that fast?

Could we keep this defense up until she did?

Nah, that was impossible. So now what should we do?

"Crap…! *Gaugh*."

Although I'd deflected the club, my stole wasn't able to block the ogre's follow-up kick.

I instantly brought up my right arm to block the kick, but the resulting pain felt as though it had been ripped out of its socket. I'd really screwed up now.

Hadn't Claris and Yukine gotten me with that feint attack a hundred times by now?

"Kousuke?!"

"Stay there!"

I had sent mana through my clothes to raise their defensive capabilities slightly, but Ludie had not. Her body would get run through like Styrofoam or be sent flying like a home-run baseball. There was no way I could have her up near the front.

The ogre closed in. He raised his club into the air again. I turned the blow aside with my convex stole, and it slammed into the ground. Then, along with a loud *crack*, it bore a hole in the floor.

I quickly pulled back and glared at the thing. His face contorted with frustration as he looked toward me. At this, a small nagging thought lodged in my mind—

Why didn't he immediately attack me back?

The question came to me after deflecting his attacks and seeing how the force behind the blow would send the club careening into the floor and nearby walls.

Then, as I saw him nursing his arms, I suddenly realized—this monster must've removed any mental limiters he'd placed on his otherworldly strength.

When he struck, he was fully prepared to injure his own body in the process.

The ogre's attacks were a double-edged sword. He was prepared to sacrifice his own body. That was why he put such ridiculous might into his blows. It made a lot of sense when I thought about it. If he knew he would just regenerate anyway, he didn't have to worry about what would happen to his body and could throw everything into his attacks with abandon.

"_____!"

Roaring, he moved his club in a sweeping arc. I immediately morphed my stole to meet his oncoming attack. The base was a convex oval. I couldn't stop the blow head-on. I could only deflect it to the side.

If I had more experience points and more powered-up abilities, I could have easily stopped the ogre's strikes like they were nothing. Unfortunately, I was a total beginner who was challenging his very first dungeon.

What should I do? Deflecting his assaults was all I had. Counterattacks were meaningless.

Though Ludie's spells occasionally hit their mark, they didn't seem to bother the ogre at all. Sadly, my moves were about as effective.

"Ludie, please get out of here!"

Still blasting magic from behind me over the past few minutes, Ludie had kept up her barrage. She hadn't pulled back at all.

"Absolutely not. I can't just leave you behind!"

Honestly, I wanted her to get away from here as soon as possible. If I lost now, the ogre would go after Ludie next. Despite this, she didn't try to flee. She couldn't just run away while someone was risking their life to fight on her behalf. I would have felt the same way in her position, and Ludie had always been that sort of person to begin with.

That side of hers was another reason why I loved her.

Well, in that case—all I could do was manage against the beast somehow and protect her. Our paths to victory were either defeating the boss, the arrival of Yukine, or running away from the monster and escaping.

That said, while taking flight was an option, the ogre was fast. We could move to different locations to some extent, but that was about it. And defeating the thing would be far too difficult.

Every card in my hand was garbage... I didn't have anything that could pose any sort of threat. In that case, what about this dungeon itself? Was there anything I saw on my way here?

Wait, on the way here...? I thought suddenly. *If we go back there...*

"Ludie!"

"What?!"

"Like I said, ignore everything else and continue on to the area right after this one."

"I'm not leaving you behind!"

"I'll follow right after. I've got a good idea!"

I was going to turn the tables. Not just that. If this worked, I'd have the upper hand.

"...Fine. You better make it quick!"

When she stopped her incantation, I heard the sound of Ludie's fleeing footsteps and felt a moment of relief. Then, while turning aside a sweep of the ogre's club with my stole, I kicked against the ground with everything I had.

"Ngggaaaaaaauuuuuuugh!"

With a loud shout, I made a great big swing and punched the ogre... or at least, I pretended to before I hightailed it out of there.

The beast was dumbstruck. Raising my hands up and shouting had convinced him I was going to attack. In the end, I'd turned around and made my getaway.

Naturally, I did this to catch my foe off guard, but it only bought me a few moments. Soon, he came to his senses and started charging after me.

"Seriously, are you a machine or what?!"

Why was there that crashing sound? Was there some pipeline construction going on in here or something?!

I peeked back to see the ogre furiously racing after me. I shouldn't have looked.

Quickly returning to the previous area, I shouted at Ludie to go further into the dungeon.

"Once I activate this trap, I'll come after you! Wait for me in the next area!"

Ludie agreed and left. While I watched her leave, I gave a soundless apology.

This was as far as I was going to run. I felt bad about tricking her, but from here on out, this ogre and I were fighting one-on-one. Ludie needed to be far from here for a variety of reasons.

"Ha-ha, I didn't think I'd end up using this."

In the center of this room was a lone treasure chest. Besides that, the place was empty. It was a normal room in between the corridors. Except with a totally average, unassuming treasure chest in the middle.

Putting one leg on top of the chest, I locked eyes with the ogre scrambling toward me. All right, time to give that thing the most fearless grin I had!

My change in demeanor seemed to make him suspicious. He ground to a halt and observed me closely.

"…Hey, ogre, you know what? In RPG-style eroge, see, there's always these annoying traps with a ninety-nine percent hit rate. I'll go ahead and show you with this puppy right here…"

At that, I kicked the treasure chest with all my strength.

"It's a perv trap."

A loud *clack* resounded at the same moment our bodies started gently floating in midair.

The area at our feet had split open, and we'd started falling down.

The ogre tried to escape, but he wasn't able to get away. Of course he couldn't. This trap was originally supposed to catch five party members all at once. Didn't he know that? It was impossible to flee at such short range.

Anticipating the impact, I made sure to activate my enhance magic, but the shock never came.

Our fall broke on top of a jellylike substance. Quickly sensing what this substance was, I got down off it. A black mist drifted faintly through the area, and each time I touched it, I felt my mana start draining out of me. I tried glancing over to see what had happened to the ogre.

He seemed confused. Unsure what he was wrapped up in, he simply flailed about and sent sweeps of his club toward the nearby slimes.

Phew. It appeared this perv trap was still in good condition.

Normally, it triggers an erotic scene.

As soon as you open the chest, the floor gives way beneath you, and you plummet to an area below that drains your mana. Then, with your mana drained and unable to properly fight, these sticky monsters known among the players as sexytime slimes surround the characters and create a naughty atmosphere. That sort of trap. In a fortunate twist, the slimes didn't have any effect on men.

Players were well aware that this treasure chest was a trap and would purposefully ignore the heroines' insistence it was suspicious to open it anyway. Even if a heroine with the Find Traps skill definitively tells us not to open it, we still do anyway. Only natural, really.

Then, faced with the heroine's seductive figures, all slimy and erotic, we can't help but lean forward in excitement. That isn't all. Certain heroines even berate the player, shouting, *"Why would you open that?! Stupid!"* which was a reward in and of itself. How could we not jump headfirst into such a wonderful ploy?

"Ha-ha-ha, still, though, why did it have to be us falling down here, you know?"

The trap had ensnared a high school boy and a male ogre. Utterly unattractive. How wonderful it would have been if my opponent were a beautiful woman. With my opponent being an ogre, I felt far more fear than arousal.

Nevertheless, I couldn't hold back a smile that bubbled up from the depths of my soul.

"All right, Mr. Ogre."

If I had one overwhelming advantage over this creature right now, what would it be? Muscles? Speed? Stamina? Regenerative ability?

No, it was my mana pool.

Mana served as the source of the beast's strength. His enhancement, his all-or-nothing attacks, and his regeneration ability all came from mana. He was already using mana to heal himself, so how did he like this floor that drained it all? How did he like a situation where his most powerful ability had started to become his biggest weakness?

I grabbed on to a nearby slime with my Third Hand and picked it up.

"Is your mana going to dry up first? Or will mine give out and leave me helpless? Time to turn this into a battle of endurance...!"

You think you can win, ogre?

Against the only party member in all of *Magical★Explorer* who can max out their mana without any boosting effects? Against someone who has been training every day to build up his mana pool? Against my overwhelming amount of MP?! Now it was my turn.

"_____!"

It wasn't clear if he could understand the emotions swirling inside me, but the ogre let out a roar and scowled at me with bloodshot eyes regardless. Based on the red mixed in with the drool trickling out of his mouth, he must have been injured during his fall. However, that red quickly disappeared.

He healed himself.

Panting heavily enough to shake his whole body, he slowly advanced toward me, one step at a time.

The monster had realized that his only route to victory was to take me out and get out of here. To put it another way, that was how I would lose this fight.

I certainly had the mana advantage. In which case, he needed to beat me down before he ran out himself. I would have done the same thing in his situation.

"_____!"

The ogre roared again. The area around us shuddered. I could see his fangs from inside his open mouth, drool trickling out between them.

He breathed heavily as he glared my way, but he finally kicked away the slimes on the ground and started charging toward me.

I threw my slime at the creature as he ran toward me. He overreacted to the ooze, unsure what exactly it was. However, it was naught but a humble pervert that tried to arouse women, and thus, didn't have any effect on us men.

Seeing an opening as he whacked the slime away like a baseball, I sent my Fourth Hand flying into his exposed stomach. I immediately picked up a nearby slime in my right hand and aimed it straight at the ogre's face.

"_____!"

He looked extremely irritated at the slime hitting him in his face. Waving his club around in anger, he sent it packing.

It made a wet *splat* as it hit the wall, probably squashed out entirely. Part of me wanted to see exactly what had happened, but I couldn't take my eyes off my opponent for even a second.

The only ones who could manage that either had to be very strong or have a death wish.

He swung his club at me. The noise it made sounded less like it was cutting through the air and more like it was blasting forward.

In that instant, I formed my stole into an oval and deflected the blow. Then it slammed into the floor and the ogre screamed. Without a moment's hesitation, I grabbed a slime next to me with my Fourth Hand and threw it at the beast.

He was certainly very strong.

Compared to Yukine's full strength—unable to be grasped with the naked eye—and Claris's full power, though, he was no tougher than a mosquito.

After this was over, I definitely needed to thank Claris. If she hadn't been coaching me every day, I would have been beaten long ago.

Dodging his forward kicks, I closely watched my opponent's movements. What I needed now was concentration. *Concentrate. Keep concentrating.* I had more mana than this monster. If I could outrun him until he expended all of it, victory would be mine. I had to keep focusing and dodge his attacks.

As I kept sidestepping, it started to feel like his movements were slowing down. No, it was more than a feeling—he was getting sluggish. Then, in contrast to the ogre's movements, which had relaxed to the point that he seemed to be in slow motion, my thoughts kicked into overdrive.

It felt as though, in the time it took the ogre to complete a single move, I could work through two different thoughts and make two different actions. I had as much leeway now as I'd had previously, when I'd first acquired my Mind's Eye skill.

At this point, the beast's movements were as plodding a caterpillar's. His defense had a ton of holes, he damaged himself with every attack, and above all else, he was excruciatingly slow.

Then I realized—his attacks were gradually getting weaker. His regeneration couldn't keep up with his wounds.

How long did I keep punching after that? It felt as though both only a second had passed, but also tens of minutes had gone by.

Observing the ogre again, I saw that what had once been the picture of fear incarnate was now a shadow of his former self. He'd just about used up all his mana. His breathing was ragged, his body covered in wounds that could no longer be healed, and he looked like he would kick the bucket at any moment.

The monster raised his fist. I gathered mana in my Third Hand and took a step forward.

The more I concentrated, the slower my foe seemed to be moving. What exactly was driving this phenomenon? I hadn't experienced anything like this back on Earth. Did Takioto have some hidden ability of some kind? In the game, all he has are his finicky skills and his monstrous mana pool.

The beast's fist was no longer anything to fear. When it slowly plunged toward me, I parried it with ease. Then, using that force to spin my body and build up speed, I slammed my Third Hand into the ogre's empty head.

His body twitched slightly before coming to a complete standstill. Then he began falling backward. After he collapsed with a deafening *thud*, I approached the ogre, remaining vigilant after seeing how quickly he'd been able to get back on his feet earlier. Then, once his body slowly dissolved into magic particles and a magic stone, I relaxed the tension in my shoulders.

Retrieving the magic stone, I returned to where Ludie was sitting ashen-faced with her legs splayed out to her sides. When she saw me, she jumped up and pounced on me as if she had been shot from a cannon. She hit me in the gut really hard, but I wasn't going to tell her that, of course.

"Stupid, stupid, stupid! How dare you go off on your own like that?!"

For some reason, Ludie's insults had a cozy ring to them. That must've been the warm feeling of being alive.

I patted her on the head. While her hair was a bit dirty, it was incomparably smoother than my own. Bringing her head close to me and breathing in, a sweet scent, almost like the smell of fully ripe peaches, wafted up my nose.

With my other hand, I held Ludie tightly up against me. Her body was slim, yet warm and soft. Finally, when reality settled in, joy came welling up inside me.

I'd been able to protect her.

Insults were still streaming from her mouth. "Stupid," "liar," "enemy of women everywhere," "pervert," and other jeers unfit for royalty. Nevertheless, she didn't try to free herself from my arms wrapped around her. The more I heard her abuse, the fuller my heart grew.

Naturally, it wasn't some thrilling reward that filled me with joy. It came simply from the fact that her words meant she'd been worried about me.

"K-Kousuke, wh-what w-were you th-thinkinnng?"

Ludie's voice was shaking. It had been normal at the start, but with each word she spoke, her tone became more and more tearful, until she ultimately stuttered on every word, and I had a hard time understanding her.

Her relentless rebukes finally came to a stop. Then, squeezing her head and body into my own, I could hear her sniffling.

"Ludie...I'm so glad...you're okay."

When I said this, she pressed her head even harder into me and squeezed me with more force. Replying to her, I also put a bit more force into my hug.

A few moments later, she lifted just her face away from my body and looked at me with her slightly swollen eyes.

"Hey, Kousuke."

"What?"

"Thanks."

I felt so glad I had risked my life.

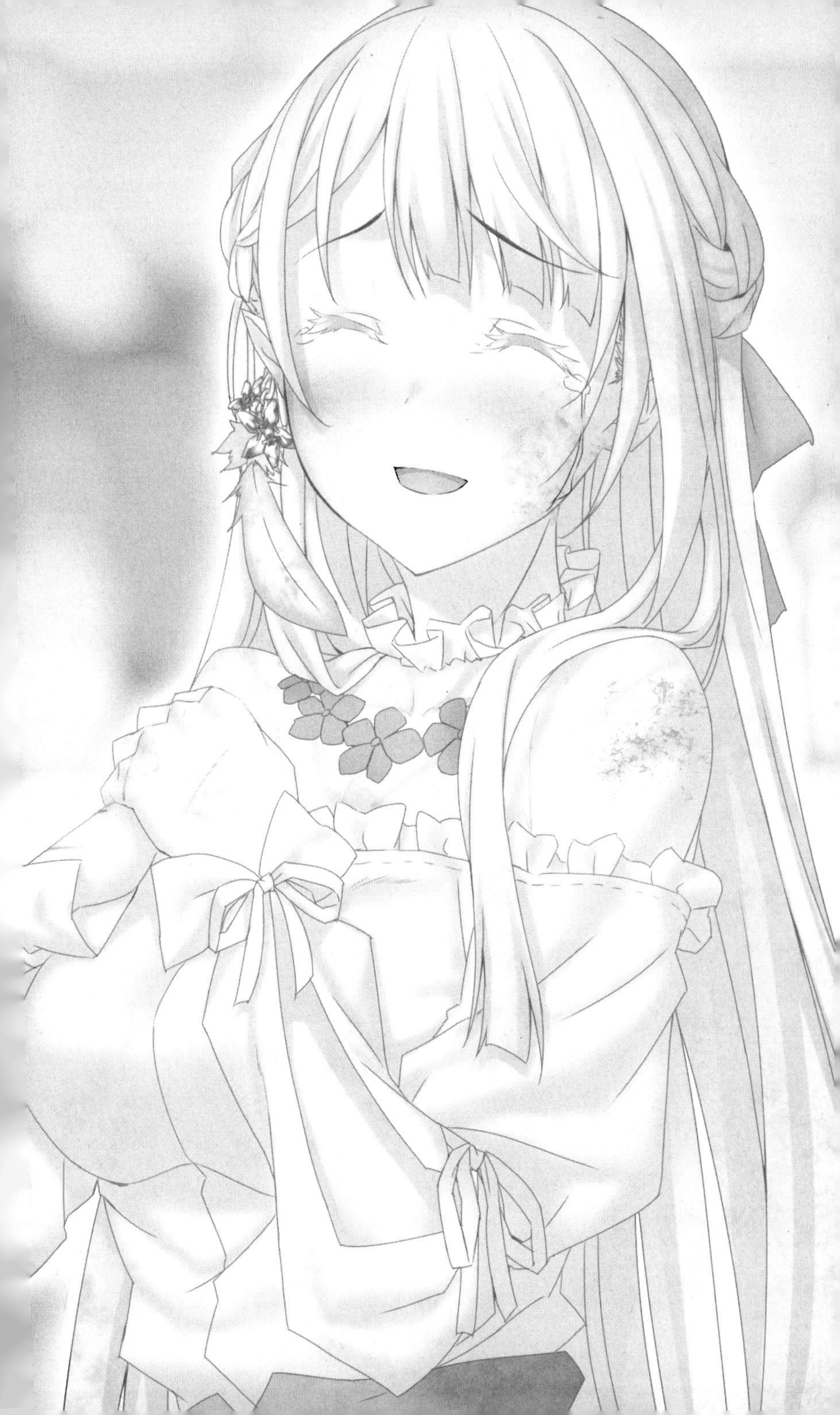

Chapter 9 (**One Thing Every Eroge Has** Magical★Explorer)

It was about ten minutes later that we were able to meet up with Yukine. As soon as she saw Ludie's puffy, tearstained face, Yukine sent a punch my way as I turned to face her that would scar me for life. Ludie immediately told her she was misunderstanding the situation, and then Yukine gave a sincere apology, praising me heartily before inevitably giving in to rage.

"Why did you leave me behind?!"

Faced with that, all I could do…

"I'm really sorry."

…was apologize. The gap between her anger and her previous words of admiration was intense. At my apology, Yukine roared with laughter.

"I'm really jealous, though, Ludie. Having someone willing to put their life on the line to save you like that."

These words, too, were another misconception on her part.

"Well, if you were in Ludie's situation, Yukine, I would definitely rush right in there, and I'm sure Ludie would come, too, right?" I said, looking to Ludie and prodding her for an answer. She gave a small nod.

Yukine gave an embarrassed yet happy "I see" before pulling Ludie and me into her arms. My head rested on her shoulder. My heart throbbed when I noticed how close I was to her nape, exposed by her ponytail, as I enjoyed her scent, which contrasted with Ludie's.

"I'm really glad you're both okay."

"…Sorry for making you worry."

"Ah, it's fine. I was being too harsh. Why do you keep worrying me so much anyway? You better make it up to me, you hear?"

Well, I mean…

"Of course."

"Thank you very much."

Now then, we couldn't very well stay wrapped up in Yukine's arms forever. If I were being honest, I wanted to turn my senses of sight, hearing, smell, and touch to max capacity and get my fill of every part of her, but I knew I couldn't do that.

It was unbearable to separate myself from the hug, but I managed to focus my mind elsewhere and peeled myself away. The manor was still active.

"Now, I'd normally want to finish off this dungeon, but I don't know how. It's unfortunate, but our primarily goal was saving Ludie, so let's get out of here."

She might not have known, but there was someone else here who did. As she tried to walk off, I stopped her with my Third Hand.

"Hold on. I actually…know how to close the dungeon."

Well, I understood how, but there would still be a few problems along the way.

"And how do you know that?" Ludie asked, cocking her head.

I worried for a moment, but after I'd given a lazily concocted excuse along the lines of *I just happened to read about it in a book at the Hanamura house*, strangely, both Yukine and Ludie totally believed me. Obviously, I hadn't seen anything about it at the Hanamura house, but except for the fact that the "book" in question was actually an eroge, I wasn't exactly lying.

It was possible that Yukine had her suspicions and just elected to stay silent. No, that wasn't just a possibility. I was sure of it. From her perspective, the actions I had taken here were far too abnormal.

While I felt slightly guilty about my lie, we decided to press on in order to deactivate the dungeon.

That said…

"Why the long face?"

"Oh, it's just, you know. Deactivating it is simple but kind of hard at the same time…"

"Well, which is it?"

Easier said than done… Actually, it was hard to say it, too. There was still something outrageous left in this dungeon, but I couldn't bring it up at all.

Our final destination was close. Partly because Ludie had been so deep inside already, it didn't take more than ten minutes from the spot where I had felled the ogre. Of course, that was in part due to my navigation keeping us on track.

"Okay, here it is."

Although I'd defeated the boss, the dungeon itself was still active, alive, and kicking. Monsters were still pouring out from the entrance. To stop them, we needed to cut off the manor's energy supply.

We arrived at a dead end. However, a magic circle had been drawn on the wall, and in the middle was set an enormous magic stone resembling polished obsidian.

On closer inspection, the obsidian-like rock seemed to be transmitting mana to the magic circle, and there was some sort of hole opened in its center.

In front of both enchanted objects were a container resembling a treasure chest, a pedestal to mount something of some kind, and a long key-like rod. The long rod also had geometric patterns drawn all over it.

A number of things caught my eye, but first, I headed toward the treasure chest. Then, upon opening it, I let out a deep sigh. Closing my eyes, I turned up to the sky and sighed again.

The contents were exactly as I'd anticipated.

"What should I do here...?"

No, after making it this far, I just had to get them to do it.

Inside were three sexy bathing suits and a single piece of paper. Though I couldn't read the characters written on the sheet, I nevertheless knew what they said. In situations where you don't have party members capable of reading this ancient language, like MKS73 or Sexy Scientist, then you'd have to return to town to have it translated and then come back into the dungeon again. Right now, there wasn't anyone here who could read it, but I already knew what it said, so that wasn't a problem.

No, if anything, there were nothing *but* issues.

Seriously, what were the game developers even thinking here? I had to assume there were worms in their brains.

...In order to deactivate this dungeon, we needed to stop the energy furnace that supplied the interior with energy.

The Church folks had confused the Energy Furnace Activation magic for the Summon the Malevolent Lord with a Human Sacrifice magic.

They'd planned on sacrificing Ludie to their god, but all they had done was sacrifice themselves to revitalize this dungeon.

The game shows you that scene together with some background CG... I couldn't know for sure without asking Ludie about the details, but something similar probably happened here.

Well then, by cutting off the energy supply radiating from this obsidian magic stone, it would deactivate this dungeon, but in the game, no matter how much the player tries, it's impossible to destroy the stone or the magic circle. I assumed the same would be true here. In any event, instead of screwing something up and making it go out of control, it was probably better to use this rod from the start to deactivate it.

This rod was also a nuisance. How so? Because of how it was used to extinguish the energy furnace.

For starters, RPG-style eroge will almost always include something after defeating a strong boss. What, exactly? Of course, experienced ladies and gentlemen know what, but even a first-time eroge player could answer that question.

A reward, of course.

Magical★Explorer is no exception. During this event, cutting off the energy furnace coming from the magic stone and circle rewards you with a sexy CG scene.

All esteemed players, including me, cooed in wonder, marvel, and admiration at this energy furnace setup, and had dubbed it the fapnace. Not furnace. Fapnace.

I showed the paper from the treasure chest to Ludie and Yukine. To be honest, I'd considered this a fantastic setup device, one that would mark a new chapter in the world of eroge. It was revolutionary enough to make you believe there'd be fapnace games numbers two and three coming out soon.

Truly, it had been too powerful, as I suppressed my current urge to throw up. Give me a damn break here.

"I can't make heads or tails of it."

"Oh, I know what it says. I know, but...," I murmured, evasive. Ludie and Yukine looked at me questioningly.

"What's wrong?"

Yeah, I had to tell them. It was necessary to stop the flood of monsters. We had already come this far. I steeled myself.

"W-well, see, to stop the energy furnace, we need to thrust this rod into that hole there…"

"Then let's just stick it in."

"Well, er, to deactivate the dungeon, we need to fill up the rod with a unique type of mana."

"A unique type of mana?"

To shut off the energy furnace, we needed to circulate a special variety of mana through the rod and thrust it into the hole in the obsidian stone inside the magic circle. However, the rod currently didn't have any of that mana. When the mana was diffused into the rod, it should have glowed with white light, but right now, it was little more than a stick.

"Yes, to fill it with that special mana, you do something with that rod placed on this pedestal."

"Let's just do it, then?"

Well, yes, but…

"Takioto, what do we need to do?"

"W-well, um, when you place the rod there, a special magic display will pop up, and it'll show a humanoid silhouette."

Yukine glanced toward the pedestal area, commenting, "There is this strange magic ring," as she ran her finger along it.

"W-well, so, if you make the same pose the silhouette's in, the magic circle on that pedestal will send the special mana through to the rod."

"That's what you have to do? What a strange contraption."

C'mon, this was an eroge dungeon. No way was that going to be all. Could I tell them all this? Should I have them just do it without telling them?

Impossible!

Of course I couldn't do that. My heart would give out if I tried to get through this without saying anything. Besides, they'd realize what was going on as soon as they started, and there was still crazier stuff to come. Saying nothing wasn't an option.

"Just what is going on? Spit it out."

My back was freezing. Yet despite my persistent cold sweat, the inside of my mouth was dry as a desert.

Still, I had to let them know what they were in for. Bracing myself, I opened my mouth.

"W-well, the thing is, the poses that, er, show up...are apparently all s-sexy poses!"

Yukine's and Ludie's faces instantly turned scarlet.

"E-excuuuuuuse me?!"

"Not only that, but you have to wear the s-swimsuits in that treasure chest, or it won't work!"

"S-seriously? This is absurd! S-s-sexy poses?! Wh-why are there swimsuits in a treasure chest anyway?!"

Her Highness couldn't be more right! But I'd expect nothing less from an eroge! Having costumes nearby and ready to use is par for the course, I'm afraid!

"Hold on, this thing's defense stats are through the roof..."

I hadn't noticed Yukine go over to the chest, and there, she held up a black swimsuit pinched between her fingers, her whole head up to the ears flushed bright pink.

I wanted to get up and scream defiantly, *You're damn right!*

We're talking about *Magical★Explorer* here—in this game, some characters' strongest armor sets look like sexy lingerie. No wonder the look and defensive capabilities of a piece of armor would be out of sync. Even a certain nationally acclaimed game has swimsuit costumes with stupidly high defenses, and one of the character designs even features bikini armor!

I immediately put my legs underneath me on the ground so that I was seated in the traditional Japanese manner. Then I forcefully bowed down, pressing my head into the floor so hard that I was ready to do a full headstand.

"It's the only way to do it! It's not my fault!"

As much as they may have wanted the nonsense to stop, it was only going to keep piling up from here. The writers and directors who thought up this scene seriously had some screws loose.

"Enough with these silly jokes!" Ludie shouted, snatching the rod next to me and shoving it into the obsidian on the wall. However, there was no reaction whatsoever.

"Is this rod broken or something?!"

Forget the rod, this whole world's logic was defective, honestly. I mean, eroge are broken and unbalanced to begin with.

"Um, well, according to what's written there, the sexy pose should immediately fill it up with mana. Two people would make it go even faster, if possible. It's not my fault, I swear!"

"W-we've got to wear this...?" Yukine mumbled, jiggling the swim-suit pinched between her fingers.

"Uuuuuugh."

Well, that wasn't the full extent of this cursed setup, either.

"So, well, on top of that, see, there's something you need to keep in mind with the poses..."

"Th-there's more...?!"

Oh boy, was there. It was just as absurd, too. If this were a normal, everyday eroge world, the situation wouldn't be this absurd. The whole *Put Them in a Bikini and Make Them Do Sexy Poses* thing would be plenty for most eroge. However, this title stuck on an extra layer of bonkers where the average eroge wouldn't. That's what *Magical★Explorer* was all about.

For starters, if this setup only involved putting the girls in swimsuits and having them make a sexy pose, the eroge veterans wouldn't have whooped as hard as they had. What got them so riled up was an additional setup added on top of everything else.

"Actually, um, if you mess up the pose, or, um...every t-ten sec-onds......it'll spew out gas that'll m-make you horny!"

"Huuuuuh?!"

It's not poison, it'll just make you horny! It's totally non-lethal! And it doesn't work on men at all! At least not in the moment. But once this event is over...

"B-but, there's no negative side effects on the human body. Appar-ently, you'll warm up after it's over, and its lasting effects include soft-ening the post-bath chill, as well as reducing shoulder stiffness and cold sensitivity..."

"I don't need any hot spring remedies right now! B-besides, just get-ting t-t-turned on is a bad side effect already!"

"Eep, g-good point!"

"This is ridiculous!"

"I—I know, but it has to be done!"

Man, I really wanted to beat the snot out of whoever came up with this setup. *Seriously, my guy, you've gone completely outside the reach of the normal person's realm of understanding. Dressing them up in swim-suits and making them do sexy poses while the room fills up with gas that makes them horny—are you out of your mind?! That's some eroge shit! Dammit, this is the world of eroge, isn't it?!*

"G-getting horny or whatever is *not* happening! Th-that's right, why don't you do it, Kousuke?!"

"No, no, no, no way, h-how am I supposed to put that on?! Imagine how indecent I'd look!"

"If you can't wear it, just do it naked!"

"N-naked?! That's crazy! I should just do it in my clothes at that point!"

"Wait…"

"You didn't even consider that?!" I complained to Ludie, who was flushed red all the way to the tips of her ears. However, she'd already made up her mind.

"Anyway, start stripping!"

"Okay, hold on, no—wait, get your hands off me! At least…at least let me keep my boxers on!"

As the two of us argued, Yukine raised her voice.

"I-I'm going to trust Takioto."

Ludie and I both craned our necks toward her. With unbelievable speed, to boot.

"I'll agree there are times when his staring can be a little—how can I put it? Hmm—lascivious, you could say."

Wait, my gaze wasn't that creepy, was it? Nah, staring hard at the nape of her neck and stuff was definitely pervy, no doubt about it.

"However, I asked myself, would Takioto really lie at a time like this? I bet he's right."

Ludie was at a loss for words. She looked at the rod, then to me, back to the rod, then back to me again, until finally sighing like she was about to chide me for something.

"……Kousuke wouldn't lie like that. F-fine, then. Kousuke's, well, someone I can trust. B-but just this once, got it?!"

I wished this would be the end of it, but this was the world of *MX*. If anything, compared to the seriously erotic dungeons in the rest of the game, this place was one of the tamer ones.

"G-got it… Thanks."

W-with that settled...

"Now, then. My humblest apologies, but can you put on these swimsuits?"

"Ughhh, fine! We just wear them, right?! Hngggh... Hurry up and hand it to me!" Ludie spat, her face bright red as she reached out her hand. However, I was in trouble. Well, see, the inside of the treasure chest...

"Well, um, there's three types of swimsuits here, so..."

"Arggghh, I don't care anymore!"

She was seriously incensed. Full of indignation, she came over to me and stared at the swimsuits inside the treasure chest. She then grew visibly flustered, plain for anyone to see.

"No... This has to be a joke! Th-th-they're all...they're all o-obscene!"

"I understood what I was getting myself into, but...w-we're really wearing these?" Yukine murmured, her whole face a deep crimson as she stared at the swimwear. Ludie took the green bikini bottoms in her hand and slammed them into the treasure chest.

"Fine, whatever! I'll wear one! I just need to put it on, right?! Kousuke! Pick one! I can't make a choice like this!"

"Sorry, but I—I can't, either..."

After looking the two girls in the eye, I shifted my gaze down to the bikinis. Then I looked up at their blushing faces once again before returning back to the swimwear.

Then it dawned on me.

I was...standing at the crossroads of my life.

A legitimate opportunity to dress Ludie and Yukine up in sexy bathing suits had landed at my feet. I doubted I'd ever have a chance like this again. I could only choose once. I also only had one chance to engrave the sight into my cerebral records. How in the world could I choose the right swimsuit here? Before my eyes were green, white, and black pieces of holy fabric. Items so profound that they could elevate angels to even higher heights of celestial splendor.

For a normal bathing suit, first, you'd check the sizes and then choose your preferred design. However, what was amazing about these ones was that they were created with special magic, so on top of their extremely high defensive ability, they would automatically adjust their size to fit whoever wore them. In other words, you see, I didn't have to worry about the size at all and simply had to choose the swim-wear that suited them the best.

This was too taxing. And the worst part was that in the real world, I hadn't been able to reload a save file at this point. Unable to preserve the sight in game CG, either, I needed to rely on the naked eye to etch the upcoming image into the ephemeral memory of my brain, as if my life depended on it. How deeply regrettable, though. Why couldn't they each wear all three? I wanted to see it all—the elven-green Ludie, the angelic Ludie in white, the coquettish black swimsuit Ludie, and Yukine, gallant in green, erotic in white, and alluring in black.

Making my agonizing choice, I handed each one of them a swimsuit and packed the leftover away in my bag.

I lost track of how much time had passed between them starting to get changed until Ludie told me, "We're done."

"Kousuke? What're you looking so worn out for?"

"Are you okay, Takioto?"

Concerned, the two girls questioned me. I was fine, I'd just been suppressing my natural masculine desire to see the two girls get changed, keenly tuned in to the sounds of their rustling clothes. And I'd been wholly dedicating my body and soul to stifling that desire as I heard them say things like "Yours are so big, Yukine..." and "You're very pretty yourself, Ludie."

None of that mattered right now, though. There were far more pressing things to worry about. Right now, in their current state, I...

"Wh-what?"

Ludie tried to conceal herself with both arms, but she couldn't hide everything.

"Beautiful..."

I had chosen her favorite color, the green swimsuit. A wonderful decision, if I do say so myself. Most of her fair and youthful skin was exposed to the air, with only her precious areas being garnished with a piece of green fabric. On top of that, that small bit of fabric was supported by nothing more than a thin piece of string, and any major movement threatened to make everything come pouring out.

Yukine was in the white bikini. A wonderful decision, if I do say so myself. The swimsuit should have adjusted its size when she put it on, so I wondered why her chest still seemed ready to spill out at the drop of a hat. It was clearly small on her. I knew what this was—it had sized itself down on purpose to emphasize her sexiness. The bottom was just as tiny, and if it shifted just a little bit…

"Takioto, I'm very happy to hear that, but, well, when you stare at me like that…it's a little, you know."

"She's right. Don't stare so much, idiot. It's embarrassing…"

"S-sorry. Let's get started right away."

After the two girls were standing where I'd pointed, I nodded toward them, mounting the rod to the pedestal.

Then a magic circle appeared at our feet, and a display screen materialized in front of us. Shortly afterward, silhouettes lit up on the screen. The shadows had white lines going through them in various places, making it easy to tell at first glance where each body part was. Also, in the bottom right appeared an hourglass, and I could see the sand slowly draining away. It showed the time left before the aphrodisiac gas was going to be pumped into the room.

"L-let's hurry, Ludie."

The first pose on the display was a simple one. They only needed to tilt their bodies sideways and make peace signs next to their faces.

But why the double peace signs?

A bell chimed with their correct input, and the rod-shaped meter in the bottom left of the display filled up about a tenth of the way. This seemed to show just how much mana had gathered in the rod.

Looking at the rod, I thought I saw a white glow, though faint.

"Nice, we got that one. Hmm? Wh-what?!"

Hearing Yukine's dismay, I looked up. When I did, this time it was Ludie who shouted in panic.

"H-hey, this isn't right! Why's the timer still going down?!"

Honestly, Ludie, you make a great point. You would think that getting the pose right would stop the clock for you, but unfortunately, that's not exactly it.

"H-hurry, Ludie. If Takioto's right, um, uh, that gas that m-makes us a-aroused is gonna come out!"

"Urrrrrrk!"

This time, the pose emphasized their chests. The suggestive stance had them scoop up their breasts under their folded arms and lean forward slightly, showing off their cleavage.

At this point, it felt like all the blood vessels in my body were about to boil over.

I wanted to throw everything else to the winds, crouch down right in front of them, and focus every nerve in my body on the sheer bliss playing out before me.

I wanted to see that unparalleled landscape from the front...so powerfully that it felt like I was going to throw up. When I considered the two girls in front of me, however, I couldn't bring myself to act so rude.

"I—I can't make a pose like that!"

"Hurry, Ludie!" Yukine shouted, already in the pose herself. Ludie hadn't mentally braced herself yet. Cruelly, though, the sands of time kept on falling.

Then, before the two could get their poses in order, gas mercilessly sprayed into the room.

"Gaugh?!?!?!?!?!?!?!"

"*Cough...* Urrrgh!"

The effect was tremendous.

Both Ludie's and Yukine's faces became red, and their eyes glazed over slightly, almost like melted marshmallows.

"Y-you two need to hurry!"

My shout brought them back to their senses, and they thrust their chests forward to make the pose. Upon successfully completing it, the mana in the rod increased a little more.

The next silhouette looked like it was crouched down and looking upward. They gratefully completed the simple position. Immediately after the chime, a new one appeared on the screen.

The next stance had them lift up their arms and bring their hair into ponytails behind their heads. The aim here must have been to show off their armpits. While relatively subdued, it was a wonderful position, able to casually pierce right through the hearts of fetishists everywhere.

Right as they finished this pose, a second round of gas jetted into the room.

Things were *really* bad now.

Not just their faces but also their bodies had now gained a lush pink glow, and they were sweating all over.

The next position...had them stick their butts out. It was possibly the sexiest pose they'd performed yet. When it came on the screen, they both looked toward me.

Neither said a word. Nevertheless, I got the message loud and clear:

Please don't look!

I was...heartbroken. I scrunched my eyes and covered them with my stole. I wanted to peek so badly. I wanted to take in every detail. I wanted to look so much that I couldn't stand it. However, I didn't want to do something they truly didn't want me to do. I couldn't...let myself...do it...

It happened as soon as I heard Ludie's seductive yelp. A divine epiphany came upon me.

Mind's Eye. I could look with Mind's Eye.

I sat myself down and honed every nerve in my body. I was after a glimpse of Ludie's and Yukine's seductive figures, here. Even if I heard the gas jets, even if Ludie or Yukine let out another seductive moan, I needed to focus.

I needed to concentrate with everything I had.

What happened when I did?

Ludie and Yukine hugging each other's sweat-covered forms came faintly into view. I remembered this pose from the game!

It was a combination pose that didn't show up unless you had two people with you. A bonus position that would fill up the rod with tons of mana if done correctly! Ludie and Yukine were tangled up with each other, exhausted and drenched in sweat.

Such beautiful and alluring entanglement!

As a fanfare echoed, Yukine happily shouted, "Th-there we go! It's full!"

I opened my eyes, immediately retrieved the rod, and ran toward the two battered girls to try and end this outrageous event once and for all.

However, when I saw them, an uneasy feeling overtook me. Had the girls looked this worn out when I'd watched this scene in-game?

Actually, to be honest, I remembered that there were two sets of CG, one with the characters a little tired, and one where they were exhausted... I *did* play through it twice with the same characters... Wait, actually, now that I thought about it, did this rod...? Uh-oh.

"Ahnnnn!"

I-it had completely slipped my mind. But hey, we finished it anyway, right?!

"Hah, hah, what's wrong...Kousuke...?"

Ludie looked feeble enough to collapse, and Yukine was trying to support her. However, it seemed the strain was too much on her legs, so I caught them both as they threatened to collapse on the floor.

Ludie's head and body rested against the left side of my chest. Her sweat-drenched hair stuck itself to my cheeks, and the combined smell of her shampoo and her body odor sank into me. Yukine's smell was slightly different. Her head rested atop my shoulder, and her chest pressed up against my body. Its magnanimity made me feel as though no matter what evils I performed, her valleys would always embrace me warmly.

Desperately trying to stay my heart from going berserk, I gently sat the two girls, still on the verge of collapse, on the ground.

A little while later, the girls had recovered. However, their faces were still a little red, and they wouldn't look me in the eye. But they didn't put that much space between us, either, tightly grabbing on to my clothes for some reason.

"Let's deactivate this dungeon."

When I announced this, they both nodded, still refusing to look me in the eye.

When I suggested that all three of us thrust the rod in together, the two women nodded in agreement. I used my Third Hand and Fourth Hand to support them as they stood up, and the three of us hoisted the glowing rod together.

Then we slowly inserted it into the pedestal.

The change happened instantly. The further we inserted, the more the light of the magic circle in front of us faded. If we inserted the

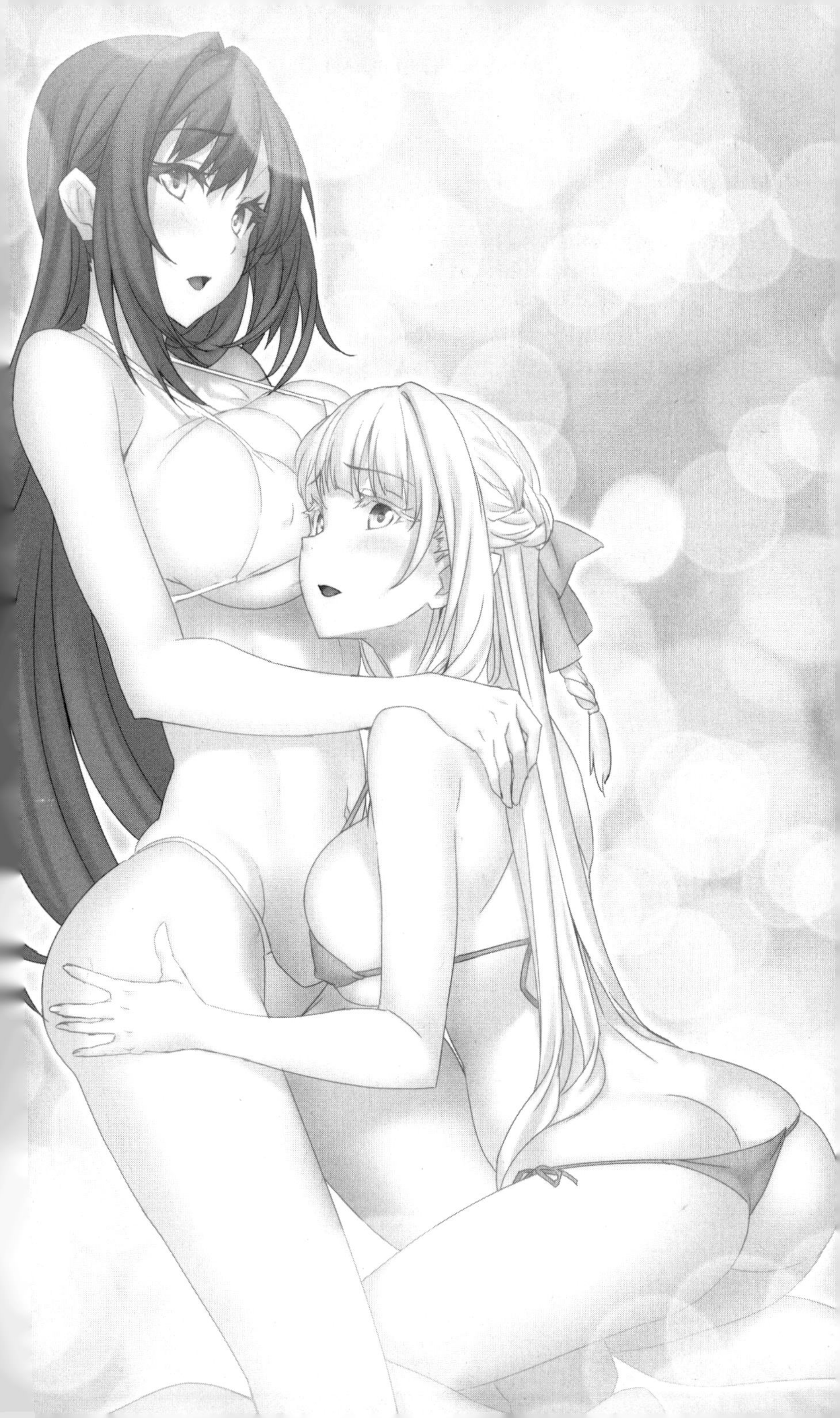

whole rod, this light would extinguish completely, and we would completely deactivate the dungeon.

As we slowly pushed the pole in, I thought back on Ludie and Yukine
growing battered and ragged as they made their sexy poses.

Man, why hadn't I remembered it sooner? If there were a character
with us who could actually read the instructions in the treasure chests,
this wouldn't have happened. The gentlemen eroge players ignored
what was written down and forced their party members to do it to
unlock all of the scene's CG anyway.

Oh well, it was in the past now, and I should just stop thinking about
it. And take the truth to the grave with me. I couldn't say anything
now.

In reality, filling 40 percent of the rod with the special mana would
have been plenty. It hadn't needed to be fully charged at all.

Chapter 10 (Resolve   Magical★Explorer)

Reborn as a Side Character in a Fantasy Dating Sim

The day after saving Ludie was a blur. Marino in particular furiously scolded me, while also praising me for saving Ludie, much as she had done after the hotel incident.

Though they commended me, I'd still been worried about Marino and Sis. When I gave Sis my sincerest apology, she pulled me into her breasts and congratulated me on a job well done. It was like I was on cloud nine. I couldn't say it out loud, but Sis was clearly the bigger of the two, no contest.

After being targeted twice, I thought for sure that Ludie would decide to put school on hold, but it seemed she wasn't going to. Despite His Majesty ordering her to return home, she'd declined. Apparently, she'd told him something along the lines of "I have Kousuke here, so what could go wrong?" However, even shouldered with those expectations, there was no guarantee I'd always be able to save her. All I could really do was keep putting my life on the line trying to protect her.

When I tried to impress that upon her, she blushed slightly before weakly replying "That's plenty, dummy" and leaving my room.

Afterward, I went to the bottom of the waterfall to restart my normal training routine, but Yukine wasn't there.

I imagined she had Morals Committee work to do. Yukine, the lieutenant of the committee, a vice presidential role, had previously said she had some work to get done before school started.

I let out a small sigh. Then, placing myself under the cold water, I took up my normal position, closed my eyes, and let the waterfall pour down over me.

Ludie popped into my mind. She's basically a heroine whose story always ends happily. The protagonist of *Magical★Explorer* always gets involved with her and winds up saving her, too. Her events trigger no matter what, and if the player fails to resolve them, they're then blocked off from continuing the story, with the exception of a special route.

That was why as long as one didn't purposefully aim for a bad ending or one of the special ones, Ludie would never meet misfortune.

However, was that entirely true this time around?

Ludie had brushed up against disaster. If things had played out exactly according to the game plot, she would've experienced a miserable series of events.

What would I need to do to ensure all the heroines had happy endings?

In *MX*, in order to make sure each and every heroine, Ludie included, winds up content, you have to trigger a number of events. Combat is also required, of course. Not only that, but you have to develop several characters to nearly last-boss levels of strength. Along the way, there are some optional events, and a few hidden ones, naturally.

Would the protagonist save the girls in these hidden events? What if multiple events happened at once? Or if things occurred in a different order, like the recent dungeon incident? What if Ludie, or Yukine, got dragged into something?

What exactly would happen to them?

If the absolute worst occurred, would I be able to forgive myself?

If I hadn't known about the game, I might have given up on the girls entirely. When it got to the point where it seemed impossible to do anything, I probably would have told myself *Well, it's winter; flowers will wither*, or some other platitude to convince myself that it was fated for things to end up a certain way.

However, just because it was winter, did that mean flowers had to die?

Being able to do all that was what made the game protagonist *the* protagonist. Where did that leave me, though?

"Hah…"

I was not a game protagonist.

Mind you, I did have knowledge. I knew there were various endings, both fortunate and misfortunate ones. That's right, I knew what brought these girls joy.

Something hot, like hissing magma, circulated through my veins.

It wasn't blood. It wasn't anything physical. It was will—a mixture of passion, resolve, and love.

Even the freezing water descending from the waterfall barely felt cold at all. I now understood that thinking about these girls would inevitably make me react this way. *If only I could just calm myself down a little*, I thought, but ultimately, it was useless. Besides, I wasn't convinced that calming down would lead me to any different outcomes.

I slowly opened my eyes.

"I...love *Magical★Explorer!*"

Ludie, Yukine Mizumori, Sis, Marino. Nanami, Monica, Ms. Ruija, Shion, Katarina, Gabby, Sakura. I loved them all.

I loved Claris, after meeting her in this world for the first time. The heroine who ends up unhappy due to circumstances in her past. The heroine cursed with sorrow. The heroine who gets sacrificed. The heroine who trades her life to save the world. I loved them all, too.

Was I okay with letting these girls end up unhappy?

No.

Absolutely not. Why should the girls I loved so much end up miserable?

They all had their own routes to joy, so how could they end up so despondent?

I wanted them to be happy.

No, I would *make* them happy.

Granted, leading them all to happiness would require about the same amount of strength needed to defeat the last boss. And what about the secret characters? Would the protagonist go and save them? He might. He might not. It didn't matter. Either way, I'd just go instead.

"I just need to get strong. If I need enough strength to defeat the Demon Lord, to protect everyone...to save them from their bad endings, then I'll just become the strongest in the world!"

I didn't give a damn about any of Kousuke Takioto's events anymore. I could do them if they proved useful and ignore them if they weren't. I was going to act however I damn well pleased.

All right, then. I needed to set a goal to work toward if I was aiming to ultimately become the most powerful in the world... Actually, I guess my goal hadn't really changed all that much.

My closest objective at hand was to surpass the members of the Academy's Three Committees—the Morals Committee, the student council, and the Ceremonial Committee—as well as the additional, powered-up heroines added with the expansion disc, the Expansion Four Kings. First, I needed to train inside dungeons. When the time was right, I would rise up and supplant the Three Committee members and the Four Kings.

Next would be the Big Three—Morals Committee Vice President Yukine Mizumori, Student Council President Monica Mercedes Von Mobius, and the ultimate weapon, the Founding Saint. I would gain enough power to surpass them all.

Then, once I had power on the same level as the Big Three...next came the dude with enough power to solo the Demon Lord himself, the protagonist of *Magical★Explorer*. But I'd outstrip him, too, and become the absolute strongest. After reaching that pinnacle, then...

...I would guide everyone to their happy ending.

So I resolved beneath the waterfall.

When someone says *entrance ceremony*, what image comes to mind?

An average Japanese person probably imagines students in brand-new uniforms and sakura trees in full bloom, as if nature itself were celebrating these students' new chapter in life. That was pretty much the exact image that came to my mind, too.

Sakura trees are a deeply familiar part of Japanese culture. Their branches, filled with lovely petals, have captivated people for generations and overlooked many a magnificent banquet held beneath them.

I adored them. Their petals, carried off and fluttering in the wind, captivate you with their beauty enough to make you forget to blink, and the scene of the grounds dyed pink with the fallen petals fills the air with both splendor and sorrow. Banquets beneath that scenery, overflowing with emotion, are truly some of the most blissful moments a person can experience.

This might just be my own personal tastes, but I also liked the trees after their petals were gone, freshly colored green. Green trees standing modestly in a deserted plaza put me in a nostalgic mood, like witnessing the end of an era before your eyes.

Now, you could say these sakura, beloved by the average Japanese person, are equally beloved in eroge and other dating sims.

Not only are there many games with sakura in the title, but many of them also have important events trigger beneath sakura trees, and countless heroines bear the name Sakura as well.

Naturally, sakura show up in *Magical★Explorer* as well. The protagonist passes through a road filled with cherry blossoms on his way to school from the nearby dorm.

"Ahhh…"

When I'd checked a few days earlier, they were all still buds. They hadn't been able to handle the warm weather recently, but now, their petals were being marvelously swept about. The sakura on each side of the row were in full bloom, making me want to stop walking and appreciate the view.

Yes, I wanted to appreciate them. Truly. If I only had the time.

"I seriously didn't expect that event to trigger like that..."

Casting sidelong glances at the trees, I hurried along.

I'd definitely left the house with time to spare. I'd left two hours after Marino and Sis, who had to prepare for the entrance ceremony, and an hour after Ludie and Claris, who said they had to make a stop along the way. By the time I'd exited the house, I should have been able to leisurely stroll to school and still arrive ten minutes early.

Now, how did it actually play out? I was walking down the street students have to take to get from the dorm to the Academy, yet I hadn't seen a single soul.

It was already time for the entrance ceremony to start, however, so really, it would have been stranger if there had been any.

I guess it was what it was. Was I supposed to continue on to school and ignore a senior citizen with an injured leg?

"Real big difference compared to the protagonist, all right..."

The main character of *Magical★Explorer* gets a text from a beautiful heroine, runs into another heroine eating bread on the way to the entrance ceremony, and begins constructing his harem. Meanwhile, I was an elderly man's hero instead. Still, I knew I had done the right thing, and the man was very grateful, so I didn't regret it whatsoever. If anything, I felt fulfilled.

"What time is it?"

I put my hand in my pocket, took out my cell phone, and opened it up to check my messages. Marino had sent a message that read *I understand. Take your time, okay?* with a ton of heart emojis tacked on the end, accompanied by a strange doodle that looked like she had tried and failed to create a cute piece of modern art. I quickly averted my eyes from the creepy picture, and upon checking the time display in the corner, groaned aloud.

"Man, and I had planned on tearing down a bunch of event flags and everything, too."

In *Magical★Explorer*, the protagonist first meets Kousuke Takioto on the day of the entrance ceremony. Oversleeping, he runs into a beautiful young heroine, a slice of bread in her mouth, and picks up the handkerchief she leaves behind. After that, he looks at the sakura trees and recalls her pink panties. That's right, a pervy flashback starts up. After coming back to reality, the protagonist goes to the Academy, but the gate is locked. There's where Kousuke Takioto makes his entrance. The pair work together to jump over the gate, but they get caught and lectured by the teacher sub-heroine. That's how it's supposed to play out.

I'd intended on ignoring that event. No way did I want to be late.

"Well, hmm, I guess maybe there's something like destiny here... Wait, why does talking about destiny with a dude sound a little sketchy?" I muttered in spite of myself. Up ahead in the distance, there was a single male student standing around looking flummoxed. He was simply staring confoundedly at the closed gate.

He had dark, short hair and a face that was neither handsome nor ugly, exceedingly average, if not a little bit cute. Sharply dressed in a brand-new and unaltered school uniform, he carried the Academy's recommended type of school bag in his hands.

There was no mistaking that utter plainness. He was the game's main character.

Keeping my smirk to myself, I walked up beside him. There, I let out an exaggerated sigh.

"Awww, man, it's all locked up," I muttered, as if I were talking to myself, and stared at the gate. Then I turned to face the protagonist.

"Hey, you a first-year, too?"

The *Magical★Explorer* protagonist looked at me, his mouth hanging half-open.

Oh well, I couldn't blame him, really. From my remark, he must've figured I was a new student, too. That first-year status was precisely what must've given him pause about my outfit. What's a brand-new student doing with his buttons undone, his shirt hanging out, his necktie loose, his tie pin stuck to his breast pocket, and with a humongous stole wrapped around his neck? I looked every bit the antithesis of his very picture of seriousness. As an aside, Kousuke Takioto in the game usually looks like this, too. Though my stole and his scarf were a bit different.

What's up with this flashy-looking dude...?

I imagined that's what was going through his mind. It was written all over his face. Hell, I felt the same way. *Today's the freaking entrance ceremony, and this guy's showing up with an outfit like* that?! or something similar. I might have even been rude enough to say it out loud.

"Y-yeah, that's right."

I nodded at his reply. Then I pointed to my tie pin, colored according to your school year.

"As you can see, I'm a new student, too," I clarified, given my unusual getup. The protagonist mumbled with confusion. I couldn't suppress a smile. He would look so attractive if he were a pretty young girl, but unfortunately, he was a boy, hardware and all. Well, he had the androgynous features typical of eroge protagonists, so I suppose he was a little cute.

What was I going to do now? At this point, I might as well push the story forward just like in the game, right? I didn't hate the full-body aromatherapy teacher sub-heroine who gets angry at us for jumping over the gate. If anything, she was one of my favorites. Having her yell and get angry at me? Hell, that was a juicy reward.

With my mind made up, first, I had to do *that*. Once was more than enough, but I did want to say it. It was a bit annoying to use the same line Kousuke Takioto uses in-game, but it had a real cringey-yet-badass ring to it.

Besides, more than anything, that line would serve also as a declaration that I would unequivocally achieve the goals I touted. It was something I had to do in order to guide all the characters of *Magical★Explorer* to their happy endings. I grinned wide and stuck out my thumb.

"I still haven't introduced myself, have I?"

Slowly turning my raised thumb inward, I put my empty hand on my waist and puffed out my chest.

All right, here we go. To you, protagonist and potentially the strongest character in the world of Magical★Explorer, Iori Hijiri—

Right here, right now, I declare to you:

"The name's Kousuke Takioto! The guy who's gonna become the strongest at Tsukuyomi Magic Academy!"

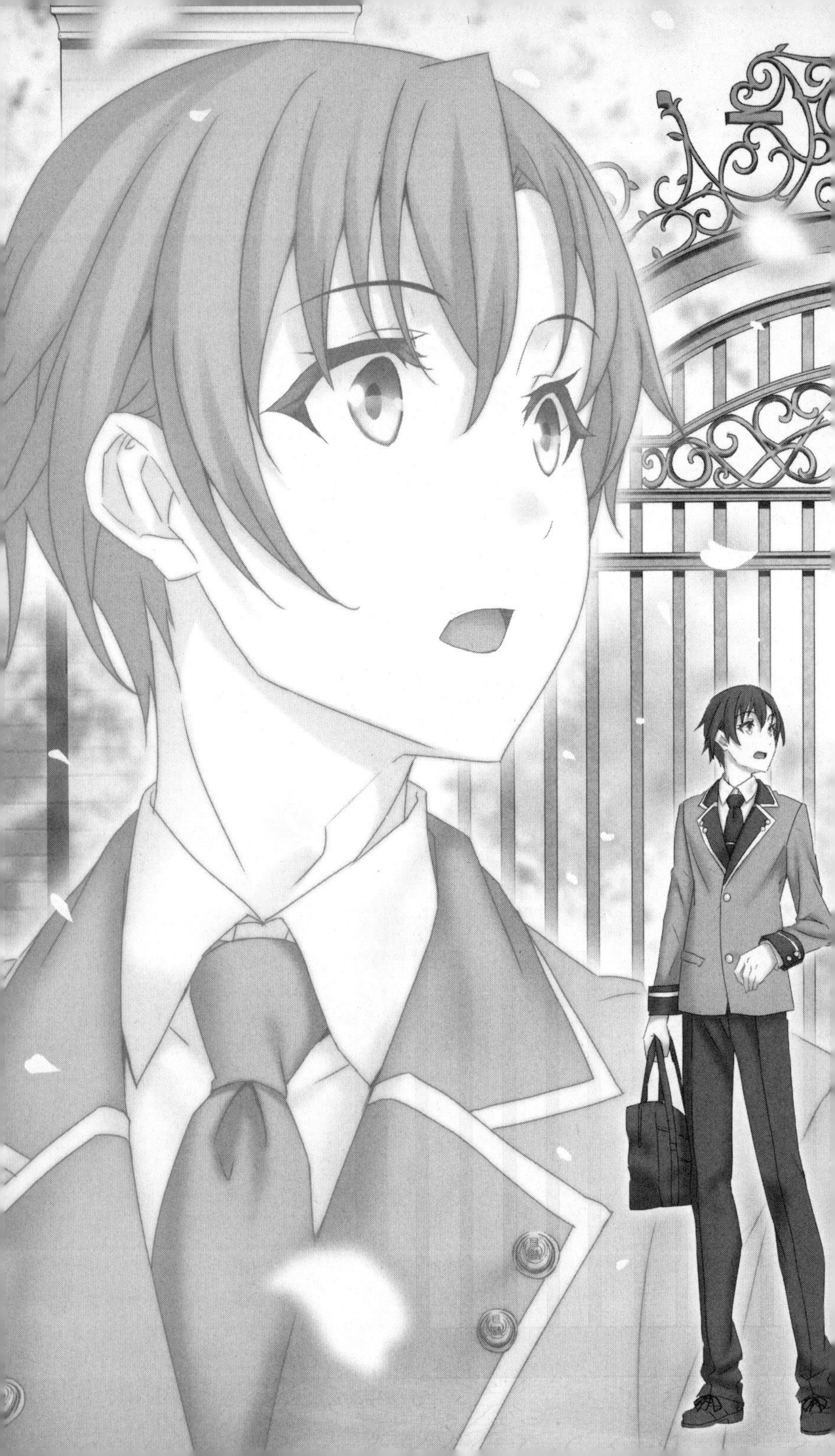

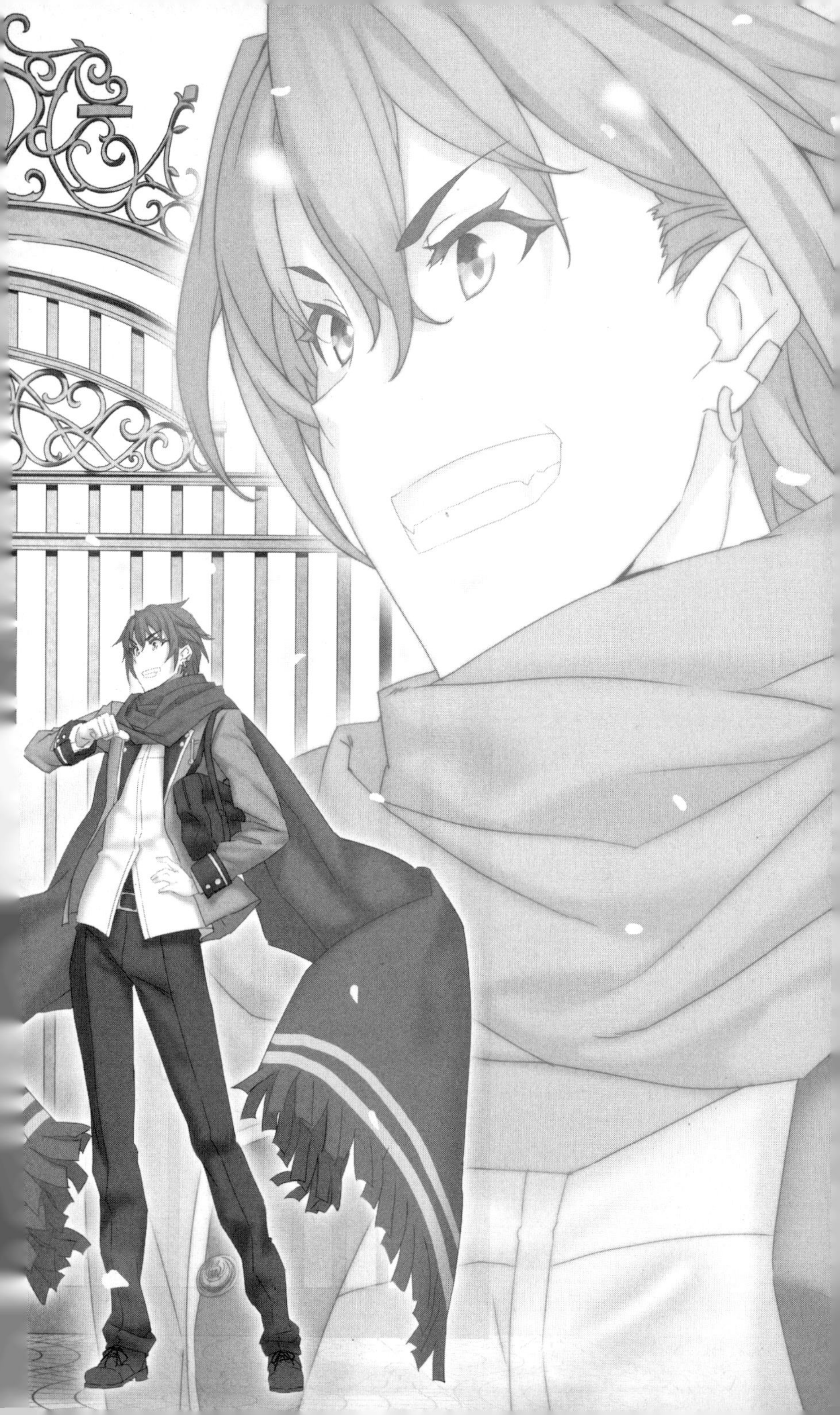

Good day. My name is Iris.

—Acknowledgments—

Thank you to Noboru Kannatuki, for your brilliant illustrations and for readily accepting my unreasonable requests. Yukari Higa, for your wonderful introductory manga. Natsuki Miyakawa, for not abandoning me, despite all the trouble I caused you. (I thought you had been rendered speechless when I handed you my manuscript with several thousand words over the limit. I've reflected on what I did and will be sure to make more touch-ups next time.)

To those who have been supporting me since the web novel, and to those of you reading this right now:

Thank you all, from the bottom of my heart. The book you hold in your hands is the fruit of my dream come true.

—Regarding *Magical Explorer*—

Readers coming from the web novel will know this, but this volume covers the prologue. Things get a lot more interesting from here, so I hope you'll keep reading on!

—Announcements—

The manga adaption of *Magical Explorer* is scheduled to start serialization in the Young Ace UP around the start of 2020.

I encourage you to support this adaption as well!

Iris

The scene shifts to
Tsukuyomi Magic Academy.

Kousuke's campus
life finally begins—

Magical★Explorer

Reborn as a
Side Character
in a Fantasy Dating Sim

2

Coming 2022!!

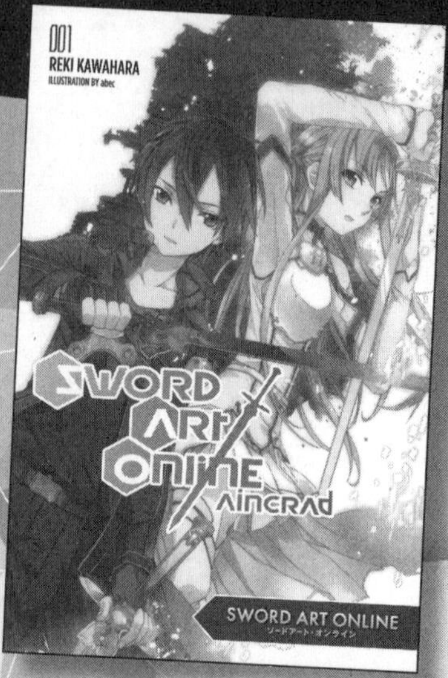

001
REKI KAWAHARA
ILLUSTRATION BY abec
SWORD ART ONLINE
Aincrad
SWORD ART ONLINE
ソードアート・オンライン

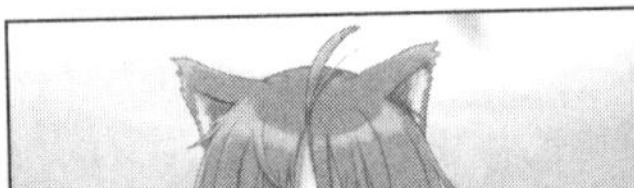

SPICE & WOLF
VOL. 1
ISUNA HASEKURA

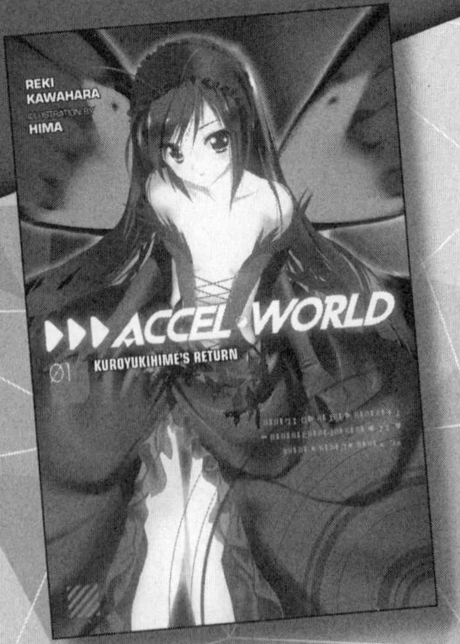

REKI KAWAHARA
ILLUSTRATION BY HIMA
ACCEL·WORLD
01
KUROYUKIHIME'S RETURN

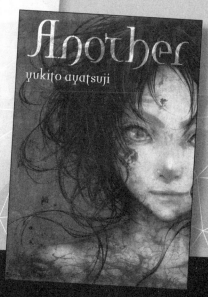